For the Love of Death

John Paul

Copyright © 2024 by John Paul

This novel is a work of fiction. The names, characters, places, and incidents are either the product of the author's imagination or are used fictitiously. Any resemblance to actual persons, living or dead, events, or locales is entirely coincidental.

All rights reserved. No part of this book may be reproduced or used in any manner without written permission of the copyright owner except for the use of quotations in a book review.

First edition, May 2024

ISBN 979-8-218-40565-6 (paperback)
ISBN 979-8-218-40566-3 (ebook)

This book contains mature content, including graphic sexual situations, brutal violence, sexual violence, drug use, foul language, and gay-themed material.

www.iamjohnpaul.com

Chapter One

The sky was bright from the midday winter sun. A thin layer of clouds swam across an ocean of pale blue. The sun's rays gave an illusion of warmth, but not enough to thaw the frozen ground. A mix of maple and oak trees lined both sides of the street, standing tall, naked, and unattractive. Like a teenage boy's growing limbs, their branches stretched in all directions. Roots from the aging trees had surfaced, disturbing the once-level cobblestone sidewalks. Leaves are scattered on the ground, some frozen to the hard soil. Dark brown and lifeless, they are void of the vibrant colors of orange, red, and amber they displayed only weeks earlier. Outside, the air is sharp and cold against the skin. Inside, Nicholas' breath fogs the window. It is going to be a cold winter, colder than usual.

Nicholas stood by one of the windows, looking out, not looking at or for anything or anyone. He was lost in a trance, thinking about everything that had led up to this day. He was hopeful that Oliver was safe, far from the chaos coming. This house, in the quaint neighborhood, was a rental. It was once Oliver's rental. Nicholas wondered what Oliver would think if he knew that Nicholas was hiding out in his old house.

The living room is warm, almost too warm. It is a hard contrast to the cold New England weather outside. The drapes are a heavy, dark-colored material; almost like velvet, and they hugged the floor-to-ceiling windows. He wonders how he never paid attention to their detail when Oliver lived here. Their chaos of dark solids and patterns is representative of Nicholas' life. As heavy as they appear, they still flutter as the hot air escapes from the floor vent.

Nicholas' face is close to the window, almost touching the glass. He can feel the cold from outside, the crisp coolness, and can see his reflection, though distorted and incomplete. He struggles to avoid the sorrow and the pain in the eyes reflecting at him. He can feel the heat of his breath clouding the window and sailing back towards his face, warming him for a moment. He holds his breath long enough for the window to clear and then pulls back just enough to lose his reflection. At this moment, he realizes that his life is empty without Oliver. He knew he needed to move quickly with this plan. He needed to be back by Oliver's side.

Outside, the dead leaves and brown grass are painted white. The last snowfall was two days ago. It was not a heavy snowfall, but enough to blanket the ground. Nicholas did not like the snow. He did once as a child, and life seemed more simple. The streets have all been plowed, but many sidewalks and driveways remain blanketed, including his. Nicholas had no real reason to clear it. He had nowhere to go. He did but would not alert anyone of his plans, least of all Oliver. He was temporarily trapped, and once again, he was alone.

The fireplace is alive with color. The wood is burning brightly, contributing to the warmth of the room. The red and orange colors dance with some blue as the wood crackles behind him. The sound would be romantic and soothing if in a different setting. But here and now, Nicholas' mind is flooded with the horrific, bloody, violent images he has left in his wake. His back is warm from the burning wood as he tries to clear his head to focus on Oliver. His focus is always on Oliver.

Nicholas knew it was only a matter of time before everything began unraveling again. It always did, but he felt like it was unraveling faster and more precisely this time. The police were getting better at cornering him, he thought. Maybe he was getting sloppier, which made it easier for the police to connect the dots. The more time he spent with Oliver, the less planning he did with his kills. He was too focused on Oliver all the time. But with his new plan, he felt that he had planned clearly and that nothing could go wrong this time. He was hopeful that Oliver was far away by now, safe from the chaos closing in on Nicholas. He knew this day would come. He is just glad that it is all happening through his planning.

Mixed with the crackling of the burning wood, the sound of music bounced from wall to wall, filling the house with quiet noise. Without it, the house would have sat silent, which it often does, even though Nicholas has lived in it for almost a year. The blood of his past still stains his hands and heart. Nicholas knew he would never be free of his sins but had been looking forward to the day it all ended. He believed that day was today.

There was not a lot of furniture in the house. The old pieces in each room were in the place when he moved in — still sitting in the same spot they were in when he signed the rental agreement online through one of his shell companies. They belonged to Howard, Camilla, and Oliver — mainly yard sale finds that were not worth getting rid of at the time. The smell of Oliver had long since evaporated, but Nicholas still envisioned how Oliver must have lived in this same house when he and his friends filled it with love and laughter not that long ago.

Nicholas never added anything to the house — he never made it home and never let Oliver know he was living in it. Since blowing up his last residence years ago, Nicholas learned to travel light; always be on the run. An oversized wingback chair sat in the front room, not far from the fireplace. Someone made it with fine craftsmanship, which you do not see in furniture today. It is wrapped in a soft fabric busy with detail. It is Nicholas' favorite chair in the house. He used to look through the window to find Oliver sitting in it, admiring the beautiful figure lost in the dark colors. The dark shades of olive, burgundy, gold, and brown stain the chair in a never-ending pattern of leaves and flowers. Nicholas has spent hours tracing the pattern with his finger, constantly losing himself in the design's splendor, beauty, and darkness. The chair is the only piece of furniture in the living room.

Still standing by the window, noticing everyone falling into place outside, Nicholas heard his doorbell ring. As he walked from the front window to the door, it took him a minute to adjust his eyes to the house's darkness. It had been exceptionally bright out, and he had been looking out the window for so long, or so it seemed. He was not sure what he was looking for outside exactly. Maybe hope. Over the years, Nicholas had seen so much through the window. He wondered how many people could see him now—how many were trying to look in on Nicholas as he used to look in on Oliver. He assumed many but could not know for sure. They changed so often, his watchers.

Nicholas had been dressed and ready to go since he had made the two phone calls almost an hour earlier. The first was to his lawyer, Lawrence. Nicholas needed to make sure that everything was ready. He was about to change his life significantly—the biggest change yet. While waiting, he pondered what finally sparked him to make the call. Maybe, for a moment, he felt remorse for what he had done to all those people—to Oliver. Perhaps, in some way, he knew that he could not run anymore. Whatever the reason, he knew that he had to stop. It was time for him to raise the white flag and come in quietly, unlike his dad Adam twenty-six years earlier. Nicholas did not want anyone taking him anywhere without him having complete control of the situation. He always had to be in control.

No sooner had his eyes adjusted to the house's darkness did he go to the front door and blind himself with light again as he broke the seal. He opened the door and looked beyond the two men standing on the porch before him. They were stomping their boots to loosen the snow. Behind them was a trail of white powder across the porch and down the stairs. Beyond the stairs, Nicholas could see the path the two men made from their car. They were the first to walk that path since the snowfall. The front yard had remained uncharted until these two men, who looked like boys, completed their journey across the smooth snow.

They looked familiar, these boys. Nicholas thought that they may have been his watchers on a previous day. Tall, pale-skinned, clean-shaven, and nicely dressed, the two stood there looking at Nicholas, almost in amazement. Nicholas thought they looked young but old enough to be considered handsome as he studied their faces. To entertain himself, Nicholas imagined that they were lovers—they just seemed too good together—so happy to be there, together. Their suits were similar, reminding Nicholas of old couples in matching tracksuits. Neither man could say anything—would say anything. When they left the police station, their captain instructed them to proceed with caution when facing the killer. Nicholas offered nothing in return. The three stood there, looking at each other, wondering who would make the first move or say the first word.

Nicholas could feel the warmth of the house escaping from behind him. His time for running was passing.

Nicholas looked toward the car that sat at the end of his driveway. It was not in the driveway but blocking it. He wondered if the men thought he had a car in the garage and would try to flee. Nicholas never knew if there was a car in the garage—he never looked and could not recall if Oliver ever had either. But that did not matter now. The driveway was buried in snow. The unmarked car looked almost brand new, crisp, and clean like the two men before him. Nicholas wondered if it still had that new car smell. He knew he would find out soon enough.

The three men never said much to each other. They did not need to. They knew why they were in this position—standing on the porch, even if none wanted to admit it. Nicholas knew that the men could smell the warmth of the house, or at least feel it, and wanted in—out of the cold, but Nicholas was not letting anyone in. This house was his space—a lasting memory of Oliver.

"Hello, fellas," Nicholas said. "Great weather we are having, isn't it?" he continued sarcastically.

"Mr. Lawson!?" one of the officers said, unsure if he was stating a fact or asking a question.

Nicholas held up a finger, indicating that he needed a moment. He turned around and left the two men standing in the cold air. He had retreated inside the house to retrieve his jacket. Oddly the men did not follow—not that Nicholas gave them a choice. He closed the door behind him as he returned to the warmth. Nicholas was gone probably longer than the officers would have liked, but they knew he was not going anywhere without them. The two men assumed Nicholas knew other officers were surrounding the house, watching his every move. Well, almost every move.

Minutes later, Nicholas returned to find both men still standing silently. It was as if they never moved while he was gone; never even spoke. Nicholas opened the door, stepped out, and closed it tightly behind him. He locked the door so he knew there was no going back. He struggled to get his hands into his gloves before either of the men could smell them. Not that they would, but Nicholas did not want to take any chances.

Anyone passing the house would probably assume these men were three friends gathering for some winter activity—maybe lunch to catch up and reminisce about their college days. The men were not in uniform, and while the streets lit up with flashing blue lights, there was no storming of the house or forceful or fast moves made by anyone. Everyone was moving slowly—carefully. The task force had already made a few blunders in Vermont and New York, so they took necessary precautions to ensure this arrest went smoothly.

"Shall we get this over with?" Nicholas asked as he motioned his hand toward the stairs. "After you, gentlemen."

One of the men began the descent while the other let Nicholas pass. They were going to keep Nicholas between them. Nicholas was escorted through the snow and to the car at the end of the driveway without handcuffs. Back in the house, he left the flames of the fire dancing to the music, still swimming through the warm air. He knew he was not returning, but he wanted that space to have peace in its final moments.

As the three men walked down the path towards the car, Nicholas looked up and smiled at the woman staring out from the upstairs bedroom window in the house directly across the street. She and her team had been watching Nicholas for hours, probably days. She knew he knew she was there. She saw him watching her watching him. It freaked her out each time, so she was glad this game was coming to an end. Nicholas watched her without remorse, without feeling now as he had since the first time he saw her. From her, Nicholas turned his attention to the dark van parked across the street a few yards from his house. No one was in the driver's seat, but he knew that there was plenty of activity in the back of the van. Nicholas looked toward it, still smiling. He knew cameras were in the front, all looking toward his house. He knew several people in the back were looking at monitors and listening through headsets. Nicholas was sure they were expecting something more exciting from him. He had assumed that the police had pieced together the suspected path of destruction he had left behind. Knowing they were in the house and the van, Nicholas kept quiet inside his house. He wanted them to think and try to understand what he was going through and what he had been through over his life. Nicholas wanted them to feel alone like he did now that Oliver was gone.

Nicholas assumed the house behind his was also crawling with people eager to know his every move. He had seen them in windows and his backyard before. He could not see them from the front of the house, but he knew they were gearing up to invade his house once they knew Nicholas was safely in the undercover patrol car, locked in the backseat. Nicholas stopped halfway to the car and looked around at the neighborhood. He turned towards his house as if to wave goodbye to someone, but he knew no one was there. There never was. Nicholas liked this house—Oliver's home—and would miss it, but like everything he had touched in the past, he had to destroy this house too. He had a suspected reputation for destroying everything and everyone he had met. He was not about to ruin his reputation now. Nicholas smiled at the two boys and quietly finished the walk to the car before slipping into the backseat without any argument.

As Nicholas sat in the car, looking out, his face was again close to the cold glass, and his breath fogged a window. He smiled. The two men were still outside the car. They met up with some people from the house across the street, and Nicholas could see more people coming from the van. Suddenly the neighborhood was alive with activity. Nicholas assumed that it would only be a matter of time before the people in the house behind his would emerge, if they had not already, and were trying to make their way in through his back door. He listened to the police radio. He could hear Dispatch sending more men to his address. In the distance, he could hear their sirens.

No one ever read Nicholas his rights. Instead, everyone cooperated as if they had played out this scene a thousand times — had memorized their lines and placement in this theatrical adventure. Everyone knew, or they hoped they knew their part. They had arrested enough doppelgängers already. They were excited to have the real Nicholas in custody finally.

Nicholas sat in the police car, trying to listen to the voices of the men and women shuffling around outside the vehicle. It still had a new car smell, as he imagined it would, which he enjoyed. He then focused on his house, watching it very closely as he inhaled the scent of new pleather. He was counting to himself silently with a devilish grin. At that moment, Nicholas felt victorious again, even sitting trapped in the back of the police car. One officer saw him smiling and hit the car window to frighten Nicholas. He did not flinch. Instead, he looked the officer right in the eyes and mouthed one word.

Before the officer could ask Nicholas what he said, everyone blocks away could hear his one word.

"Boom!"

The house, once a place of warmth and security for Nicholas, exploded with a loud bang. Flames shot out of most windows, and the now-melting snow was sprinkled with glass. The house to the left caught on fire while the one on the right had its roof caved in from the collapsing chimney of Nicholas' house. An officer flew into the side of the car with such force that it broke his spine. His body was Nicholas's only protection from the explosion, the flames, and the glass.

The force of the explosion pushed the police car into oncoming traffic. Hit by a passing truck, the police car plowed toward the undercover police van. Soon the truck, the police car, and the van were a pile of twisted metal. Windows shattered in the neighboring cars and houses. Bodies were wrapped in flames, dancing around the front yard without direction. Flames rose two stories into the air above the house. The colors were bright and beautiful, like the fire Nicholas had watched earlier in his living room. Screams and cries filled the warming air as dozens of officers worked to save their burning coworkers.

The house was destroyed—erasing any evidence, and one more chapter of Nicholas's life ended. For the police, the explosion happened so unexpectedly. They had assumptions about how Nicholas might hurt or even kill them, so they took precautions with him that day. But what they never planned for was Nicholas blowing up the house. The killer they had been tracking—had been studying, never used explosives. At least none of their reports mentioned explosions. They never knew of Eric. Knives and guns were all they had on file, which was the worst of what they expected from Nicholas if he started a fight with them. They never expected Nicholas to have a plethora of homemade explosives in the basement that would cause enough damage so nothing could be salvaged or identified.

Over the last four years, Nicholas had gotten a little sloppy in his killing, and there were times when he was confident that the police were beginning to connect the dots, but he knew that everything played out the way it did today because of his doing. The stakeout was all because of a plan that Nicholas put into motion — not because the police had finally connected enough dots between Nicholas and all the murders. The police had already botched a few arrests — wasted enough taxpayer dollars, so they were taking extra precautions now to ensure they finally arrested the right person. But, for all the assumptions and fuzzy video footage the police had, if it were not for Oliver helping them and Nicholas calling them, they would not be any closer to solving any of the murder cases of the last few years. Nicholas was found now only because he wanted to be found. It was all part of his plan.

Nicholas had thought most of this plan through but had not anticipated being trapped in the police car, now a pile of hot metal, plastic, and pleather. He thought he would have been able to cause a diversion and slip away like he always did. Turning himself in was only supposed to be part of the fun. Watching the chaos from a distance as he escaped was supposed to be the main fun.

Nicholas could have escaped from the windows, which were nothing more than piles of glass pellets, but he did not go anywhere. He sat crying to himself. He was not crying because he was hurt, although he was hurt badly. He was losing a lot of blood. He was not crying because of what he had just done. He was not upset that he had killed more innocent people. He was not afraid of what might happen to him now. Instead, Nicholas was crying because he missed Oliver. The heat and the chaos had Nicholas thinking about his life before Oliver—before he knew anything about Oliver, but all he could think about were the times after he first set eyes on Oliver. He wished, at that moment, that he could feel the warmth of Oliver's body-hugging him—holding him, but instead, Nicholas felt the warmth of the blood from the cut on his head as it poured down his face and the bar in his leg. He was not sure what would happen next. For once, he was no longer in control. He could feel life escaping him. Was this the end, he thought? Is this what his victims felt, he wondered.

Nicholas could not stop the blood, so he took comfort in its warmth. He could taste it in his mouth. Within minutes everything went black.

Chapter Two

Four years ago.

Oliver stood, looking at Nicholas—looking deep into his green eyes. He found their beauty—his beauty paralyzing. Fear rose within him, causing him to blush and sweat simultaneously. Oliver had only been this close to the "real" Nicholas—as far as he knew—one other time, and that was Peter's funeral, and even then, it was not 'this' close. Looking at Nicholas closely, Oliver was struggling to remember every other time he thought he saw Nicholas. With each memory, he could remember the place—the time, but not the face, at least not enough to believe that the Nicholas before him was the same Nicholas that he and his friends had been obsessing about for the past year.

"Hi," was all Oliver could muster, and even that sounded like a teenage boy going through puberty. "You are Peter's son?!"

As those words fell out of his mouth, Oliver wondered if they sounded more like a question or a statement.

"Yes," replied Nicholas. Then after a long pause, "I wanted to talk with you at the funeral, but it seemed like the wrong place—wrong time to let you know how we were… I mean, we are connected."

"But that was months ago," Oliver shot back accusatorily. "Why now?"

"There were several times when I wanted to find you. I knew you lived in town. Peter's lawyer told me that much, but he would not—he could not give me your address or other contact information. I asked him to check with you to see if it would be okay if I reached out. Clearly, he never asked you."

"I am sorry," said Oliver. "I need to sit down." Oliver sat on the bench—the same one where he first met Eric—where he first felt the soft warmth of Eric's hand. Oliver was quite aware that he was on the same bench; so was Nicholas. Nicholas planned this meeting, but unlike the last time the two shared this bench, Nicholas had been waiting patiently for this moment to arrive when he could be himself finally. He was done being Eric. He was done being anyone other than himself, especially as he worked Oliver into his life.

"I wanted to tell you about Peter—about our past, yours and mine," Nicholas continued without skipping a beat or giving the impression that he feared Oliver was beginning to make the Eric/Nicholas connection. Their hair was styled and colored differently—Nicholas and Eric had different colored eyes. They even dressed quite differently. Nicholas had gone to great lengths to ensure that Oliver would never discover that Eric and Nicholas were the same person. Nicholas felt confident that Oliver was still not connecting those dots—he might never connect them. As Eric, Nicholas shared parts of himself with Oliver that Oliver would never link back to the real Nicholas. He did not lie, but Nicholas did not share whole truths when posing as Eric. He was saving those moments for when he could be his true self with Oliver.

Nicholas had all but killed off the idea of Eric, the kind, alternate persona he had used to lure Oliver closer earlier in the year. The character of Eric had lived out its usefulness. That final text he sent to Oliver, as Eric, all those months ago made it clear that Eric would not be returning. It was time for Nicholas to be himself with

Oliver. Nicholas was very focused on going forward, getting to know Oliver, and letting Oliver get to know him.

Nicholas did not put his hand on Oliver's as they sat quietly on the bench. Instead, he was waiting for Oliver to speak. It had to look like they were meeting for the first time—that Nicholas was meeting Oliver for the first time. Nicholas could not let on that he loved Oliver—he had loved him for a long time. All those revelations would come in time. As the two sat on the bench, a cool breeze sent dead leaves sailing through the air as Autumn showed its colors, taking over the sky and the ground. Oliver looked ahead, then at Nicholas, almost studying his face. Nicholas looked back at Oliver, staring into his eyes, trying to see his reflection. Nicholas finally broke the silence.

"I've known about you for years," Nicholas began. "Peter talked about you, but not until I was in high school. I think he wanted us to meet. I am almost sure of it. He said so one time when we were in London. I think he was overly sentimental about the city where we were born. Did you know we were both born in London? In the same hospital at almost the same time, in fact."

"I did," Oliver lied. "My mother told me everything, well I thought everything. She had to; she felt compelled to tell me something after we went to Peter's funeral." The truth was that Oliver's mother only told him part of the story. She did not tell Oliver that he and Nicholas were born in the same hospital on the same day, almost within the same hour. Oliver would learn over the coming months that there was quite a bit of the story that his mother left out. On the other hand, Peter left a wealth of truths in the written word for Oliver to read over and over.

Oliver did not feel that now was the time to tell Nicholas about the journal. He was unsure if Nicholas knew about the journal, but he thought it was something he was not ready to discuss. He wanted to learn more about Nicholas—about why he was here, on this bench now. It had been a week since Camilla had left, longer since Eric had left. Oliver spent the last week wondering where he and his friends went wrong and how so much pain and suffering wove into their lives. Oliver had been abandoned. He was left to clean up the mess—to make sense of it all as the dust settled. Everyone else was gone.

"I don't want this to sound creepy," said Nicholas realizing that starting a sentence like that would only make his words sound creepier. "I went looking for you once Peter told me about you. I was mad at him for telling me that I could have grown up with something—someone like a brother. I wanted to find you and tell you everything he told me so maybe we could be mad together. I was just a teenager then—we both were.

"I know that sounds ridiculous when I say it out loud, but it is what it is, right? I almost talked with you. I almost approached you at a coffee shop, but you were always with some girl."

Oliver knew what girl Nicholas was talking about, and he started crying as the memory of Elizabeth was slapped back in his face by the very man who killed her. Oliver wanted to say her name, but he could not. He was not ready to let Nicholas that far into his life, and he had no idea that Nicholas already knew everything.

"Anyway," Nicholas said with more enthusiasm. "Without sounding like a complete ass or being too forward, would you be interested in grabbing dinner sometime? You did not grow up with

Peter, but he was your father, and he was my dad. I think that is something we should talk about."

Oliver wiped his eyes and looked at Nicholas. His green eyes, bright and alive, looked back at Oliver with excitement and with kindness, trying to project some innocence. Oliver got lost in the green momentarily and then looked at the rest of Nicholas—still struggling to place him outside the funeral. Still no luck.

"Sure," was all Oliver shot back.

"Give me your phone," Nicholas said with authority and confidence. At that moment, Oliver thought of Eric—he said the same thing, and that did not end well. Oliver looked at Nicholas for longer than he meant to before pulling his phone out of his front pocket and handing it to Nicholas. Nicholas looked at the locked screen and admired the photo of Oliver, Camila, and Howard. The three were smiling. They were happy or at least looked happy.

"It's locked," Nicholas said as he returned the phone to Oliver. "Cute photo."

Oliver ignored the comment about his screen saver as he entered the code and handed the unlocked phone back to Nicholas, who quickly tapped his digits into the phone. Nicholas' own phone buzzed. He pulled it out and promptly typed back to Oliver.

"Got it," said Oliver looking at the smiley face emoji on his screen.

Nicholas did not want this first meeting to go longer than necessary. He wanted it to be the foreplay to a longer, more intimate time together. He stood up, and Oliver followed like a puppet pulled off the bench. The two boys shook hands like strangers rather than hugging like brothers and walked off in opposite directions.

Chapter Three

Oliver had not walked far. He found another park bench just yards from where he had left Nicholas. He needed to sit down. His entire life had been thrown into the spin cycle over the last year, and he had lost too many friends. He thought about the conspiracy theories that he, Camilla, and Howard had concocted, but now that he was alone, he was unsure what was real and what was just a conspiracy. If the three friend's conspiracies were just that, then Nicholas was not a threat. He was someone who shared a dad with Oliver, sort of, and Oliver could live with that reality. Of course, if the theories were real, and Nicholas was a killer, then Oliver just came face to face with the person who killed his friends. At that thought, Oliver leaned over the back of the bench and threw up.

When he finished, he wiped his mouth with the embroidered handkerchief he always had in his back pocket. Instead of his initials, the embroidery was a detailed image of his family crest. At times he thought it was gaudy and over the top—his mother flaunting her wealth, and at other times he loved looking at its colorful details and uniqueness. Oliver questioned his existence and relation to the crest as he studied it, covered in vomit chunks and smelling horrible. That was the crest of his father's name—his paternal father. He lifted the trash can lid next to the bench and threw the hanky into it. Oliver was mortified that he puked on the ground—in a public space. If the trash can did not have a lid, he would have thrown up in it, but now nature was soaking in his breakfast and lunch.

Sitting alone on the bench, convincing himself that the conspiracy theories were just theories, Oliver started thinking more about what he and his friends went through and how Nicholas couldn't have been the killer. Oliver was conjuring up facts that helped justify this thinking. The more he talked to himself, the more he began to accept that Nicholas was not the evil person he and his roommates believed him to be. He needed and wanted this to be true. He wanted Nicholas to be something other than the killer. As he sat, convincing himself of this new truth, his phone rang, startling him back to reality.

"Hello, mother," Oliver said as he placed the phone to his ear. "Everything okay?"

Oliver's mother, Jessica, never remarried after her husband, James, Oliver's paternal father, died. The only other man ever to share a bed with Jessica was Peter, Oliver's biological father, and she lost track of him after their affair—soon after Oliver took his first breath. She enjoyed the freedom of not having a husband, but when cornered and with a few too many martinis warming her mind, she would confess to wishing she had reached out to Peter when her husband died. Jessica was mainly hoping for a second chance with the only other man to excite her, but these moments would pass when her hangover would kick in.

With Oliver out of college and not living at home, his mother lived the life of a wealthy widow. Between her clubs, charities, and girlfriends, she managed to stay quite busy. That did not stop Oliver from worrying about her being alone in her big house, fast approaching her 60s. Oliver was mostly concerned about his mother because of her health. He had good reason, too. His mother smoked a lot when she was younger—everyone smoked back then. She had long since quit, but that, combined with her excessive drinking, affected her organs. She had a baby and lost a kidney in her 30s, and had a heart attack in her 40s. She had liver issues in her early 50s, and as she prepared to turn 60, she was diagnosed with stage four breast cancer.

Jessica had survived the other battles with her body and was determined to survive this latest one, too. Oliver knew she would not. Battle scars aside, she had to step back from most activities. She had a full-time nurse living in her guest house at the insistence of Oliver — for his peace of mind.

In these, her final days, Oliver's mother spent more time closing out her estate and hosting friends rather than going out with them. She did not see Oliver nearly as much as she wished, but they often talked — more so now with her latest diagnosis. Oliver had been so immersed in conspiracy theories over the last year that outside of Peter's funeral, he had neglected his duties as her son and had visited his mother only a few times since the funeral.

"Yes, dear," she sang back through the phone. "Everything is fine. I think that nurse is getting bossier by the day, but we are surviving.

"I am calling because I want you to come to dinner this weekend. It seems I have not seen your smile in months, and I miss you. Besides, I am old and dying. You should want to visit your mother more often." She liked to try and guilt Oliver, but it rarely worked.

Oliver wanted to correct her and tell her they had seen each other two weeks ago, but he did not want to argue with her. He knew she was not well enough to remember such details. He was silent momentarily, still thinking about his meeting with Nicholas. His mother felt compelled to interrupt the silence and force him to give her an answer.

"Oliver?"

"Sorry, yes, of course, I can come around this weekend," Oliver sputtered, almost annoyed. "How about Friday night? I can pick up something from that Italian place you like so much, and we can play a board game—maybe Trivial Pursuit or something to work our brains."

Moments after Oliver hung up, he received a calendar invite from his mother for Friday night. She was always doing that—putting their time together on Oliver's calendar as if he would never remember to visit her without it. He accepted the invite and was about to put his phone back in his pocket when he got a text from Nicholas. Oliver was surprised the text came so quickly. They had just seen each other thirty minutes earlier.

"Hi. Great bumping into you today. Do you want to grab dinner Friday night? I know a great Italian place in town."

Oliver kept rereading the words on his screen. Friday night? Italian? He had just made those same plans with his mother. It was eerie. He did not want to blow Nicholas off so quickly after their formal introduction, but at the same time, he knew he could not cancel on his mother.

"Sorry, but I have plans Friday," Oliver typed back. "How about coffee Tuesday at Cup of Joe?" He hit the send button and put his phone away. The time had gotten away from him, and he still had to get home to clean up his place. It had been too long since Camilla left, and Howard had died. Oliver had spent the time ignoring both of their rooms for as long as possible. But his lease was up next month, and he still had a lot of cleaning to do. He had no intention of staying in his rented house. It had too many bad memories.

Chapter Four

Nicholas looked at Oliver's text but did not respond right away. He wanted to think about his next move. He was determined to make things work between him and Oliver and did not want to mess up their second first date. After test-driving their relationship last year under the disguise of his alter ego, Eric, which he felt went well, Nicholas felt ready for the real deal. He needed Eric gone, so Eric ghosted Oliver, and Nicholas erased all evidence of Eric ever existing. With that persona gone, Nicholas was finally ready to get to know Oliver as himself and share himself—his authentic self now and forever.

* * * * *

It was through the window of the local coffee house that Nicholas first saw Oliver. It feels like a lifetime ago now, but Nicholas remembers that moment like yesterday. He had been stalking Elizabeth for months by then. For all the 'homework' Nicholas did while stalking Elizabeth, he had not yet discovered that she and Oliver were cousins. He just saw two beautiful people sitting across from each other, enjoying each other's company in a way that enraged Nicholas with jealousy.

While watching Elizabeth, Nicholas saw a handsome boy sitting across from her in the coffee shop. The boy was the most beautiful person Nicholas had ever seen, even more so than Elizabeth. All those years ago, Nicholas had the most challenging time understanding his feelings as he looked at Oliver from a distance. His heart raced. His breathing was irregular. He could feel goosebumps consume his body as he shook, trying to understand how one person could spark such a feeling in another. Nicholas had never felt like that, not even when he killed people. Cupid's arrow struck him in a way he never thought possible. Nicholas had not come to terms with his sexuality then, yet at that moment, Nicholas knew with every fiber of his being that he was in love with the boy sitting across from Elizabeth. He had to know more about the mysterious boy. It had become his new mission. Nicholas was speechless when he later learned that the boy he fell in love with turned out to be Oliver.

Nicholas was just beginning to expand his killing beyond animals when he first saw Oliver sitting with Elizabeth. Nicholas had recently taken Toby's life and had been looking for his next victim. He found it easy to prey upon people that he found attractive. He was able to build a fantasy around the kill. One day long before he first saw Oliver, Nicholas sat in the coffee shop reading a book about serial killers. He looked up and saw Elizabeth walk through the door. Looking back, Nicholas could not say what it was about Elizabeth. Maybe it was how the sunlight reflected off her body as she walked in, or how she smelled as she walked past him, completely ignoring him. Whatever it was about Elizabeth does not matter now. She is dead. But beginning that day years ago, Nicholas became obsessed with Elizabeth. He would eventually have sex with her, but not so much out of an attraction, but as part of his mutilation—violation of her.

Nicholas had learned about Oliver a few months before first seeing him with Elizabeth. Peter finally felt Nicholas was old enough to know the truth, so he told Nicholas he was not his biological father. He told Nicholas that his biological father was dead, and his name had been Adam. Peter also told Nicholas about Oliver, his other child with another woman. As any teen would respond, Nicholas was angry to learn about Adam and Oliver. He was more furious with Peter than he was with Adam and Oliver. He did not know them, after all.

Nicholas wanted to know more about the man who killed his mother and the boy who had captured part of Peter's love. Peter was not entirely neglectful of Nicholas as a child, but he was not entirely focused on Nicholas either. Nicholas always thought it was because of work or the loss of his mother until Peter admitted it was because of Oliver. Peter never had the opportunity to see Oliver grow up—to be part of his life. He felt that void in his life every day until he died, and as a result, Nicholas felt a void, too. Nicholas felt anger towards a boy he did not know for stealing love from a father he learned was not his. With this newfound knowledge and anger, the teenage Nicholas embarked on a journey of discovery—of his birth father, himself, and Oliver.

Nicholas always knew he was different from the other kids around him. He kept to himself in school—excelled in his classes but did not bring any attention to himself. When possible, he avoided most social settings. When he was not studying, teenage Nicholas would find solace in the woods behind his house, masturbating or killing animals cruelly, then masturbating over the dead carcass. While most teen boys would shoot a pellet gun at a squirrel or bird and think it was fun—never really wondering or caring if they killed the creature, it was different for Nicholas. He found pleasure in trapping animals when he was a teenager. He would build elaborate traps and then torture the animals to death. He never understood why he did it—why he killed them, it just seemed to be a natural part of who he was as a person.

Nicholas had captured, tortured, and skinned more than a dozen animals by his teen years. He started small—rabbits and squirrels but evolved into dogs and deer. As he aged, he grew tired of the animals and wanted to hurt something bigger—someone, bigger. Eventually, he killed his first human—Toby, and the feeling he got—that euphoric rush was like nothing he had ever experienced when killing small animals. Taking someone's life—dominating and killing a human became his new obsession.

As Nicholas spent more time stalking Elizabeth, he would think about Oliver and how he might go about finding him. At that point, all those years ago, Nicholas still did not know that the boy in the window—the one he fell in love with, was Oliver. Nicholas was confident that Oliver would be the next one on his list once he could take Elizabeth's life.

When Nicholas eventually learned that the boy across from Elizabeth is Oliver, he was no longer focused on killing Oliver but on killing to be with him. No one else—nothing else mattered to Nicholas other than spending the rest of his life with Oliver, and he was prepared to kill to make that a reality.

*****

As Nicholas looked at his phone screen, studying the message from Oliver, he smiled at the thought that the two were going to meet up at the very spot where it all began for him. Nicholas was confident that Oliver did not see him outside the window that day all those years ago, so this meeting spot had much more meaning for Nicholas than for Oliver.

"Sure, that sounds great," Nicholas started to type before erasing it. Then he typed "okay," only to delete that, too. In the end, he fired back a thumbs-up emoji, turned off his phone, and put it in his pocket while he watched Oliver's silhouette get smaller and smaller as Oliver walked farther away from Nicholas. Oliver had no idea that Nicholas had been watching him—had even seen him throw up. When Oliver was out of sight, Nicholas turned and headed back towards the abandoned warehouse park on the outskirts of town. He had to put his plans in motion to kill the next two people on his list.

Chapter Five

Oliver sent another text to Camilla—his third one this week, and still no response. He had just finished emptying her room, clearing it out for the next tenant, and was getting overly sentimental. He desperately wanted to talk with his dear friend. A lot of crazy stuff had gone down—he did not deny any of it. But they had gone through it together, so Oliver thought they would get through the recovery part together, too. When he put her on the plane six months ago, he thought Camilla would be gone for a week or two. He was not aware that she had no intention of returning. There was too much blood on the town for her to ever want to return, but she could not tell Oliver that then. She knew that news would crush him—to lose the one living person he needed most. She knew he could be that selfish. So, she did the next best thing she could think to do. She ghosted him. Periodically she would text back something short. A "Hi, all is good here—still need time," just to let Oliver know she was still alive and still his friend.

The rented house sat empty for most of the past six months. Oliver slept in his bed a few times, alone, and sometimes he fell asleep on the couch, but the house's silence was deafening. He felt violated whenever he entered the house—like someone was watching him. With no friends in the house to combat the uncomfortable silence with him, Oliver spent many nights sleeping at his mother's house or his family's cottage on Martha's Vineyard—isolated, trying to heal.

While on the island, Oliver met Harold, a young city boy from a middle-class family who was spending his first months out of college decompressing from all his studies. He had worked as a part-time beach lifeguard but was more focused on relaxing, having fun, and meeting boys. Oliver and Harold met at a farmer's market one Saturday morning. The air was crisp—salty, and the breeze made it clear that the end of summer was approaching. The grass was still wet with dew, wet enough to feel the moisture on his toes as Harold walked to the market in his flip-flops. Harold always wore flip-flops, board trunks, and a tank top—his island uniform. He had the body to pull of that look. The colors were bright and branded. He did not care. He liked wearing as little clothing as he could get away with—the tank top was often hanging from the back of his shorts.

Oliver had not noticed Harold the morning they met—he had not noticed many things around him since losing so many friends. He should have been more in tune with the world around him if only to keep himself safe, but he wore his depression like a heavy blanket, concealing him from the world. Harold noticed Oliver a few times prior but lacked the courage to say anything to Oliver, which he found odd because Harold never considered himself shy. He was typically quite boisterous.

That Saturday was different. The two were almost next to each other, examining peppers, corn, and other fresh vegetables grown on a farm from the island's west side. Oliver was there to pass the time and get some fresh air. Harold was there for his weekly supply of veggies. Harold was a vegetarian. He was highly focused on what he put into his body and how well he cared for it. That morning Harold took advantage of the moment he was standing next to Oliver. Harold commented on an oversized green pepper Oliver had been holding. Startled, Oliver looked to his right to find a handsome, shirtless, tanned, unshaven boy standing beside him. Harold's smile was intoxicating. He was bigger than Oliver—more muscles and only slightly taller. Oliver looked a little too long into Harold's eyes before finally speaking.

"I'm sorry," said Oliver. "I did not mean to stare, but what did you say?"

"No big deal, dude," Harold replied, trying to sound hip. "I was just saying that was a good-looking pepper you were studying so intensely."

Oliver handed the pepper to Harold and said, "oh, you can have it. I was just looking and got lost in thought."

"Care to share the thought over a coffee?" Harold asked without thinking. Oliver did not respond immediately. He looked at Harold and then back at the vegetable stand as if looking for something—maybe the answer. Eventually, he turned back to Harold, looking at his tanned physique. Oliver noticed a few pellets of sweat sliding down Harold's chest and wondered why this stranger was shopping shirtless.

"I am Oliver," he said, extending his hand to Harold.

"Nice to meet you, Oliver. My name is Harold, but my friends call me Harry."

The two shook hands, and Harold took the pepper out of Oliver's hand. Oliver agreed to grab a coffee that morning at the farmer's market. He thought it would be easier to get away from a quick coffee while he was at the farmer's market. Harold paid for his peppers, and the two walked a few stalls down to a stand selling organic coffee.

That was the first of many dates for them over the month they were both on the island. Harold invited Oliver to the carriage house he was renting so he could serve Oliver a home-cooked meal packed with ingredients from the farmers market. Oliver would return the gesture with a few overnight stays at his cottage but without the home cooking. Oliver preferred they dine out or order in and then end up naked for dessert. Oliver was not much of a cook.

The weeks they had together went by too quickly for Harold's liking. He had enjoyed Oliver's companionship and was beginning to fall in love with Oliver, which he had not expected. When the summer ended, Harold had to return to the city and start his post-college life, even though he was not entirely sure what he would do. He had completed some internships during his last couple of years at Boston College, but he remained lost when it came to what he wanted to do with his business degree.

Harold was the first person in his family to go to college, so he had very little guidance from his parents regarding the path he should take outside of getting a college education. His father ran a successful plumbing business, but that was not the line of work or the life Harold sought. While Boston was not that far away, Oliver felt confident that he and Harold had nothing more than an end-of-summer fling. He never expected to hear from or see Harold again and certainly had not fallen in love.

That adventure was two months ago.

Oliver put the last of the trash bags on the curb of the house he called home for the last couple of years—a place that was once filled with laughter and joy. His heart sank at the thought that this chapter of his life had ended. He was deep in thought about how to get Camilla to come back when his phone buzzed. It was Harold.

"Hey buddy," it displayed, followed by three dots.

"I am moving to the Big Apple next month. Want to grab lunch?"

Oliver smiled at the screen. He loved when people called New York City the Big Apple. It was a term that had been around for more than a century but was not used as much anymore, at least not by the locals. Oliver dropped the last bag on the curb and then started typing back.

"I am about an hour outside of New York City," Oliver typed back, trying to remember if he had lied to Harold and said he had lived in New York. Oliver was thinking about eventually moving to the big city, but he had not finalized any plans. Greenwich was stained with too much blood and death, and with his mother counting the days until her death, the idea of a fresh start in a big city—a place he could get lost in, totally lose himself, sounded perfect.

"Oh, I thought you were in the city. Where do you live? If you are on my way, it would be great to see you again," Harold typed back almost immediately. Oliver gave the message a heart emoji and then typed "Greenwich" in response.

"Right on my path from Boston. How does Sunday work for you?

Oliver looked at his typically empty calendar and noticed it filling up with activities—his mother next Friday and Nicholas on Tuesday. Sunday was blank. He typed back that Sunday would work for him and looked forward to seeing Harold, too.

Back in the house, Oliver was packing up the last of his clothes. He was planning on spending the next few days alone in the house and then a week with his mother, although she did not know it yet.

Chapter Six

On two different floors of an abandoned warehouse, Nicholas had been holding two innocent people captive in two separate rooms. He had not purchased this building, nor had he leased it. A lot of graffiti covered the building through layered murals spread across the decaying interior walls. Nicholas knew that he was not the only one who had frolicked in the building, so he had spent a lot of time scoping it out and determining which floors of which building he felt safest to paint his murals—in red.

In his ongoing mission to be with Oliver, Nicholas was still tying up loose ends—at least, they were loose ends in his mind. Nicholas was confident that anyone connected to any story that included him, Oliver, and any of Oliver's friends was an obstacle to his being with Oliver forever. With Howard and Reed most recently out of the picture permanently and Camila missing, Nicholas continued to find anyone he thought could be a wedge between him and Oliver, becoming a couple. Nicholas was increasingly obsessed with the idea of him and Oliver being together, so much so that he was beginning to connect people to his plan obscurely—people he would not typically consider a threat. Right now, that included Jennifer and Mike.

For all her good intentions, Jennifer was not a great police officer. Too many of her life decisions were led by her heart, which resulted in her getting drunk and giving away confidential police investigation information—on more than one occasion. This behavior worked in Oliver's favor when Camila reluctantly flirted with

Jennifer to get information on Reed's death to help Howard cope with his loss. Still, it did not work out so well for Jennifer. When she compiled a lineup of people, she thought might have been Nicholas; based on the information Camila, Howard, and Oliver gave her, the entire lineup was a bust. Her boss came down on Jennifer hard. Jennifer had been wasting taxpayers' dollars on a witch hunt, presumably because she had a crush on Camila. When Jennifer looked back at the lineup she presented to Camila, Howard, and Oliver so quickly, she realized just how bad the options of men were, and her boss knew it, too. Nicholas knew it, and he did not like how determined Jennifer was to find Nicholas if only to impress Camila.

Soon after the failed lineup, Jennifer went on administrative leave again. And the only way Jennifer could cope with these moments was to drown them in alcohol. Thankfully for Nicholas, Jennifer always chose a lesbian dive bar called Ginger's two towns east—mainly so no one who knew her would find her.

Nicholas had been watching Jennifer since the police showed up at the front door of his father's house—when he barely got away with his lie about having been in London. Believing he might have been so close to being caught, Nicholas stepped up his game of monitoring the police activity around any of his murders. That is how he discovered Jennifer. She was an easy target to follow, and before he knew it, Nicholas was posing as a taxi driver outside Ginger's, waiting to convince Jennifer she was too drunk to drive home.

Nicholas was slightly surprised at how easily Jennifer believed him and how much more cooperative she was in the back seat than Reed had been months earlier. Jennifer sat at the old wooden counter in the dimly lit bar drinking alone, waiting for a friend. She ended up drinking too much, flirting poorly, and leaving the bar alone, which worked well for Nicholas. As she sat in the back of the stolen taxicab, slumped back in the seat, mumbling nonsense, Nicholas convinced her to drink from one of the bottles of water he had placed in the backseat cup holders.

"The water will hydrate you," Nicholas said to Jennifer in a British accent as he cautiously drove the stolen car. He was not sure why he used an accent to disguise his voice. He had not disguised anything else about himself, mostly because he knew that Jennifer would not escape him. He had nothing to hide from her now.

Jennifer removed the cap from one of the water bottles and guzzled the entire bottle, oblivious that she was ingesting a large amount of GHB. Before they made it through the neighboring towns, Jennifer passed out in the backseat, and Nicholas was one step closer to ending another life. A good detective would have realized she did not break the seal when opening the bottle, but this was one more example of why Jennifer was not a good detective.

That was a few days ago.

Since that night, Jennifer has hung from a meat hook in the abandoned warehouse. Her head was wrapped in silver ducted tape, covering her eyes and mouth, while her wrists were taped together and handcuffed. The handcuffs hung over a large, rusted hook suspended from the ceiling. Her entire body was upright, her arms stretched over her head, and she was suspended just high enough for her feet to be flat on the floor. Her ears wore headphones that were also duct taped to her. As Jennifer stood with her arms over her head, she could see nothing, hear nothing, and say nothing. Her arms grew sore from being up over her head, and she was weak from not eating. Thanks to the hook, her knees would buckle, but she could not fall to the ground. On the second day, she shat in her pants—the smell was foul enough to make anyone gag, but she couldn't with her mouth shut. The front of her pants was soaked with urine—all that alcohol finally making its way out.

On the third day, with her body completely exhausted, too weak to even struggle anymore, Nicholas took the handheld sickle he found on the warehouse floor and swung at Jennifer's stomach, almost slicing her thin, frail body in half. Jennifer tried again to scream, but she had no energy, and even if she had, the tape would have kept her voice trapped. The tears in her eyes rolled out and stuck to the tape, never really escaping. The amount of water backing up into her eye sockets hurt. There was nothing she could do; nowhere for her to go. Nicholas watched Jennifer bleed out. The sickle was lodged in her body, and Nicholas left it there. It was by luck that he found it on the warehouse floor. It had a broken handle and a rusty blade, crusty with reddish-brown metal flakes bubbling all over it. Nicholas believed that when the police would eventually find her, they would find someone else's fingerprints; many other prints blurred together on what remained of the handle. He knew to wear gloves and did not want Jennifer's blood staining him.

Jennifer bled out. Her urine and shit-stained pants were painted brown in the back and red in the front. Her bare feet stuck to the warehouse floor, glued in place with the thick puddle of red liquid. Nicholas left Jennifer for dead. His thrill was in the kill, not the cleanup.

Chapter Seven

One floor up, almost directly above Jennifer, hung another body, this time from his ankles. From the moment Nicholas noticed Mike outside of Hunter's apartment the day after Nicholas poisoned Hunter, he knew that Mike would be a problem. Nicholas saw Mike talking with the other residents and the police. While Nicholas could not hear the conversations, he felt confident that Mike was a third party helping Camila, Oliver, and Howard connect the dots between Nicholas and Hunter. In a way, he was. When Nicholas saw how easily Mike exchanged numbers with one of the police officers, he knew then that Mike had to be on his kill list. After that day, Nicholas spent many weeks stalking Mike.

One week ago, Nicholas followed Mike into New York City. Keeping his distance, Nicholas got on the same train as Mike and then switched to the subway once in the city. The two got off at the Washington Street station and walked a few blocks to a gay club called The Monster. As Nicholas approached the club, he smiled at the name of the club. He considered himself a monster sometimes, and his father, Adam, was often referred to as one in the articles Nicholas read about Adam.

Nicholas watched Mike drink and dance alone in the club in a sea of half-naked men. No one was alone, though. It was a gay club, after all. Nicholas knew he was there to bring Mike home, but as he stood in a dark corner watching Mike and the other men, he could not stop staring at all the beautiful bodies. It had been some time since he had sex—real, passionate sex. Thoughts of his escapades in the cemetery in London filled his head, and excitement started to tighten his pants. He could have taken any man in the bar—he knew that. Nicholas was that confident with himself—in himself. He thought about taking one of the guys closest to him into the bathroom and ravaging him, but he could not risk losing sight of Mike. Tonight was a work night; he convinced himself. He could come back any other night to play.

After a few hours of watching Mike get quite drunk, Nicholas stepped out of the darkness and purposely bumped into Mike, spilling his drink down his naked, hairy chest. It felt good to Mike—cooling him down as it mixed with all the sweat and heat that had matted his hair. Nicholas apologized and bought Mike a replacement drink which he spiked. Mike appreciated the drink but was more interested in putting his hands all over Nicholas. Nicholas had no interest in having sex with Mike, but he would not let Mike know that, so he played along. The two danced seductively close to one another. Mike tried to get Nicholas to remove his shirt, but Nicholas refused. He was performing another outstanding performance so that Mike would go home with him.

After more drinking and dancing, Nicholas convinced Mike to leave with the promise of sex. Mike jumped at the idea that he and Nicholas would get naked together, even if he felt that he was too drunk to get hard. The outside air was cool, almost sobering to Mike, but not entirely. The two caught a cab to the train station and boarded a train back to Greenwich. Mike was excitedly drunk because he was going home with someone from the club who also lived in the suburbs. That rarely happened to him in the past. Typically, Mike would end up waking up in some messy bedroom of some dumpy apartment on the fifth floor of a walk-up. He would spend too much time separating his clothes from piles of others, often leaving in someone else's underwear, then strutting his walk of shame through the city and then the train and the burbs, too. Each time he did, and it was often, Mike told himself it was the last time. With Nicholas, it finally would be.

The train car was empty except for the two men giving Mike the green light to get handsy again with Nicholas. He sloppily kissed Nicholas on the mouth, face, and ear—anyplace he could land his drunken lips while his hands groped Nicholas' crotch. Nicholas got aroused a little, which excited Mike even more. Those moments were brief as Nicholas repeatedly pushed Mike off him and said they should wait until they arrived at his apartment. Mike gave Nicholas a frowning face which Nicholas changed with a whisper of lies about what he would do with Mike once they were naked at Nicholas' apartment.

"Here, drink this," Nicholas said to Mike, pulling a water bottle out of his backpack. "You want to be more alert when we get naked."

Mike guzzled the bottle of water at the empty promise.

At the station, Nicholas broke into the first car he found. Once in the vehicle, Nicholas pulled another bottle out of his backpack and offered Mike a second GHB-laced treat. Dehydrated, Mike opened and drank the second almost as quickly as the first. Before the two men reached the warehouse, Mike passed out in the passenger seat.

Nicholas drove the car right into the warehouse's first floor, so it was not visible from the outside. He didn't want anyone to know that there was activity in what was supposed to be an abandoned property. Once inside, Nicholas pulled Mike's limp body out of the car and carried him up several stairs. Mike was heavier than Nicholas had anticipated. On the dark third floor, Nicholas carried Mike across the room to where a table sat with some supplies and laid Mike on the table. Mike looked like he was ready for surgery.

Nicholas grabbed a pair of heavy-duty scissors and cut off Mike's shirt and pants, exposing his naked body to the cold air. Nicholas was not surprised that Mike was commando. He removed Mike's shoes and socks and stuffed all the clothing into a paper bag. Looking at the completely naked body, Nicholas admired Mike's skin—his muscle tone. Mike was not fat, but he was far less muscular than he looked when he was all sweaty and shirtless in the club.

With the same roll of duct tape he would use on Jennifer days later, Nicholas bound Mike's hands together and sealed his mouth with the tape but did not cover his eyes or ears. Then Nicholas put Mike's feet into a wooden shackle device hooked to two long chains. Once Mike's feet were securely in place, Nicholas walked across the room and pulled on the far end of the chains. Mike's body slid across the table as he did, rising into the air. Within minutes Mike was hanging upside down. His head was about three feet from the dirty warehouse floor. As Nicholas secured the chains, Mike's limp body swung, and he hit his head on the side of the table, slightly jarring him awake.

It was dark, so Mike could not see much, but he could feel the tape around his hands and sensed that he was hanging upside down. The air was cold, and he could feel that he was naked, but he could not see much around him to gauge where he might be or who he might be with if anyone. In a moment of panic, Mike started to pee. It sprayed out in front of him, running down his chest and across his face, then splattering the floor around his head. He could not understand what was happening, and then he saw Nicholas step into what little light was in the room. When Nicholas appeared upside down to Mike, he immediately recognized Nicholas from the club, from getting on the train with him. He tried screaming, but his voice was muffled.

"Don't scream," Nicholas said calmly. "There is no need to panic or thrash. You are tied up tightly and hanging upside down in an abandoned warehouse. No one will bother us here. It is just you and me now."

Nicholas touched Mike's leg then and ran his finger toward Mike's crotch. Along the way, he tickled the ball sack hanging upside down and tugged on the limp dick, naked and exposed. Nicholas could feel the stumble of the freshly shaven area and wondered how often Mike manscaped. Then Nicholas pushed Mike, so his whole body swung away and back towards Nicholas a few times like a human pendulum. Mike wiggled his body, thinking he might be able to loosen what held him suspended in the air. He could not.

"Stop struggling,' Nicholas said. You will only make it worse. Nicholas was already tired of Mike and ready to end his life.

As Mike's body swung backward and forward, Nicholas set up a battery-operated circular saw he had fastened to a stand. The blade sat at the same height as Mike's neck. Mike could not clearly distinguish what Nicholas was doing but could see something shiny. Nicholas moved out of the way, and then Mike's body swung over and barely bumped into the saw. The motionless blade nicked Mike's neck. He let out a loud mumble of pain through the tape. Seconds later, a few red dots appeared on his neck and started getting more prominent as the blood escaped. Nicholas smiled.

Nicholas did not say anything else. He flicked a switch on the saw, and the quiet hum of the electric motor filled the otherwise silent air. The blade was spinning quickly, silently. As Mike's body swung toward the blade, Mike could see it as light reflected off the metal. The first few times, his body swayed in a direction that avoided the blade, but then the blade contacted Mike's skin with the next swing toward it. The blade sliced a clean cut into Mike's neck. It was deep enough that more blood started spewing out and up his neck toward his face. Nicholas stood out of blood splatter range, watching his human pendulum slowly open. He hoped the blade would do enough damage to kill Mike before the batteries died and the motor stopped.

While Nicholas packed up anything that might have his fingerprints on it, he looked over to see if the blade was doing more damage to Mike. It nicked Mike's neck a couple more times. More and more blood spilled onto the warehouse floor. As Nicholas prepared to leave, he approached Mike and punched him in the chest as hard as possible. The contact made a loud bang that echoed across the empty space. Mike's body swung far from the blade and back towards it much faster than Nicholas had expected. At that speed, the blade got lodged into Mike's neck, striking his neck bone. The blade stopped spinning, but the machine was still whizzing. Blood was spraying around the room like a Jackson Pollack painting in the making. Nicholas laughed.

Mike screamed, but again the tape trapped it in as he wiggled to escape the blade.

"You are going to make it worse if you keep fighting it," Nicholas said to Mike as he watched Mike free himself from the blade, only to swing away from it and back towards it with even more speed. This time the blade made direct contact with Mike's forehead, getting stuck in his skull for a few minutes before grinding through the bone and puncturing his brain.

Brain and blood escaped onto the floor, and Mike's body stopped struggling; he stopped screaming. Nicholas watched Mike's limp body for a few minutes longer as the area was painted red. When he felt confident that Mike was dead, Nicholas walked away, leaving Mike's body exposed to decompose. He left the blood-covered blade in Mike's head. Nicholas knew that no one would find a decent print on it.

With Mike and Jennifer out of the way, Nicholas finally believed that he could now spend the rest of his life with Oliver without any more distractions. As he drove away from the warehouse, all he could think about was holding Oliver. Nicholas knew he had these feelings over and over. He knew that each time he thought he could stop killing people to be with Oliver; finally, more people would come into focus, and the idea of being with Oliver would get clouded. This time will be different, he told himself.

Chapter Eight

"Olly," Harold yelled as he stood, waving his arm so Oliver would see him in the back corner of the coffee shop. Oliver preferred to be called Oliver, but Harold was big into 'y' names. He liked Harry, even though Oliver continued to call him Harold.

Oliver maneuvered through the coffee shop privately, thankful that most of the younger patrons were wearing headphones and were clueless about the production Harold made to get Oliver's attention. The coffee shop was not that big, and Oliver had visited it hundreds of times, so he knew that Harold would not be somewhere he could not be seen. Once Oliver reached the table, the two hugged.

"Man, you look fantastic," Harold sang to Oliver, admiring what Oliver thought was a tired body, but he accepted the compliment with a simple 'thank you.'

While it had been less than a year since Oliver had come to terms with his sexuality—being gay, he was still quite reserved in public spaces. On the other hand, Harold had come into his sexuality in high school and spent most of his college years exploring the gay underworld of Boston and other bigger cities around New England. As a graduate now, Harold was a confident, out, and proud gay man. His confidence was often mistaken for arrogance.

Much of their conversation involved Harold bringing Oliver up to speed on his life. Oliver shared little about his and almost nothing about the last year's chaos. On the island and in the coffee shop, Oliver enjoyed conversations that did not revolve around the deaths and the conspiracy theories he and his friends spun up. Oliver had been trying to move on. Harold was still clueless about the death and destruction that wove through Oliver's life, and Oliver was hopeful that he would not have to share that part of his life with anyone ever again.

Harold told Oliver about his plan to take on New York. He had accepted a job at a hedge fund in Manhattan and was looking forward to living the big city life. Oliver learned that Harold would be renting a tiny apartment in Greenwich Village with two other people Harold had not met yet. All three were starting at the same hedge fund, and the apartment was in a company-owned building.

"We will each have private rooms, of course, and so I am hoping you will come to visit," Harold said to Oliver as he blew on his hot coffee before taking a sip. "I have missed you, missed our time together. We had a lot of fun, at least I did, this past summer, and I would like to see more of you, Oliver McPherson."

"I did, too," Oliver replied. "I had a good time. You were the distraction I needed that became something more than I expected."

"Thank you, I think," Harold said with a confused look.

Oliver smiled back and put Harold at ease with a pat on the knee under the table. Oliver had made that same move many times over the summer, a lovely touch to say that he was happy to be with Harold.

"You know," continued Oliver. "New York could be fun. I have not been there in a while, which is sad, considering it's in earshot from here. My lease just expired. I am spending a little time with my mom for the next week or so. She is ill, and I am unsure how long she has left in this life. But then, after that, the world is my canvas. I am ready for a fresh start somewhere different."

Harold smiled at the idea of Oliver joining him in New York or at least being in the same city for a change. He knew their time together over the summer was not a serious commitment; they were not boyfriends. But at the same time, he was looking forward to an opportunity to spend more time with Oliver and maybe become something more than just friends. Maybe actually becoming boyfriends.

"Well," Harold said with some excitement in his voice. "I would be super excited if you visited or even moved to the big city. I really do; I did enjoy spending time with you this summer. I like you, Olly, and I would like to continue to hang out and see where things go beyond a summer fling.

"And you can stay with me to start; get your bearings and figure out where you want to live and what you want to do."

Oliver smiled, unsure how to respond to Harold's over-excitement without sounding like a complete jerk. "Sounds like fun," was the best he could force out.

For all the time Harold and Oliver spent together on Martha's Vineyard, Oliver never told Harold about his inherited wealth. Oliver was still uncomfortable with that amount of his own money and certainly was not one to go around flashing it. He grew up wealthy, but that was his parents' money. This newfound wealth was all his. For all that Oliver had endured the past 18 months and for all his newfound fortune, Oliver did his best to remain himself, the demure but confidently quiet kid.

Oliver agreed that he would stay in touch with Harold. He would tell Harold when he had wrapped things up in Greenwich and was ready to head to New York City. And with that cheerful note, they both stood and hugged. Harold took the initiative and kissed

Oliver on the cheek, but Oliver did not reciprocate. They both walked out of the coffee shop, hugged again, and turned to walk away in opposite directions. Harold was almost skipping away, a giddy schoolboy thrilled at the thought that his crush might still be interested in dating him. Oliver watched Harold for a moment before finally turning around and walking towards the parked car he had ordered from his phone while listening to Harold say his final goodbyes.

Oliver and Harold were clueless about Nicholas sitting on a bench across the street from the coffee shop. The same bench he warmed many times over the years while watching Oliver.

Chapter Nine

For a man who usually oozed confidence and stayed in control of every situation, Nicholas was perplexed at the feelings that swirled in his head and heart as he sat on the bench outside the coffee shop, waiting for Oliver to arrive. His hands were moist, and his heart was racing. He could almost taste his heartbeat in his throat. He had arrived a few minutes early, as he did with everything in his life, and while he was surprised Oliver was not early, too, he was secretly glad that he was not. Nicholas needed a few minutes to compose himself before his brother arrived.

"I am SO sorry," Oliver said to Nicholas, reaching out his hand as he crossed the sidewalk and walked toward the bench. Oliver was a few minutes late as he stepped out of the taxi.

"It's all good, man," Nicholas said, trying to sound calm and unfazed at the tardiness of the man he was hoping to spend the rest of his life loving.

"Do you mind if we skip the coffee," Nicholas asked. "I am quite hungry," he said, pointing to the sandwich shop across the street.

Oliver admitted he could go for more than a coffee and pastry, so the two boys crossed the street, playing Frogger with the traffic.

Sitting at a table, silently reading menus with too many choices, Nicholas was the first to speak. Not knowing where to start the conversation, he apologized to Oliver for never getting the chance to meet Peter, as if Nicholas was to blame. It took Nicholas many years to come to terms with his father having a child with another woman and getting over hating the unknown child. But, as he got older, Nicholas realized that he needed to put that petty behavior aside if he was ever going to get close to Oliver.

"It is weird," Oliver responded. "My mother never mentioned Peter once, at least not until he died. My dad, I mean, my paternal father, died years ago, so my mother had many opportunities to tell me about Peter and you. But she never did.

"So, I guess you don't need to apologize. It would have been one thing if I knew he existed but could not meet him, but since I never knew of him, it seems okay. Does that make sense?"

"Sure, it does," Nicholas replied. "Without being intrusive and inappropriate, I hope Peter left you something in his Will." Nicholas already knew the answer.

"Yeah, well, that was one of the odd parts to all of it," Oliver continued. "He did. He left me too much, I think. Not sure if it was guilt-driven or not."

"Peter did quite well for himself, and he always had my mother's inheritance in reserve, so we were never hurting for money. And he is no more my father than I am your brother, so if we all scored, it's all good, right?" Nicholas continued, almost letting out a nervous laugh, but held it back.

"No more, your father?" Oliver asked with a confused look.

"My mother was a victim of rape, and I am the product of that violent experience," Nicholas shared, not thinking he would get this deep into his past on their first date. "According to Peter, my mother was one of those die-hard pro-life people, even back then, and could not imagine terminating my life just because some crazy asshole violated her personal space.

"Anyway, I guess my mother and Peter had marital issues, and it sounds like your parents did too since your mom and Peter hooked up and gave life to you. Peter told me that you and I were born on the same day, in the same hospital. Can you imagine how awkward that must have been... for everyone?"

They both chuckled as the absurdity of the story was coming together. Here they were, two young men, brought together by the strangest series of events... one learning new information about his past while the other painted the picture he wanted Oliver to see.

"Anyway, so the good news is that while we shared a dad, you and I are not blood-related in any way, which is good," Nicholas said. "Because I think you are hella cute."

Oliver blushed. He could not remember the last time he blushed. He had spent the previous couple of years sleeping his way through his pain and struggling to understand what love was or could be that he never took the time to blush. The closest he came to having feelings for anyone was with Eric. Harold was just a fling as far as Oliver had been concerned.

"Oh, man. I am so sorry," Nicholas apologized. "That was way out of line. I didn't mean it. Well, I did mean it, but I did not mean to say it now, here, with ..."

"It's okay," Oliver interrupted. "I've had a rough 18 months, so hearing sweet words for a change is nice. And, if I am being honest, you're kind of hot yourself."

Nicholas smiled in a way that said, 'yeah, I know,' and reached out to grab Oliver's hand but was interrupted by the waitress returning to take their order.

With their orders in, Nicholas reached back out to grab Oliver's hand. He had felt it before when he pretended to be Eric, so he was not surprised by how smooth it felt. He missed that feeling, missed touching Oliver. He was beginning to think that he would finally be able to be himself with Oliver.

"You've got soft skin," Nicholas said as he rubbed his fingers over Oliver's hand. "It's like a baby's bottom." He laughed as he spoke, and Oliver joined in the laughter, trying to hide his blushing yet again.

"Is it weird that I want to get out of here right now and go to your place and get naked?" Oliver asked Nicholas, almost regretting the words as they ejaculated out of his mouth. "Never mind. That was super weird. We are brothers, or well, kind of, but not really, but you are hot, and as I said, it has been quite the year. I could do with a good fuck."

Oliver was not being totally honest with Nicholas. He had enjoyed a month of nakedness with Harold recently. Then there was Hunter last year, but that was before the shit storm that became his life. As he thought about how much sex he had engaged in over the previous year and how many boys he had kissed, Oliver remembered that he and Howard never actually had sex. Even more surprisingly, he and Eric never had sex. There was a lot of kissing and oral excitement with both guys, but never any naked, all-night, sweaty sessions that would make his mother blush.

"I do not think it is weird at all," Nicholas said calmly, trying to hide the excitement that was bubbling up inside his pants. "But let's eat first. Something tells me we are going to need our energy."

As their food arrived, the two sat smiling, excited about the dessert they would share later. Minutes after they dove into their meal, they were interrupted by the buzzing of Oliver's phone. He pulled the phone out of his pocket and saw that the caller was his mother's nurse.

"Sorry, but I have to take this," Oliver said as he excused himself from the table. Nicholas watched Oliver walk out the door and stop just on the other side of the window from where Nicholas sat alone again. Nicholas watched Oliver's body shake as he fell into the bench crying before he hung up the phone. It was the same bench Nicholas often sat on, watching Oliver in the coffee shop across the street.

Nicholas went out to join Oliver on the bench; to find out what had happened. He sat beside Oliver and put his arm around him, pulling Oliver into his chest. He had no clue about who was on the other end of the phone or what the conversation could have been about to upset Oliver, which Nicholas found discomforting since he had spent years working to know everything about Oliver. Nicholas held Oliver, trying to comfort him.

"I've got to go," Oliver spat out through tears as he pulled away from Nicholas and wiped his face on his shirt sleeve. "My mother just passed away. I am sorry, but I need to go. I will call you later."

Nicholas sat alone on the bench again. Now neither of them had any living parents, freeing Nicholas to pursue this relationship even more. He was sad that he would not get dessert that afternoon, but he knew their time would come. His thoughts were interrupted by the waitress tapping on the window, indicating that Nicholas needed to return and pay the bill. She had seen Oliver go out and Nicholas follow, so she took the initiative and packed the sandwiches and handed a "to go" bag to Nicholas as he paid the bill in cash.

Chapter Ten

A week had passed before Nicholas heard anything from Oliver, and even then, it was a short text saying that he had finished all the funeral arrangements, of which there were little. Oliver's mother was the last living child in her family. While she had a handful of friends in her later years, she had no intention of having them dress in black and mourn her, so her instructions were simple; cremate her body and spread her ashes along the beach on Martha's Vineyard near their family cottage.

Oliver finally had his mother's ashes and was packing to go to the cottage when his phone rang. The number appeared as "unknown," so Oliver ignored it. After a few rings, the phone stopped for a few seconds and started ringing again with another "unknown" displayed on the screen. Oliver was not in the mood for any sales calls, so he ignored the ringing.

Nicholas was surprised that Oliver was not picking up the phone. It took a few rings to realize that he was using his burner phone, not the phone he had set up to communicate with Oliver. Instead of making a third attempt to reach Oliver, Nicholas decided to go to Oliver's mother's house.

Once he was packed and had his suitcase by the front door, Oliver sat in the living room, listening to the silence of the empty house. He looked at all the furniture, artwork, and other collectibles his mother had around the room and suddenly felt the weight of her death. He was alone. The air felt heavy like he was being crushed by an invisible force squeezing the tears out of him as he let the wetness run down his face. He screamed as loud as he could, pushing all the pain out.

After giving in to his new reality, Oliver wiped his arms across his face to dry the remaining tears. He felt he could sit in his mother's empty house forever, but he knew that would not help him heal or move on. He was hopeful that his visit to Martha's Vineyard would provide the comfort he needed now, more than ever. With this new felt wind of determination, Oliver stood up and headed for the front door. He opened the door and saw Nicholas standing alone at the end of the walkway, holding a bouquet. Oliver grabbed his suitcase, and the urn then closed the door behind him and walked towards Nicholas, trying hard not to drop the urn.

"I am so sorry," Oliver said before reaching Nicholas. "It has been a crazy week, but it's almost over." He held up the urn. "Mother, meet Nicholas, and Nicholas, meet my mother."

"Dude, it is okay," Nicholas replied with a laugh, raising the flowers to Oliver. "These are for you."

Oliver shrugged his shoulders in thanks and asked Nicholas to walk towards the driveway where Oliver's mother's car sat waiting with its top down. Oliver put the urn and his luggage in the trunk, safely securing the urn so as not to send ashes everywhere; then, he turned and finally accepted the flowers from Nicholas. The bouquet was an extensive collection of Gerber daisies wrapped in a white paper, making the orange pedals shine. Oliver leaned over the back of the car and placed the bouquet on the back seat. When he turned around, Nicholas was within a few inches of him; he reached out and hugged Oliver. Oliver reciprocated, and the two stood there locked in each other's arms for longer than most people would embrace, but Oliver liked it. He needed it. Nicholas loved it.

"I am talking my mother's ashes to Martha's Vineyard. She wants them spread across the beach behind our cottage. I am not sure that is even legal, but who cares.

"I am sorry that I have not called you back. I was enjoying our lunch together. Leave it to my mother to interrupt a date," Oliver continued.

"Oh, so it was a date, was it?" Nicholas asked with a smirk on his face.

"You know what I mean," Oliver shot back with laughter as he delicately slugged Nicholas in the shoulder. "What are you up to?"

"Nothing. I just wanted to bring you some flowers and let you know that I was thinking of you," Nicholas said. "I know how hard it can be to lose a parent." Oliver knew that both of Nicholas' parents were dead, but he had no clue that Nicholas killed his paternal father decades after he killed his mother. Nicholas would do everything he could to keep those secrets to himself.

"I know this might sound crazy, but would you want to come to Martha's Vineyard with me?" Oliver asked, almost regretting the words as they came out of his mouth. "I mean if you want and have the time. I am planning on staying out there for a week." Oliver was torn as he let all those words linger in the air. Part of him wanted Nicholas to come so he could get to know him better, and part of him wanted to enjoy the week alone.

"I'd love to," said Nicholas, "but I have some business I must attend to over the next few days. Can I take a rain check? I'd love to see the cottage sometime." Oliver had no idea that Nicholas had seen the cottage often and had been inside.

Oliver agreed and hugged Nicholas again before getting into the car and pulling out of the driveway. As Nicholas watched the car pull away, he hated himself for not kissing Oliver goodbye but knew there would be plenty of opportunity for kissing soon. Besides, he did have some unfinished business. He figured that the bodies of Mike and Jennifer had hung out to dry long enough. He knew they would not be found for weeks or months if he left them hanging, but he knew he needed to get rid of the bodies.

Chapter Eleven

Nicholas was confident that he could have disposed of both Mike and Jennifer and made it to New York to start looking for Harold by the time Oliver arrived on the island. He needed to start tracking Harold to better assess how much of a threat Harold would be to him. From where he stood, watching Harold and Oliver interact on Martha's Vineyard over the summer, it was clear to Nicholas that Harold was keen on dating Oliver, and Harold was one more obstacle Nicholas did not need. Nicholas remained convinced that anyone who befriended Oliver would be a potential threat to his plan of being with Oliver forever. Such a plan would sound crazy to anyone hearing it, but his plan made total sense to Nicholas. He believed that if he could have Oliver all to himself, they could live a long, happy life together.

Nicholas approached the warehouse to find flashing blue and red lights bouncing off the building walls. He knew that this would mean postponing his trip to New York and ultimately postponing killing Harold. He was concerned that the bodies he believed were safely isolated were now the center of a police investigation—something Nicholas had been avoiding since the death of Elizabeth all those years ago.

Nicholas knew he would have some explaining to do if the police were to see him at the warehouse, but he needed to know if they found the bodies of Mike and Jennifer or if they were at the warehouse park for a completely unrelated matter. Nicholas turned the car around and parked it a few blocks away from the complex and off the main road. Then he walked the short hike back towards the warehouse, where he left Mike and Jennifer. The abandoned property included several buildings. Nicholas never counted them all, and there was no guarantee that the police were in the building where Nicholas left Mike and Jennifer, but with the lights bouncing off so many buildings, it was hard to tell without getting very close.

Nicholas slipped behind one building and, without being seen, ducked into the building where he had left Mike and Jennifer. As he walked up the stairs to the third floor where he had left Mike, he kept ducking down each time light filled the broken windows of the building. He had been close to the police before— many times at murder scenes of his own doing, but in each case, he could blend in and watch as the police investigated without them knowing their killer was watching. He felt that it would be difficult to pretend to be a bystander tonight, given the deserted surroundings.

When he was safely on the third floor and saw Mike's lifeless body, Nicholas diverted his attention to the neighboring building. He needed to know if the police were investigating something else or if they were going building by building looking for something or someone. That is when he saw him—a silhouette of a figure in the next building looking back at Nicholas, or at least looking in his direction. What Nicholas did not know was that the figure was trying to determine if Nicholas or the figure standing by the window one floor above Nicholas was the friend he was supposed to meet that night. The person in the other building stood still, almost lifeless, so Nicholas knew it was not a police officer. They were frantically moving around on the ground. Soon Nicholas could see that the police had lit up the first floor of the neighboring building, and they were working their way up, floor by floor. The silhouette would be cornered soon. Nicholas knew that if he tried to warn the figure, the police would see him and investigate the building where Jennifer and Mike were still publicly rotting.

As the second floor of the neighboring building lit up with police lights, Nicholas watched the figure finally move. They were gone almost instantly. A few minutes later, the figure appeared two floors above. As the police lit up the third floor of the neighboring building, Nicholas heard the explosion; he felt it. All the buildings shook. Nicholas held on to the wall to keep from falling over. When the dust settled a little, Nicholas could see that the entire second floor of the neighboring building was on fire. He could hear police crying out in pain.

He knew that this would draw more people to the complex, and he needed to get out before getting caught. But Nicholas needed to understand who the silhouette was, and why they appeared to be watching him. When Nicholas scanned the building for the person after the explosion, he could see that the person was running on the roof. Then with one giant leap, the figure jumped off the top of the warehouse and caught a wire that he used to silently glide down to the ground to a corner where the police had not yet investigated. Nicholas watched the figure reach the ground, stop, and look back up in Nicholas' direction, confirming Nicholas' concern that this person was watching him. The figure waved and then was gone. Again, Nicholas had no idea that this person was waving to a stranger one floor above Nicholas. This was the closest he and Juan Diego had been in a long time.

Nicholas took that as a sign and started running through the warehouse, past Mike, and down the stairs. He was determined to catch the person and discover who and why they were watching him.

Nicholas had no idea if this mystery person knew or had been following him. He did not like the coincidence of them lurking in abandoned warehouses, especially when the police were present. Nicholas believed that the mystery figure caused the explosion, whether planned or done out of panic, which only intrigued Nicholas even more.

As Nicholas moved down the stairs, Juan Diego did the same thing, staying one floor above Nicholas. Juan Diego stopped to admire the decomposing body of Mike. He was admiring Nicholas' work of art and fondly remembered the time years ago when they murdered together. Juan Diego knew he needed to go find his friend, the one who Nicholas' assumed was watching him, but Juan Diego was more interested in finding anything around Mike that wore an odor of Nicholas.

Once outside, it took Nicholas a minute to notice that his mystery friend was waiting for him. This figure was watching from the edge of the property, away from the buildings, still thinking he was looking at Juan Diego, not Nicholas. They could hear sirens getting louder, and they both knew that the entire complex was about to be swarming with more police and many fire trucks and ambulances. Nicholas then started running towards the figure, who stood still, almost waiting for Nicholas to reach him, but then in a blink of an eye, he was gone again. Nicholas stopped running. He looked all around but could no longer see the figure.

Frustrated and concerned that he might come face to face with the police, Nicholas ran into the brush and out of sight of anyone as he tried to understand what had just happened. He was unhappy that he got so close to the stranger only to lose them. Nicholas had too much to do and was unprepared for this distraction. He was trying to clean up one mess and did not have the time for another when all he wanted was to focus all his attention on Oliver. Frustrated and defeated, Nicholas headed back toward his car, but it was gone.

Through the brush, Nicholas watched more police cars and fire trucks pass him as they headed to the burning warehouse. Nicholas knew that Jennifer and Mike's bodies would be discovered now. He was furious because he did not necessarily want them found in their current positions. He had not killed other humans like he killed Mike and Jennifer—not since his murderous days with Juan Diego. He knew that when the police found the two bodies, the story would be all over the news, and the town would know a sadistic killer was on the loose—yet another distraction he did not need.

Nicholas decided that he could not focus on that problem right now. He needed to find the person who saw him in the warehouse—who possibly knew that Nicholas killed Mike and Jennifer. Nicholas needed to find this person. He believed that they either knew him or knew enough about him to have caused the chaos at the warehouses as if to point the police right at Nicholas. He pulled his phone out of his pocket. It was the same one he used to text with Oliver and opened an app that, after a few seconds, showed precisely where the car was. It was in motion, but Nicholas knew he would eventually catch up to it. Being on foot now would slow him down, but he would reach the car and hopefully find his mystery fan with it.

Two hours later, Nicholas finally reached the car—it was a car he had stolen before it was stolen from him. Nicholas found it sitting abandoned in the middle of a strip mall parking lot just off the highway. It was late now—the sun had long since gone to bed, and most of the dimly-lit parking lot sat silent. Most of the mall tenants and guests had gone home for the night. The only activity was in front of the movie theatre and neighboring arcade, filled with teens trying desperately to act like adults. Nicholas could see they were failing at both as the mall security car patrolled the parking lot. The security guards inside were pretending to uphold the law as underaged boys who looked like men drank beers out of paper bags, almost taunting the guards to stop them.

Nicholas knew that most of the towns' malls just off the highway were home to poverty-stricken families. He avoided these parts except for when he was desperate to kill. Most of the people Nicholas encountered in these parts of the state could go missing for days before anyone would miss them or even care. The opioid crisis was rampant, and if young people were not pregnant or drunk, they were undoubtedly strung out on some cocktail they bought behind a convenience store, convinced they were buying some premium product at bargain basement prices. Nicholas had purchased a few drugs in similar surroundings many times before, never for himself.

As Nicholas scoped out the parking lot, looking for anyone who might be out of place, he realized that, in a way, everyone here looked out of place. The one-screen cinema had three shows daily and had been screening the same movie for almost a decade — Porky's II. The arcade was a small retail space next to the cinema with a few dozen video games made popular by a different generation and just now returning to fashion. They were machines that took actual quarters, not tokens or cards, like most modern arcades. Nicholas approached the car slowly in case his new friend was hiding inside. When he got to the driver's window, Nicholas could see wires dangling under the steering wheel — a mess he had created, not his fan. Nicholas opened the driver's door and was attacked by an overwhelming wave of mint and rosemary. He knew his fan was swimming in Axe body spray—just the clue he needed to hunt him down.

Nicholas left the car and headed for the cinema and arcade, hopeful that the person who stole the vehicle, who had been watching him at the warehouse—who might have known what Nicholas did, was stupid enough to be still nearby. There was the chance that this person had convinced themselves that Nicholas would not find them, so they hung around to play video games or get drunk with the locals who might be their friends. But the more Nicholas thought about if he had been the one in the shadows—the one to be lurking, he would still be watching, waiting to strike.

As Nicholas opened the door to the arcade, he was once again overwhelmed by the potent smell of body odor hiding behind mint and rosemary. The combination of teen body odor and various scents of body spray and cologne attempting to cover the body odor was almost too much for Nicholas. The stench was so pungent that it hurt his eyes and his nostrils. After walking around the small arcade for a few minutes, Nicholas became numb to the smell and realized it would be hard to identify the car thief in the sea of odors. He made a second loop around the games, decided he would not find what or who he was looking for inside, and headed back for the door. As he did, Nicholas noticed a man—more of an old boy standing near the door, looking right at him.

The two stared intently at each other, neither prepared to look away. Nicholas held the boy's stare as he passed him and walked out of the arcade. He knew this boy was the person he had been chasing. Nicholas did not expect his fan to be Harold, or at least

Harold's doppelgänger. He walked out the door and headed straight towards the car without looking back. He was hopeful that if Harold were the person that he had been chasing, then Harold would also come out of the arcade and follow Nicholas to the car. When Nicholas got to his car, he turned around and leaned against the passenger door, facing the arcade. He could see the boy only a few steps behind him, moving towards him quickly.

"What were you doing at the warehouse," the boy asked, still many feet away from Nicholas. At that moment, Nicholas believed that there was a chance that Harold had not been following him, but the two just happened to be at the same place at the same time. But he was not about to show all his cards just yet.

"I could ask you the same question," Nicholas responded.

"I was just having a little fun," the boy chuckled.

"By blowing up a warehouse?" Nicholas asked, trying not to sound like the adult in the conversation.

"When you feel trapped, you got to do what you got to do," he shot back with a hint of arrogance. "You the police or something?"

It was then that Nicholas felt an overwhelming sense of relief. Even though he did not know why Harold caused an explosion at the warehouse, he was more confident that their meeting was just luck. He was excited but did not show it. Nicholas was relieved he no longer had to trek into the big city to find Harold. Nicholas was confident that the idiot was standing right in front of him. Nicholas did not say anything for a few minutes. Satisfied that he was back in control of the entire situation, he knew his silence would push the kid to start talking and saying things he might not otherwise confess. Silence always makes people talk too much. It was a ploy that Nicholas often used with his victims.

"Of course, you ain't the cops," the boy started. His Boston accent came in and out as he tried to sound both gangster and refined at the same time. "Not that it is any of your business, punk, but I had to get rid of some things. I didn't know what to do, and the explosion seemed, at the time, to be the quickest way out."

As he spoke, the boy watched Nicholas stare back in silence, his green eyes both calming and scary. The boy was in awe at how someone's eyes could be so commanding and intoxicating simultaneously. The young man stood before Nicholas taking in just how handsome Nicholas was now that he had a clear view of him. He had noticed back in the arcade, but rage and panic blurred his vision until now when he was standing face to face, paralyzed by Nicholas' beauty; and his eyes.

"It wasn't even my stuff, man. You know?" he continued, unable to stop his mouth from spewing facts he never intended to share. "It was my friends' lab—not a lab, but a small setup. He had been working on a new batch of ecstasy—a new formula he had concocted. He was there with me, but he heard the police and bailed without me. As I was gathering what I could sell, the place lit up like Christmas, and that is when I knew my supposed friend had ratted me out or something—I don't know. I saw him in the building where I saw you looking back at me. Nicholas was suddenly furious that there was someone else at the warehouse, and in the same building as Mike and Jennifer, but he could not think about that right now.

"I'm a good guy just trying to make a buck, man. I do not even know why I am telling you all of this." His last few words were muffled by tears rolling down his face. The boy was scared— nervous. Nicholas could see that, so he reached out his arm, pulled the boy towards him quickly, and kissed him. The kid resisted for a few seconds and then reciprocated, enjoying Nicholas's passion for the kiss. He could taste a faint toothpaste flavor, then felt a large tongue in his mouth before tasting blood as Nicholas bit his lip. He pulled away, pushing Nicholas back against the car.

"What the fuck, man?" he spat, sending the words and blood into the air. He wiped his mouth and looked at the blood on his sleeve. "Geez, that fucking hurt."

Nicholas stood there, leaning against the car staring at the boy, smiling at the pain he caused him. The car was far enough from the arcade so no one could hear them, and the car was under a streetlamp that lost it's light weeks ago when kids threw rocks at it. Anyone looking in their direction could only see two bodies entangled as one.

Nicholas reached out and pulled the boy closer and apologized with a sarcastic, condescending tone. He resisted at first but gave in and accepted the hug that Nicholas was trying to give him. Nicholas pulled a switchblade out of his back pocket as he reached around the boy. Nicholas was sure that Harold was no real threat to his future with Oliver. He felt confident that Harold had been nothing more than a poor distraction for Oliver. Nicholas opened the knife and started kissing Harold, more gently this time. With his left hand, he held Harold's head close to his, lips locked. He felt a rise in the boy's pants as he pushed into Nicholas. Nicholas opened the blade with his right hand and stabbed the boy multiple times in the lower back and side. The boy tried to escape, but Nicholas was much stronger. The boy could feel the pain in his back—far greater than the lip biting. He tried to scream but could not free his mouth from Nicholas'. In all, Nicholas stabbed the boy 24 times. He managed to pierce several organs in the process. Long before he stopped stabbing, the boy had gone limp—had stopped fighting.

Nicholas's hand was soaked in blood. Thanks to the blood spewing out of each wound, his clothes stuck to the boy. A puddle was forming around them, and Nicholas knew that everything he was wearing was swimming in evidence.

Nicholas opened the car door and dropped the boy into the passenger seat. The inside of the car was a mess, but not from Nicholas. He had stolen the car a week earlier. With the boy securely sitting in the seat, bleeding into the cracked faux leather seats, Nicholas opened the glove box, pulled out the Tile he had put there a couple of days ago, and slipped it into his pocket. His bloody fingerprints were all over the car, but he was not in the police system, so he was not too worried. He was confident that there were dozens of fingerprints in the junked car, and he felt sure some of them had a record. They would take the blame for Harold's death, not Nicholas.

Nicholas wiped his red-soaked hands through the thick head of platinum hair of the kid. Nicholas did not remember Harold having platinum hair, but it was a detail that he did not care about now. He was pleased that he ended Harold's life without having to trek into the city. Nicholas closed the car door and walked away calmly as he always walked away from his murder scenes. He contemplated blowing the car up but remembered that there was still too much activity in the parking lot. Nicholas did not need the added attention. He licked the remaining blood off his hands and headed towards the highway.

Chapter Twelve

Oliver expected it to be easy to spread his mother's ashes across the beach. He was not sentimental, and he knew that his mother had not been either when she was alive. He was happy she did not want a large, drawn-out ceremony celebrating her life. Just the thought of planning such an ordeal sounded exhausting to him. Of course, knowing his mother, she would have planned it all out, down to the smallest detail, but then he would have to execute her plan. Nothing sounded more exhausting and uninteresting than living through one more of this mother's master plans.

Oliver's feet sank into the soft sand as he stood alone on the beach. His face was warmed by the setting sun as a low white noise of the birds and ocean-created music together. Oliver found himself crying quite heavily. He needed to sit in the sand. Oliver cried more for her — for the loss of yet another loved one. He was overwhelmed with the realization that he was truly alone now. No parents. No siblings — unless he included Nicholas, but he did not want to think of Nicholas as a sibling.

As the sun set and the ocean breeze picked up, sending sand dancing through the air Oliver took advantage of the moment and reached into the urn. He threw a handful of his mother's ashes into the air. Some fell immediately, but most were caught in a passing wind as he watched the ashes sail through the air. He repeated this process until the urn was empty. With each thrust of ash into the air, Oliver felt more alone. When the urn was empty, he turned it upside down to let any lingering ash out into the world — to let his mother fly away for good. He continued sitting in the sand, hugging the now-empty urn. His moment of peace was interrupted by the buzzing of his phone.

"Well, well, well. It is about time you called me back bitch," Oliver sang into the phone, seeing Camilla's name displayed on his phone. "Where have you been?"

"Oliver is that you?" the woman on the other end of the line asked. Oliver instantly realized that it was not Camilla. His face warmed with embarrassment.

"Hello, Mrs. Kennedy," Oliver responded with a hefty dose of innocence. "How are you? Is Camilla okay?"

"Oh, good. It is you. Hello Oliver. Thank you for taking my call," Mrs. Kennedy replied in her typical, overly formal way. "I am sorry to bother you, but I was hoping you might know where Camilla is or how we can reach her. She left a week ago. She would not say where she was going except to say that she was going to stop in Greenwich to see you. We just now discovered that she had left her phone behind, which is how I found your number. From what we can tell, she did not take any of her clothes with her either."

"Holy crap… I mean, sorry, um, wow, this is not good," Oliver stuttered, trying to stay composed. "I have not heard from her at all, even though I have been texting her with almost no reply. I am on Martha's Vineyard right now. My mother passed away last week."

Oliver continued to ramble—a mechanism he often used when flustered. Eventually, he stopped talking long enough to let Camilla's mother finish telling her story, including Camilla being very upset about something. Mrs. Kennedy told Oliver that Camilla refused to tell her mother what bothered her so much. Oliver could tell that Mrs. Kennedy was upset. He could hear her voice quivering as she spoke. Oliver agreed to call Mrs. Kennedy the moment he heard from Camilla, hoping he would hear from her.

When he ended the call, Oliver decided that he needed to be back in Greenwich. If Camilla was working her way to him, he better be there. Camilla left Greenwich quite upset after everything she, Oliver, and the others had been through. Oliver knew he needed to be there for her, assuming she would show up. He stood up, brushed the sand off his shorts, and carried the urn back to the cottage. Inside he put his mother's empty urn on the fireplace mantle. He was unsure why he chose that spot, but it seemed the right place. Then he headed to the bathroom to shower. Oliver felt a film from the beach covering his body. It was a feeling he did not enjoy.

Oliver stepped out of the shower only to realize he had forgotten to grab a towel. Rather than stress about it, he shook himself somewhat dry and moved around the cottage naked, tidying it up, knowing that he would not return for a few months. While cleaning up, he found a pair of boxers and stepped into them. He did not mind walking around the cottage naked, but he figured putting the boxers on was easier than carrying them to the bedroom and packing them. As he continued to move around the house, he heard a knock on the front door. Oliver was startled because no one ever visited unannounced. He tip-toed around the cottage in hopes that whoever was at the door — maybe a solicitor, would move on, but the knocking continued. It was not loud or forceful. The knocking was paced, almost polite. Oliver decided that he would have to answer it, and the unannounced guest would just have to deal with Oliver being almost naked.

When he opened the door, Oliver was surprised to see Imani standing before him with a friend. If Oliver were a shy man, he would have jumped behind the front door and stretched his head around to have a conversation hiding his body, but instead, he stood proudly in the doorway in just his boxers.

"Hi, Oliver," Imani said, almost matter-of-factly. "You are a tough one to track down."

"Imani!" Oliver sang back with excitement and confusion. She was the last person he would expect to knock on his door in Greenwich, let alone Martha's Vineyard. "What brings you out here."

"Camilla is missing."

"Yes, so I have heard. I spoke with her mother earlier," Oliver responded. "Wait, how do you know she is missing?"

"She was supposed to meet us in New York three days ago but never showed up.

"Oh, this is Jackson, by the way," she said, pointing over her shoulder to the man behind her.

Oliver and Jackson shook hands. Jackson was a tall, young black man with sweaty palms. Oliver could not decide if that was just how his palms were all the time or if Jackson was nervous—uncomfortable standing before a half-naked man he had just met.

Jackson and Imani had only been on a couple of dates, so Jackson was quite surprised when Imani called and asked him to accompany her to Martha's Vineyard. At first, he thought Imani was taking their relationship to the next level with a romantic overnight trip, but he quickly discovered that she asked him because she did not have a driver's license or a car. He liked spending time with Imani, so he did not mind. Imani gave him gas money and bought a couple of meals. Their relationship was very balanced, treating each other as equals. Imani would not stand for any man who treated her in a condescending way. She and Jackson always paid their own way when on dates, and she would not allow Jackson, nor any man, to treat her like a woman from the fifties. She was a modern woman and made sure that everyone knew it. Jackson was reminded quite regularly.

Imani and Jackson had been on the island for two days trying to figure out where Oliver's cottage was located. Imani remembered Camilla talking about the cottage, but the details were fuzzy. Ultimately, they made it, and now they stood before Oliver in his pair of dirty boxers. Imani was a little embarrassed but enjoyed looking at Oliver's sculpted body. She heard stories about Oliver's smoking hot body from Camilla, but this was the first time she was getting a front-row seat to the show. Though taller than Oliver, Jackson was heavier and suddenly felt insecure as he watched Imani quietly droll over Oliver.

"Her mother says she left for Greenwich a week ago," Oliver continued after letting go of Jackson's sweaty hand. He did not want to be rude by wiping his hand to dry it, so he left it hanging in the air before putting it on his hip.

"This is not like Camilla," Imani continued. "She is my girl, you know, and if she says she is going to do something or be somewhere, you can count on it—count on her."

"I know," Oliver said as if the two were verbally fighting over who knew Camilla better. "I was packing to return home in case she shows up there. When did you two get to the island, and when are you leaving?"

"We arrived two days ago. It has taken us this long to find you. We planned to leave once we found you and got some answers."

Oliver asked Imani and Jackson into the cottage. He explained that he was ready to head back that evening. He was going to catch the last ferry off the island and asked if they wanted to join him. Imani and Jackson would need to check out of their hotel first, so they all agreed to meet at the ferry dock. Oliver told them that he could leave his mother's car on the island so he would have something to drive next time he visited and that he would ride back to Greenwich with them. Jackson had been looking forward to more alone time with Imani but accepted that he would have to drive three hours listening to two people talk about a third person he had never met.

Chapter Thirteen

Camilla left her phone at home on purpose, as well as all her personal items. She did not mean to have her mother panic, but she needed to get off the grid if she was going to try and expose Nicholas for the fraud and murderer she believed him to be. While she agreed with Oliver that they had been on a goose chase, she did not think she was entirely wrong. With all her heart, Camilla still believed that Nicholas was killing her friends, and she would prove it at any cost.

After spending some time with her parents, decompressing from the anxiety and stress of losing Miles, Reed, and then Howard, Camilla became more convinced that Nicholas was behind all the killings. Oliver, however, had waned from their conspiracy theories, ultimately refusing to believe that the deaths were connected and that Nicholas was at the center of them all.

Even though she told Oliver she had given up blaming Nicholas, she had not. When she got to her parent's house, Camilla was already hard at work reviewing all her notes and thoughts about why and how she believed Nicholas was to blame. As hesitant as she was at first, Camilla did agree to keep in contact with Jennifer. While Camilla was not entirely comfortable with how aggressive Jennifer was at trying to date her, Jennifer was still a police officer, which Camilla believed would give her an 'in' to solving the murders of her friends, even if Jennifer was on administrative leave.

Oliver never knew that Camilla made multiple visits to town so that she and Jennifer could talk more about the murders in person. She often asked Jennifer to meet outside of town and places where

Camilla felt sure she would not run into Oliver. Camilla was not mad at Oliver, but she knew that if he knew what she was doing, he would try to talk her out of it. He would tell her to get on with her life. Oliver was undoubtedly trying to do that—move on. He had Harold as a distraction for a while, and now even Nicholas himself, which Camilla would not be pleased to learn.

Camilla planned to meet Jennifer for a drink at Ginger's bar on her most recent visit. As she stood across the street, waiting to cross, Camilla noticed a man standing against a taxi in front of the bar. It took her a moment before she convinced herself that the man was Nicholas. She wanted to walk up to him and punch him—scratch his beautifully intoxicating green eyes right out of their sockets, but she did not. Instead, she froze—stood motionless, almost lurking in the shadows, to see why he was at the same bar where she was supposed to meet Jennifer. Camilla quickly concluded that Nicholas was hunting for his next victim, and she felt like a police officer on a stakeout—like the ones you see in the movies. Camilla was not entirely wrong. Nicholas was at the bar for a specific reason, but not to find his next victim. He already knew who it would be. He knew Jennifer was inside, and he had every intention that night of getting Jennifer into the taxi he stole at any cost.

Camilla stood in the shadows, leaning against the window of an abandoned bakery, waiting—watching. She was afraid to confront him. Nicholas never moved. He was laser-focused on the front door of the bar. It was a popular bar, so the door opened and closed often. When it opened, Nicholas could see inside—could see Jennifer at the bar drinking away her sorrow. Nicholas had no idea that Jennifer was waiting for Camilla, and he certainly did not see Camilla across the street watching him. After too many drinks, Jennifer finally decided she had been stood up by Camilla and decided it was time to leave the bar—to head home. Had Camilla not left her phone at home, she would have received the text messages Jennifer slurred—spell check was no help. After what felt like hours for Camilla, she finally saw Jennifer emerge from the bar, swaying left and right like a good drunk. As she reached the sidewalk, and the bar's front door had closed, Jennifer tripped. Nicholas was there to catch her and offer her a ride home. He had turned down many others who were looking for a taxi as he waited for Jennifer.

    Camilla tried yelling out to Jennifer, but Jennifer was too drunk to make sense of any screams. Nicholas did hear Camilla and looked quite startled when he looked across the street after securing Jennifer in the car. He slammed his hand on the car's roof with rage as if to signal Camilla that he was coming for her next. Camilla jumped at the sound. Even though she feared Nicholas, Camilla knew she had to do something because she believed Jennifer was in danger. Seconds after Nicholas pounded the car, Camilla started walking towards him. Her rage gave her the strength to stand up to the man she once loved. Before she could reach the vehicle, Nicholas jumped in the driver's seat and sped off. Continuing her "movie-like" adventure, Camilla hopped into the taxi behind Nicholas and yelled, "follow that cab," before she could comprehend how cliche it sounded.

    Camilla followed Nicholas in her cab, albeit with a little distance between them. She studied the road before her to be sure not to lose sight of Nicholas. After some time, she noticed Nicholas turn into the warehouse complex. She asked her cab driver to stop at the edge of the entrance and let her out. She knew a second cab going onto the property would undoubtedly alert Nicholas to her proximity, and she wanted the element of surprise.

Once her cab pulled away, it struck Camilla just how insane she was behaving. She was alone, and about to walk into an abandoned warehouse park chasing someone she suspected to be a killer, even though she had no proof. She had no phone or idea how to stop Nicholas from doing whatever he was planning. She realized she might have made a big mistake, but she knew she could not turn around. Camilla believed that her friend was in danger.

When Camilla found the car Nicholas had been driving, it was empty. She looked around at the buildings trying to determine what direction Nicholas and Jennifer had gone. It was dark. None of the streetlights were on. Her only light was the moon which filled the night sky with a three-quarter glow. Eventually, Camilla noticed a bouncing light reflecting off the broken windows of the building closest to the car. She quietly made her way toward the lights, hoping she could stop Nicholas from doing whatever he was planning. She could not.

By the time Camilla made it to the first floor, Nicholas had appeared to be gone again. Jennifer, however, was hanging alone. Camilla did not run up to Jennifer for fear that Nicholas might be in the shadows watching. She could not take the risk to save her friend for fear that her own life would be in danger. Instead, Camilla stood still, quietly crying in the dark corner, watching Jennifer struggle. She felt helpless, and the silence was more frightening than when she first noticed Nicholas earlier in the evening. Camilla decided the best thing she could do to help Jennifer would be to go to the police and get them to rescue her. With that decision, Camilla slowly backtracked her steps out of the building and off the property.

Standing at the entrance where the taxi had dropped her off earlier, Camilla remembered that she had passed a convenience store a few minutes down the road, so she turned and began walking.

Back in the warehouse, Nicholas wondered what he would do with Camilla. He had not planned for her. When he watched her through the camera lens all those months ago, soon after Howard died, as she got into a car and headed off into the sunset, Nicholas was hopeful she was gone for good. As he stood in a different dark corner of the room looking at Jennifer's body sway with panic, Nicholas thought about going after Camilla immediately and ending her life quickly. He knew those kinds of kills were often messy, and he was not ready to deal with 'messy' right now. He was too busy tying up loose ends in hopes of spending the rest of his life with Oliver. As he contemplated what to do, he looked out a window and watched Camilla move through the night, making her way to the street. He assumed she would call the police, so he knew he needed to speed up his plans. He turned his attention back to Jennifer.

By the time Camilla made it to the convenience store, it had closed. The phone booth that sat in the parking lot was layered with graffiti. The door had been broken off the hinge and hung to the box by one screw. I looked like it would come tumbling to the ground at the slightest touch. She almost gagged at the urine stench as she stepped inside the booth. She screamed when she saw the receiver lying in a pile of debris on the booth floor.

Camilla sat on the sidewalk in front of the lifeless store and cried. She was tired, hungry, and beginning to regret leaving her phone at home. All Camilla could see was the image of Jennifer suspended in the air with her eyes, ears, and mouth wrapped in the tape. She struggled to understand how Nicholas knew about Jennifer and why he would want to hurt her. She wondered if there was anything she could have done that could have protected Jennifer.

At that moment, Camilla knew that she needed to do something bold, something very un-Camilla-like. She assumed it would take hours to walk to any place with activity at this late hour, and she had no idea where to locate the police station, so she did the next best thing she could think to do. She picked up the large rock that she had been staring at for the last five minutes and threw it at the convenience store window. She was hopeful that it would set off an alarm and make a lot of noise. Camilla figured that if she could not get to the police quickly, they might get to her instead. As the rock landed on a bed of broken glass inside the dark store, Camilla stood waiting, hoping for a loud siren or something that would call for help. There was silence. After a few minutes, she looked around, hoping that a silent alarm had gone off and she would be rescued, that Jennifer could be saved. Camilla looked at her watch, and after another 15 minutes of silence, she was convinced that she had lost—that no one was coming to help, so she sat back down and cried some more.

"What the hell?" she heard moments later.

Camilla looked up to see a tall, skinny boy standing before her. He wore an old baseball cap tilted back on his head of long blonde hair. His faded jeans had large holes in the knees and hung below his small waste. Camilla could not get over how skinny the boy looked. Looking up at him, she wondered if he just did not eat or had an addiction to meth. She thought he sounded like a country bumpkin.

"Where did you come from?" Camilla asked. "I have been out here alone for what feels like forever."

"I am parked around back," the kid responded. "I was at home chilling with my boys when I got the call from the alarm company. I work here.

"Did you break my window?"

"Oh, thank goodness," Camilla exhaled. "I am so sorry about the window, but I had no phone or way to get help."

"Seriously, lady?" the kid fired back, telling Camilla that she would probably be in trouble. She did not appreciate the 'lady' comment even though the more she thought about it, the more she realized she was probably talking to an 18-year-old stoner. At 23, she must seem ancient to him.

The kid pulled his phone out of his pocket and called the alarm company to tell them he was on the scene and that it was not a false alarm. He also asked to have the police sent out, explaining to the customer service person on the other end of the line that the person responsible for setting the alarm was still on site. Once finished, he dropped his phone back into his pocket and explained to Camilla that the police were coming. He said it as if she had not heard the whole conversation or that she might try to flee the scene, which Camilla found odd, considering she was waiting for someone to help her when he arrived.

"Thank you. I have been trying to figure out how to get the police to come," Camilla said. "I am Camilla. What is your name?"

"Tucker," he responded, a little confused. "What do you mean you have been waiting for the police to come? Where did you come from, and why are you out here by yourself?"

Camilla proceeded to tell Tucker the whole story. After a few minutes, she realized that she had started the story too far back. Tucker was looking at her like she was speaking a foreign language.

Camilla stopped and sped her story forward to that night, bringing Tucker up to speed by the time the police arrived. Even after she finished talking, Tucker still looked at Camilla like she was the one on drugs. He could not decide if she was full of shit or if she was for real. His high had kicked in when the parking lot lit up with flashing blue lights.

"Officer, this girl is bat shit crazy," Tucker shouted as the officers stepped out of their car. "I work here. The silent alarm went off when this lady put a rock through the window. I got here as quickly as I could, and she has been going on about some crazy man or something."

Tucker was doing all he could to deflect any officer's attention away from him and towards Camilla. He was stoned and did not want the police to focus on him.

"Ma'am, is everything okay here?" one of the officers asked Camilla as if he did not hear a word Tucker had just said to him. "Is this man bothering you?"

"Oh, come on, are you kidding me?" Tucker fired in the direction of the officers. "I just told you that she tried to break into MY place of employment."

Camilla interrupted the men and got them all focused on her. She explained to the officers that Tucker was telling the truth and did what she did because she needed the police. It took a little longer than she wanted to explain why the night played out as it had, and she was furious when the police told her that they would not investigate the warehouse. Instead, they put her in the back of their patrol car and took Camilla into town so she could file a report at the station.

As the police car drove off, Tucker unlocked the store and searched for something to board up the window so that he could get back to his friends and his drugs.

Chapter Fourteen

At the police station, Camilla sat waiting for someone to listen to her. She needed any police officer who came and went—who moved around her almost as if she were invisible to stop and listen. The more she had to wait, the more convinced she was that Jennifer would die.

"For the love of god, people," she heard herself yell through tears. "He is going to kill her. You need to stop him."

"You tell 'em," she heard a drunk man yell out. He was sitting in a chair across from Camilla. He was missing his right shoe. His nose and left eye were black and blue, and he was missing four front teeth. Camilla looked at the man and wondered what had happened to him and why no one was giving him any medical attention.

"Shut up, Sam," an officer behind the front desk yelled to the drunk man. "Leave the little lady alone, and you think about what you will tell Lucy when she gets here." Camilla had no idea that Sam was a regular at the police station. He lost his accounting job two months ago. His wife, Lucy, was a waitress and was tired of bailing Sam out of jail every week. While Camilla waited impatiently, Lucy walked into the station, already yelling at Sam as if she started yelling at him the moment she got out of her 20-year-old, rusted Honda Civic. It has been a long time since Camilla heard a woman cuss as badly as Lucy did. When the Sam and Lucy show had ended, and Camilla was once again the only civilian in the room, she resumed her soapbox screams for help,

Her words finally got her the attention she had been looking for all night. One of the older officers, a man in his late 50s, who was just coming on duty, stopped and sat on the bench next to Camilla to find out who she was, who 'he' was, and who 'he' was going to kill.

Camilla started to tell the story yet again; she was beginning to feel like a broken record. The officer let Camilla tell her whole story without interruption. He had been on the force long enough to know that you must let people get it all out. He knew Camilla would feel better for it, and he also knew that once Camilla could say everything she thought she needed to say, he could then get to the root of the matter and find out what was going on. In his experience, people are hysterical in the heat of 'the' moment and typically do not think clearly. Logic and reason are clouded with rage, fury, or confusion — sometimes all three. He had been down this road with many other young girls who showed up at the police station crying, screaming, and appearing quite confused.

When Camilla finished talking, she sat silently, looking at the floor. She was so exhausted from crying, speaking, and feeling unheard that she had little strength to look up at the officer now. He decided that Camilla would be okay if he touched her, so he put his arm around her shoulders and pulled her in for a hug. Camilla responded by wrapping her arms around the officer and squeezing him tightly. She felt like she was hugging her grandfather, and it was comforting.

When she finally let go, she wiped her eyes and looked at the officer.

"So, will you help me?" she asked, flashing swollen, red, puppy dog eyes.

"Well, young lady, you tell a fascinating story. There is a lot to digest. Where do you think you need the most help, first?"

"You need to save Jennifer, of course," she said, angry that maybe the officer did not hear her.

"Okay, okay. Calm down. Can you tell me more about who Jennifer is," the officer continued as he singled to a few other officers to join him and Camilla.

"These officers here will take you into a quieter space so we get more details about Jennifer and where she is right now. Can you do that with us?" The officer sounded more condescending than supportive, but Camilla agreed. Every little step forward was a good step, she thought.

Hours went by before Camilla finally felt that the police understood her story. For all Camilla knew, Jennifer was already dead. The officers took a more serious interest once it became clear that Jennifer was also a police officer. One officer left the room to confirm Jennifer's identity with a different precinct. When he returned, he nodded to the other officers about the validity of Jennifer's profession but further expanded that no one had yet reported her missing.

"I am reporting her missing asshole!" Camilla screamed. "I am telling you that I saw her hanging from the ceiling, all taped up. You need to do something right now!"

The police officers calmed Camilla down by telling her that they would send a car out to investigate, and in the meantime, she should go home and get some rest. Camilla lied and said that she was staying at a hotel in town. She had nowhere to go, but it was becoming clear to her that she had to get out of the police station if she was going to maintain any form of sanity and decorum. The officers released Camilla and told her they would call her once they had investigated. She told them she had lost her phone and would return later for an update.

Camilla left the police station in search of something to eat. She was upset at the lack of help she was getting but knew that she was in no condition to argue if she did not maintain her strength. As she left, she told the officers she would return in the morning, hoping they would have rescued Jennifer by then.

After exceeding her caloric intake for the day at a local diner, Camilla checked into a motel on the edge of town. She was exhausted from the adventure of the last 24 hours and needed to rest. The motel was clean enough, but Camilla still felt a little dirty staying in the room. It had a musty odor, and the walls were relatively thin. The neon sign at the front of the motel that advertised room rates by the hour assured Camilla that she was checking into a total dump, but she had no choice. The motel was the only option around, and she was exhausted. Once in her room, Camilla could hear the sexual escapades happening in the neighboring rooms. Fortunately for her, she was so tired that she was in a deep sleep within minutes of her head hitting the pillow.

When Camilla woke, she felt refreshed, revived. She could not remember the last time she had slept so well, especially considering she was in a cheap motel room with an unidentifiable lingering smell and an uncomfortable bed. Camilla had been hoping for a 5–6-hour nap so she could get back to the police station and help Jennifer. She could not believe that she had slept for 22 hours. Camilla was angry that she had lost an entire day and felt she had let Jennifer down.

Back at the police station, still in the same clothes from two days earlier, Camilla was, once again, trying to convince the police of what she saw and where. She was still annoyed that no one was taking her seriously, especially since she was talking about the life of a police officer. It was not that she was not being taken seriously, but more so that this police station, small and lightly staffed, to begin with, had been given a load of cases recently. Dead people had been popping up everywhere lately in random acts of murder or suicide. Sometimes the young officers could not distinguish between the two. Juan Diego knew, mostly because he was responsible for a number of the deaths. These cases had the police officers of this small-town doing work they felt untrained to do.

The one officer who had been the most helpful to Camilla when she first arrived the other day was there that morning to help her. He told her officers went to the warehouse park as promised but found nothing unusual. Camilla was unsatisfied with his answer, so he said that he was going to check out the warehouse himself. She wanted to go with him. Under normal circumstances, such civil involvement would not be allowed, but this officer felt confident that Camilla would not accept 'no' as an answer.

"I promise I will not interfere," Camilla said, fearing that Jennifer was dead.

When the officer and Camilla arrived at the complex, it was still daylight, but the sun was beginning to set, allowing Camilla to see how large of a complex it was. She felt small and lost. And when the officer asked Camilla which building Jennifer was in, Camilla could not answer. There were so many, and they all looked the same.

"She is here. I just need to remember in which building," Camilla heard herself saying, almost trying to convince herself as much as the officer.

"I am going to call for backup. There is no way we can get through all these buildings before dark," the officer responded.

Within an hour, several more cars showed up. They were all flashing their blue lights—local, county, and state police since the town was short-staffed, and the complex was in a district that allowed all of them to participate in the hunt.

Camilla looked up and saw Nicholas standing in the window—well saw a person. She did not know if it was Nicholas but wanted to believe it was him. She also noticed another person one floor above Nicholas. She was about to point them out to an officer when a team of officers started moving towards a different building, where they saw a shadowy figure moving around.

Nicholas looked down at the commotion caused by the police, and that is when he saw Camilla looking up at him. He was confident she could not make him out but was not pleased about feeling cornered. With Camilla on the ground and another stranger looking at him from another building, Nicholas believed he was about to be caught.

The explosion changed everything. Camilla took cover and lost sight of Nicholas and the other figure, and all the police were trying to save their co-workers. Nicholas went off searching for his admirer, leaving Camilla with the police. He would have to deal with her later.

* * * * *

Exhausted from the chaos of the evening and furious that the police raided the warehouse complex before he could properly dispose of Mike and Jennifer, Nicholas wanted nothing more than to get some sleep. His clothes had a lot of blood on them, from stabbing Harold to death. He walked a few miles further down the road to the motel where he had set up base to deal with Mike. Once he reached his motel room, Nicholas took a long, hot shower rinsing off all the blood, hair, and other DNA he had all over him. As he was drying himself off, he heard someone making a lot of noise getting out of a car. Nicholas looked out the window and saw Camilla talking to the police officer, dropping her off.

"Yes, ma'am, we will let you know when we find out more information, but as my captain told you, you could not stay at the warehouse. It became a live investigation. You will be safer here at your motel. Just get some rest, and we will update you soon."

"Fine, but you need to let me know when you find Jennifer," she said, closing the passenger door. She did not notice Nicholas looking at her through the window as she walked to the room next door to his. She opened and slammed the door closed. Nicholas's room rattled.

Nicholas could not believe his luck. Camilla was in the room next door. She brought the police to the warehouse and now to the motel. He was unsure when he would have an opportunity like this again—when he would have Camilla so close and isolated.

As tired as he was, Nicholas knew he could not sleep now. He needed to take advantage of this opportunity to dispose of Camilla once and for all. He put on the same clothes he had worn before he showered, soiled with the blood of one person who

Nicholas believed stood between him and Oliver, so why not one more, he thought.

Nicholas picked up the large butcher's knife in the room, initially intended for Mike. Nicholas had originally planned to bring Mike back to his motel room and chop him into pieces, or at least chop off his dick and maybe another limb or two. That never happened, so he decided to put the knife to use on Camilla instead.

Nicholas quietly stepped out of his room onto the landing. He tucked the knife into the back of his pants and walked ten feet to Camilla's door. He put his finger over the peephole and knocked. Camilla quickly swung the door open, expecting it to be a police officer bringing her good news, but was shocked, and suddenly scared, that Nicholas stood before her.

"What the hell!" she yelled. "How did you find me?"

"Hello, Camilla," was his only response as he lunged through the open door pushing Camilla to the floor. Once inside, Nicholas slammed the door behind him, trapping Camilla in the room. Laying on the floor, Camilla was kicking up at Nicholas, doing anything she could to keep him away from her. Their little dance moved them deeper into the room, and before she realized it, Camilla was almost in the bathroom. Nicholas sauntered toward Camilla, forcing her to move back. He did not try to touch her or say a single word. He was savoring the moment—her moment of total panic.

Camilla scrambled to stand up when she realized she could go no further. She wanted to be more level with Nicholas, as if she thought she had a fighting chance.

"You look a little frazzled, Camilla," Nicholas finally said. "These past months have not been good to you."

"Shut the fuck up, you psycho," she shot back at Nicholas, hoping words would sting. "Why are you here? I know you have been killing my friends. You cannot fool me."

"I am not trying to fool you, Camilla," Nicholas said calmly. "You are the one who seems to have figured me out and is a gnat that will not get out of my way long enough for me to complete my mission."

"Mission to do what? Kill everyone I love?" Camilla asked as tears ran down her face. Camilla believed that she had been the center of Nicholas' killing spree. To her, that was the only logical explanation since they dated in college.

"Oh Camilla, you have it all wrong. Yes, I am killing to get to the one I love. However, you and your roommates, and others who were in the wrong place at the wrong time, are just obstacles to my true love—to Oliver seeing that I am his one true love."

"You are talking nonsense. Oliver does not love you. He doesn't even know you. You are completely delusional."

"That is where you are wrong. Oliver and I have been dating for some time—on and off," he lied. "We would have had more time for falling in love if Howard had not gotten in the way. But he is not a bother anymore. Oliver and I are together now or will be soon, and no one can stop us this time."

Camilla started laughing at the absurdity Nicholas was spewing at her. She teased Nicholas for being crazy to think that someone as kind, sweet, and honest as Oliver would find him attractive. As best she could, Camilla started rambling on about what a fantastic person Oliver was to everyone and how well she knew Oliver, enough to know that Oliver would have nothing to do with Nicholas.

Nicholas moved closer to Camilla as she chatted away until she went silent, seeing him so close to her that she could almost feel his breath on her face. She stood silent, inhaling the smell of cheap soap that tried to cover up the stench of his last kill.

"What do you want from me?" she whispered.

"Why I want you to die, of course," Nicholas said in a deep, sinister voice as he pulled the knife out from behind him and jammed it into Camilla's chest.

Camilla shot a mouthful of blood all over Nicholas as she felt the large butcher's knife carve through her breastplate and into her heart, slicing the organ. As Nicholas let go of the knife, Camilla's body fell to the floor. Camilla hit her head on the porcelain vanity as she collapsed. Blood flowed from her chest, staining the worn, warping, discolored beige carpet. She never said another word, and within a few minutes, her eyes glazed over. Camilla had stopped breathing.

Nicholas was not expecting that one blow would kill her. He wished to do more, but Camilla was not a big person. Her body was exhausted from the activity she had put it through recently. Nicholas stepped back to watch the contorted body bleed onto the rug. He pulled the knife out of her chest only to release a waterfall of red, then turned around and walked away.

He walked outside and felt the cool evening breeze. The sky was dark—almost starless, and there were no lights in the parking lot. They had burned out or been smashed long before Nicholas arrived. Before returning to his room to clean up again, he walked across the parking lot to an in-ground pool protected by a low, rusted chain-link fence. The water looked dirty and lifeless, and Nicholas could smell the chlorine. The water was dark, almost black. A few beer cans floated silently across the almost still water. The stench of cigarettes lingered from the piles of ash and butts lifelessly scattered around the pool's edge. Nicholas threw the butcher's knife over the fence. It made a loud splash as it cut through the water and sank to the bottom. The blood added a swirl of color to the dark water. Nicholas knew that by the time the knife was discovered, the chlorine would have taken care of any evidence linking him to Camilla. He did not linger. Once confident that the knife was sitting at the bottom of the pool, Nicholas returned to his room, cleaned up, then went to sleep.

Chapter Fifteen

One month after releasing his mother's ashes and learning of Camilla's disappearance, Oliver, Imani, and Jackson were no closer to finding Camilla. Any lead that Imani thought she might have found was a dead end. Jackson was growing tired of listening to Imani go on and on about Camilla and began questioning whether their new relationship would survive this missing third wheel. Oliver was less obsessed than Imani with finding Camilla. It was not because he cared less, but because he knew that Camilla did this sort of thing—went off the grid to 'find herself' periodically. Even though her mother told Oliver that Camilla was coming to Greenwich, and she had not yet arrived, Oliver still saw that as a typical Camilla move.

Oliver believed Camilla was off finding herself, exploring what life could be after all the recent deaths. On the ride back to Greenwich weeks earlier, Oliver told Imani about some of the adventures he and Camilla dealt with before Camilla left Greenwich. Imani heard some of them from Camilla directly but not to the level of detail that Oliver shared. Oliver told Imani that he would be concerned if Camilla did not reach out in the next couple of weeks, but a couple of weeks was too long to wait for Imani.

Meanwhile, Oliver and Nicholas continued to text each other. It had been a few weeks since they hugged in the driveway before Oliver threw his mother's ashes all over the beach. Oliver had not told Nicholas about Imani and Jackson showing up to the cottage or Camilla supposedly missing. He was not sure their relationship required that level of sharing just yet. Instead, Oliver kept the conversations with Nicholas short and guarded, as if he were working hard to show only the good parts of his life. Oliver believed this was typical new dating rules of engagement.

With Oliver leaving the worrying about Camilla to Imani, he decided that it was time he and Nicholas had a proper meal together, an actual date. Oliver was ready to learn more about Nicholas and Peter, although he felt the journal Peter left for him contained quite a bit of history. Nicholas was equally as excited to spend quality time with Oliver finally. Nicholas let Oliver pick where they should have their first full meal together, and Oliver picked The King & Queen, a quiet, family-owned American-style restaurant in downtown Greenwich. Nicholas was initially apprehensive, mainly because The King & Queen was the last place he had dinner with Oliver, albeit as Eric. For Nicholas, that night last year was terrific. It was one of the few times he relaxed and enjoyed being in the moment with Oliver. He was, however, a little nervous about going back there with Oliver. Nicholas was afraid he might slip up and talk about their last time together at the restaurant or be recognized and called out as Eric. Nicholas tried to suggest elsewhere, but Oliver wanted The King & Queen. Oliver knew it would conjure up memories of the night he spent with Eric, but he also knew that it was a place where he could relax with Eric, so Oliver felt it would be where he could relax with Nicholas, too.

A few days later, Nicholas and Oliver met at the restaurant, and the two had a wonderful time together. While Nicholas started the date worried about saying or doing the wrong thing, by the main course, he was focused entirely on Oliver and enjoying the conversation. Nicholas was also hoping that dessert would finally include the two of them naked.

"I am so glad we are finally doing this," Nicholas said while Oliver studied the wine list.

"Me, too. I am sorry it has taken so long," Oliver said without looking up from the menu. "For some reason, every time I think we are finally going to get together, some drama resurfaces in my life. And trust me, I have plenty of it."

"No worries, and I get it."

"Do you prefer red or white?" Oliver asked as he continued flipping through the abnormally thick wine list for such a small restaurant.

"Whatever you want is fine with me." Nicholas was trying to make the evening as accommodating as possible. He wanted Oliver to be comfortable—happy.

They started with a bottle of Viognier and emptied an Oregon Pinot Noir before draining an old bottle of Sonoma Valley Cabernet. The conversation flowed like wine, and before they knew it, they were outside the restaurant hailing a cab. Oliver only had his mother's house—big, empty, and full of memories—to invite Nicholas back to, and the idea of having sex in his dead mother's house did not sound appealing. Before Oliver could speak, Nicholas offered to host, but not at his father's house. He did not want Oliver to get distracted by photos and mementos of Peter.

Nicholas had an apartment on the south side of town. He kept it on the off chance he needed a place to hide out, but he figured he needed to stop holding his secret hiding spaces and start living with Oliver. When the two arrived at the apartment, Oliver could not help noticing how sparsely decorated the place was. It looked more like a showroom than a home.

Before Oliver could question Nicholas about his decorating, the two were already kissing. They both had been looking forward to getting the other naked for a long time—much longer for Nicholas. When Nicholas was pretending to be Eric, he did not have sex with Oliver because he did not want Oliver to become comfortable with or familiar with his body while he pretended to be someone else. He was saving that for when he could be himself, and tonight was that night.

Nicholas was unbuttoning Oliver's shirt while Oliver was trying to do the same to Nicholas. The two of them fumbled like teenage boys tackling a new bra. Their arms kept getting twisted around each other. They were in such a rush to get the other naked that they were both moving too quickly, almost unable to enjoy the moment. With shirts finally off—thrown into the air without a care of where they landed, Oliver stopped and thought they might be moving too quickly. His pause caused Nicholas to pull away and study Oliver's face for an indication of what might be happening. Oliver smiled and pulled Nicholas' lips back to his. Soon a series of loud thuds echoed off the empty walls as they both kicked off their shoes.

Oliver reached down to try and pull off his socks while still trying to kiss Nicholas. Their midair game of Twister was quite complicated as they tumbled over each other and landed on the floor. Oliver hit his head hard enough to scream out, but seconds later was back to sucking face with Nicholas. With his back against the floor, Oliver looked up and saw Nicholas hovering over him, frantically unzipping Oliver's pants. They got stuck around his ankles. Nicholas stood up and pulled Oliver's pants off; then, he stripped out of his pants. Nicholas was not wearing any underwear.

Still, on the floor, Oliver looked up at the naked man standing over him. He was bigger than Oliver expected and was saluting Oliver, almost pointing to the bedroom. Nicholas grabbed Oliver by the arm and pulled him off the floor and towards the bedroom. As the two trotted across the apartment, Oliver escaped out of his boxers and followed Nicholas—two naked bodies bouncing towards the warmth of the bedroom.

Oliver woke hours later, wrapped in Nicholas' arms. Their bodies were knotted together like a pretzel, and Oliver liked it very much. He needed to pee but did not want to get out of bed or pull away from Nicholas. He held it for as long as he could, but eventually, his bladder won, and Oliver had to untangle himself from Nicholas. When he returned to the room, Oliver saw Nicholas, still in bed, looking at him.

"Wow," Nicholas said as he watched the naked work of sculptured art return to the bed. "You are so beautiful."

"Awe, thanks," Oliver spat back, embarrassed a little.

"I am being serious, man. You are so fucking hot. How are you still single?" Nicholas continued. "Are there some skeletons that are going to come out only after we move in together or get married?" Nicholas said with a nervous giggle.

Oliver laughed as he got back into the bed and under the warm covers with Nicholas—their bodies once again merged.

"Without sounding too forward," Nicholas started. "I like you, Oliver. I mean, really, really like you. I know this is our first, whatever we want to call it, but I would like it to be the first of many."

Oliver kissed Nicholas' forehead and then tightly hugged Nicholas without saying anything. He was enjoying the moment. While also enjoying their time together, Oliver tried not to rush anything. It had been a long time since he was 'himself,' and since he felt good about his life—except for Camilla missing—he wanted to move slowly.

"I know this might be too soon, but I am going to New York next week for business. I know it is not that far away, but would you like to come with me? I plan to stay in the city for a week or two."

"Seriously?" Oliver asked. "I have been thinking about moving to New York. With all my friends gone and my mother dead, nothing is holding me here except maybe you. I was going to head to New York soon to start looking at places to live."

"Great, let's go together," Nicholas said, almost singing joyfully.

A week later, Oliver and Nicholas were in a car heading to Manhattan.

Chapter Sixteen

They spent much of the past week wrapped in each other's arms, snuggling on the couch and watching movies together. They walked through the park holding hands. Under the table, when eating at a restaurant, their feet would be tied in a knot together. Nicholas was in heaven. He was finally living the life he had spent years chasing. Oliver was just living in the moment. He had not been looking for love; for someone who 'completed' him the way Nicholas had, but he welcomed it. He was relishing in the warm, compassionate kindness that he so desperately believed he deserved after the awful stench of death that lingered behind him. If he only knew that Nicholas was responsible for it all; the kindness and the killing.

When they were not together, Oliver was busy sifting through the lifelong collection of stuff accumulated in his mother's house. No one else was going to clear it out, and as much as he did not want to either, he used the 'downtime' when he was not with Nicholas to downsize the mess. Nicholas was busy continuing to set up his web of plans that he hoped would ensure that he and Oliver could have a long, happy life together which included the continual monitoring of too many people. Right now, the only person getting almost as much attention as Oliver was Imani.

Neither Nicholas nor Oliver asked the other about their work. Nicholas knew that Oliver did not work and that he had money from Peter. On the other hand, Oliver had no idea what or if Nicholas worked. He assumed Nicholas had money. He was pretty confident that Peter would not leave money to him and not Nicholas. Work had not interfered with their new romance, so Oliver never questioned it.

After a week of romantic bliss, Oliver and Nicholas drove to New York City. Nicholas had been to the city much more often than Oliver but still let Oliver pick out their hotel. He wanted Oliver to have the best time in New York, and to Nicholas, that meant letting Oliver feel like he was in charge.

Once in the city, they checked into the Hotel Geoffrey, a boutique hotel in the heart of Chelsea. Oliver had spent hours researching dozens of hotels before settling on the Geoffrey. He wanted someplace quiet and romantic, not a large chain hotel. Soon after the handsomely young bellhop left Nicholas and Oliver in their room, they were both naked. Nicholas wanted to ravage Oliver before leaving him alone in the room while he returned to Greenwich to keep tabs on Imani.

They had sex, ordered room service, showered together, and then had sex again before Nicholas let Oliver soundly sleep. Nicholas left a note to say that he would be back in time to take Oliver out to dinner. The message did not say where he was going. When Oliver read it hours later while he sat alone in the room, he began to question, for the first time, what Nicholas did when they were not together.

Oliver did not question Nicholas when he returned. He knew they were in the city for Nicholas to conduct some business. Rather than wallowing alone in the hotel room while Nicholas was out stalking Imani, Oliver searched for an apartment. He did not need roommates, so he was looking for someplace more upscale than where he would typically want to live. He figured that he had to enjoy his new wealth eventually. Oliver also knew or planned that he was not moving to the city with Nicholas or Harold. Oliver and Nicholas were having a great time together, and Oliver certainly enjoyed the sex and the company, but he was not ready to settle down with anyone. He had always lived with someone, his parents, Howard, and others, and he felt he was now prepared to live alone. He needed to live alone.

Nicholas would be gone for hours, never telling Oliver where he was going or what he was doing other than to say it was 'work-related.' Their newfound friendship was still early enough that Nicholas did not feel he needed to explain his every move—not that he would, and Oliver did not feel it was right to ask just yet. It did not bother Oliver because it gave him time to explore the city. Oliver enjoyed getting lost in the towering steel, glass, and brownstone maze.

While Oliver was absorbing the energy and organized chaos of the city, winding through busy streets and quiet alleyways, he stumbled upon a local coffee shop—a nice escape from the big chain coffee shops he found on almost every corner. Oliver stepped inside, and the freshly ground Columbian beans' aroma filled the air. He was taking in the scent when he heard his name called.

"Olly!" Harold yelled more loudly than he wanted. "I cannot believe you are here!"

Oliver waved to Harold, skipped the coffee line, and went right over to him. They shared a hug tighter than Oliver usually received from Harold, which was saying something since Oliver was used to Harold giving long, tight hugs as if he were squeezing the love right out of you.

"It's so great to see you, Olly. I mean it. You are the sight I needed today," Harold rambled as he released Oliver from his bear hug.

"It's great to see you, too, Harold," Oliver said. "Is everything okay? How have you been settling into the big city?"

They both sat down, and Harold told Oliver how much fun it was having a few roommates in a strange city. Harold said that he and his roommates were getting along well enough. They did not socialize much outside of home or work, but they did enough together to consider themselves all friends. One of them was gay and had a partner. The second was straight, single, and very quiet. Harold talked about how cute the quiet one was and how much he wanted to find out if he was quiet in bed. Harold knew nothing would ever happen between them unless maybe a lot of alcohol was involved. Work was good, too, Harold told Oliver. It was more 'grunt' type of work than he expected, but he understood it was all part of a grander plan for his growth.

"That all sounds wonderful, Harold," Oliver said when he thought he heard Harold stop to catch his breath. "But something sounds off. You are as talkative as always (laughs), but your tone is sullen. What is wrong?"

"Olly, you know me so well," Harold replied through laughter and tears as he gently slapped Oliver's wrist.

After a few seconds of silence, Harold added, "my brother died recently."

"What the fuck!" Oliver almost screamed back at Harold. "I am so sorry. I did not know you even had a brother. What happened?"

Before he could answer, Harold was crying again. Oliver pulled him in for another hug while Harold incoherently mumbled into Oliver's shoulder. Oliver just let him cry. There was no point in asking questions now, he thought. Oliver had been in this position before—not because of death—but crying into a dear friend's shoulder was something Oliver knew well. He shed a tear for Howard at the thought.

"Sorry," Harold said as he pulled away from Oliver and wiped his face dry. "I didn't mean to cry on you like that." He started patting Oliver's shoulder with a napkin.

"Stop that," Oliver said, almost scolding him. "You can cry on my shoulder anytime. When you are ready, you can tell me what happened."

Harold smiled, grabbed Oliver's hand, and held it tight as he told Oliver the story of his twin brother, Shane. As Oliver sat there listening to Harold tell the story about his brother and what little he knew about his death, Oliver could not help thinking about having sex with twins, especially a pair as hot as Harold. He knew he should not have been having those thoughts as his friend shared such a personal moment, but as Oliver held Harold's hand, he realized that he was horny. Suddenly, having sex was the only idea on Oliver's mind. He felt his pants get tight.

"And so, we still do not know who killed him," Harold continued, with Oliver now more focused on Harold's words and not his looks. "But the police tell us that there were some security cameras in the parking lot, so they are hopeful they will get some leads soon. We only buried him a month ago, but it feels like yesterday. We were close—more so when we were younger."

"I am so sorry, Harold," Oliver said as he squeezed Harold's hand. "So, were you two identical or fraternal? I mean, was he as handsome as you?"

Harold laughed and blushed. He needed that laugh. "We were identical. Even our parents had trouble telling us apart sometimes. If it were not for his white hair, you could not tell us apart."

"White hair?"

"Well, maybe more platinum," Harold continued. "He was more extreme than I in almost every way. By the time we were in high school, Shane had been dying his hair in different colors for years. He wanted to be an individual and was tired of always being a twin.

"He was more adventurous, more risk-driven, and a lot more outgoing than I was in high school," Harold said, almost with a tone of disdain or regret. "He came out before me, dated before me, and even got a tattoo before me. In a way, Shane helped me out of the closet and helped me become the person I am today."

"Well, I am sorry I never got to meet Shane," Oliver said, still wide-eyed at the idea that there were two of Harold not that long ago. "He sounds like a wonderful brother. Did you two ever fool around with each other, or is that just some gay boys' fantasy?"

Harold was quiet for the first time in a long time and looked at his and Oliver's hands clasped together, getting sweaty.

"You didn't?" Oliver said with excitement in his voice. Harold shook his head 'yes.'

"Just once," Harold confessed. "I had just come out. Our parents were out of town. It was common for us to share a bed—we shared a room for so long, in bunk beds. I always slept in the top bunk. By the time we reached high school, we had moved to more traditional beds, but now and again, one of us would climb into bed with the other if we were scared, had a bad day, or just needed a brotherly snuggle.

"One night, we took the snuggling a little far. Please do not think I am some freak now."

"I would never think any such thing, Harold," Oliver reassured him, hoping to get more details about their encounter.

"Thank you. It was just that once like I said, and it was the first time I ever gave or got a blowjob. But that was it. There was no penetrating," Harold said, half laughing, half embarrassed.

Then, Oliver let go of Harold's hand and gave him another tight hug. Harold accepted the silent hug. Oliver then changed the topic and told Harold he was in the city with a friend, looking for places to live. Oliver felt obligated to give Harold more details after his revelation, but he did not have much time. He was supposed to meet Nicholas back at the hotel within the hour.

"I want to tell you the whole story, but the abridged version is that I have a brother. He is not blood-related, which is good since we already slept together," Oliver said nervously. "He is in town with me, and I need to go meet him, but you should come out to dinner with us tonight.

Harold thanked Oliver for the offer and agreed to join him and Nicholas for dinner. Oliver told Harold that he would text him when he returned to the hotel.

Oliver got up from the table, and they hugged one more time. Harold kissed Oliver's cheek as Oliver walked away, leaving Harold alone in the coffee shop.

Chapter Seventeen

Oliver arrived back at the hotel to find Nicholas already in the room. Nicholas had arrived moments before and was getting ready to take a shower. He was naked when he greeted Oliver. As Oliver entered the room, Nicholas had an overwhelming burst of excitement fill his entire body. The idea that he and Oliver were alone in the same room again filled Nicholas with joy. He sometimes struggled to put the feeling into words, and now was no different. Nicholas ran over to Oliver, hugged and kissed him like they had not seen each other in years. Oliver welcomed the affection and reciprocated, accepting the tongue penetrating his mouth. Nicholas went from kissing Oliver to removing Oliver's clothes. He wanted Oliver naked as quickly as possible, almost to ensure that Oliver would not walk out of the room and leave Nicholas.

An hour later, Nicholas lay naked on the bed, covered in fluids. He could not remember the last time he had such great sex. In the bathroom, Oliver drowned himself in a hot shower, a little sad to be washing Nicholas off. He looked up to see Nicholas open the shower door and join him as the two bodies were one, yet again.

After their shower, they got dressed for an evening on the town. They were making small talk like strangers after sex. Nicholas was not giving in to Oliver's questions about his work, so Oliver changed the topic and told Nicholas that a friend was going to join them for dinner. Oliver left it vague only because he often felt that Nicholas kept some of their conversations the same way. Nicholas did not pry. He said that he was excited to meet any friend of Oliver's.

Of course, that was not true at all. Nicholas was angry at the idea that he would have to share Oliver. Nicholas did not like it when Oliver talked about any friends because, for Nicholas, that meant one more person who had to die. As much as Nicholas was trying to stop killing so that he could entirely focus on Oliver, he felt mad at Oliver for continuously introducing new obstacles.

Oliver sent a text to Harold with an address to a restaurant that the hotel concierge recommended. Oliver was a little nervous about introducing two guys he had had sex with over the past few months and both of whom he found attractive. Oliver kept telling himself that the sex he was having with Nicholas was just sex and that a relationship would not be possible since they had the same father. But the more he reasoned why he and Nicholas could not be a couple, the more he reasoned with himself why it could be possible if they both wanted it to happen. At the same time, Oliver was attracted to Harold and would welcome a relationship with him. He was conflicted. He knew the dinner would be complicated for him, but he had no idea it would be equally as tricky for Harold and Nicholas.

Harold was already at the restaurant by the time Nicholas and Oliver arrived. He was at the bar with his back towards the door, but Oliver spotted him quickly, and he and Nicholas joined Harold at the bar for a drink while the three waited for their table to be ready.

"Olly!" Harold yelled with the excitement of a child on Christmas morning. The excitement in his voice and the shortening of Oliver's name were still something Oliver was getting used to, even after all the time the two had spent together. Hearing Harold's voice was like listening to fingernails drug across a chalkboard for Nicholas.

Oliver and Harold hugged.

"Harold, this is Nicholas," Oliver said as he let go of Harold.

"Nice to meet you, Nicky," Harold said as he tried to hug Nicholas.

"It's Nicholas," Nicholas shot back as he extended his hand before Harold could hug him.

The two shook hands, and the three sat down for a drink. Harold talked about nothing in particular—just filling the air with noise. Nicholas felt like he saw a ghost. Aside from the hair color, Nicholas was pretty sure that the young man before him was the one he had killed not that long ago and left him for dead in a parking lot.

As Nicholas continued to stare at Harold, who had not come up for air since the three sat down, he wondered if it could have been possible for anyone to survive more than a dozen stab wounds only to be as chatty as Harold was now. Nicholas kept looking at Harold intently, almost studying him to see if Harold recognized him. Was he looking at some doppelgänger, Nicholas wondered.

"I'm sorry," Harold said, diverting from his story to Nicholas. "But are you okay?"

"Sorry," Nicholas responded. "It's just that you look so familiar. Have we met before?"

Nicholas was about to reveal a clue about Shane's death when Harold interrupted him.

"No, but maybe you knew my twin brother," Harold started to say before tears cascaded down his face.

Oliver put his arm around Harold and filled in the gaps with information Harold had already shared. He told Nicholas that he had run into Harold earlier that day and learned that Harold had a twin brother, Shane, who had been murdered recently.

"I am sorry for your loss," Nicholas said with little emotion or empathy. He was momentarily relieved that he was not seeing a ghost and frustrated that he would have another person to kill to keep Oliver to himself.

The three finally moved to a table and washed a particularly awkward and quiet dinner down with four bottles of expensive wine. Harold offered his fair share of chatter, but each time Shane came up in the conversation, Harold would get quiet. Nicholas was his typical quiet self—not shy but not adding much value to the discussion. Oliver filled in where the other two faltered. The evening was not the fun time Oliver had envisioned when he invited Harold. The more he thought about it, the more he realized he should not have invited Harold. He knew that afternoon that Harold still had some healing to do. The freshness of his brother's death was still too painful for him to be socializing, Oliver thought. Oliver apologized to Harold and Nicholas and suggested that they end the evening so Harold could go home—maybe go back to Boston to spend more time with his family so he could mourn completely.

Harold stumbled into a cab, telling Oliver he would text him soon. Nicholas and Oliver watched the taxi drive away, and once it was out of sight, Nicholas grabbed Oliver's hand and held it tightly. Then he tugged Oliver in the opposite direction for the short walk back to their hotel.

"He seems like a nice guy," Nicholas said as they walked hand in hand, enjoying the cool evening. "I am sorry about his brother." Nicholas knew he was being polite and admitting to killing Shane without Oliver knowing the truth. Nicholas felt the guilt escape as he confessed.

Chapter Eighteen

While in New York, Oliver fell in love with what he called the perfect apartment. He found it on his own while Nicholas was away at 'work.' He then waited for the next few weeks to hear if the board would approve his purchase. The apartment was in an old building in the center of Gramercy Park, which is not where Oliver thought he would end up. Still, there was something romantic, something extraordinary about the neighborhood, so much so that he stopped looking once he found 'the one.'

Nicholas continued to cross people off his kill list when he was not with Oliver. It was not a list he had written on the back of a napkin or a post-it note stuck to his fridge. His list was internal, and at times it was hard to manage. Nicholas refused to write any of their names down. He did not want to leave a paper trail for anyone to find, but lately, he was having trouble keeping track of the list. Oliver continued adding more people to it without realizing he was digging so many graves.

Nicholas' latest focus was still on Imani and Jackson. He was not yet convinced that Jackson was a real threat, but he followed him to be sure. Nicholas had been watching Imani and Jackson since seeing them with Oliver on the island months ago. Nicholas was already aware of Imani. He remembered her, at least by name, from when he briefly dated Camilla in college. In the short time that Nicholas and Camilla were together, Camilla would talk about Imani a lot, but Nicholas did not see them together often. Nicholas did not know back then that he did not see much of Imani because Camilla did not want to introduce Nicholas to any girls that Camilla believed were prettier than she. Her insecurity would not be able to handle the competition. Through all the time Nicholas spent tracking Camilla over the years, he never saw Imani dating or spending time with anyone other than Camilla, so he was surprised to see her with Jackson.

The more time Nicholas spent with Oliver, learning more about who Oliver engaged with, even just periodically, the more he understood that not everyone had to die. He was accepting that some of the people in Oliver's life were distant enough that they could live, that they would not be a deterrent to their relationship. Nicholas began believing that Imani and Jackson were good examples of this new belief.

* * * * *

"I got it!" Oliver texted Nicholas soon after learning that his apartment of choice had come through. He spent a couple of weeks fielding questions, participating in interviews, and enduring extensive background checks by several board members and residents. A few older residents seemed tougher on Oliver than some of the younger ones, so he was not sure how the vote would go in the end.

Fortunately for Oliver, the board president, Mrs. Longfellow, was a long-time friend of Oliver's mother and one of the oldest residents in the building. Mrs. Longfellow enjoyed the luxury of one of the four penthouse units and remembered seeing Oliver when he was just a toddler. He had often visited her with his mother more than a decade ago, but Oliver did not remember the visits or the building that he would now call home. Mrs. Longfellow and Mrs. McPherson went to college together, and in their later years, they would get together for high tea around the holidays each year. Mrs. Longfellow, when interviewing Oliver, told him that she would not play favorites, but she would put in a good word with the rest of the board because she had enjoyed spending time with his mother and was sorry to hear of her passing.

And just like that, Oliver was the new owner of a high-rise apartment in the big city.

"Got what?" Nicholas responded, almost forgetting that Oliver had been obsessed with finding a place to live in New York for the last month. "Just kidding," he continued.

"Congrats! When do you move in?"

"Two weeks from tomorrow," Oliver sent back. "I am finishing up packing my mothers' house until then. I put it on the market yesterday and already have a few interested buyers. Come over, and let's celebrate."

An hour later, there was a knock on the door. Oliver opened it expecting to see Nicholas, but instead, he saw Imani. She was crying, and as the door opened, she ran into Oliver's arms and started babbling as she drooled all over Oliver's shirt.

"Come on in," Oliver said sarcastically. "What is wrong, Imani? Where is Jackson?"

After a few minutes, Imani stopped crying long enough to tell Oliver that Camilla was dead. As the words came out of her mouth, she cried more hysterically than before. Oliver hugged Imani's little frame, almost engulfing her.

"How do you know she is dead?" he asked, holding back his tears.

Oliver closed the front door and moved Imani to the living room, where they both sat. Once Imani had settled down, she told Oliver about how she had been going to the police station every day, asking if they knew anything about the disappearance of Camilla. She did not know if Camilla was in town but figured he had to start her search somewhere. She said that all her nagging finally paid off. The police received a call while Imani was at the station. Imani described Camilla to one officer while another listened to a caller describe a dead body found at a motel on the edge of town. The two officers were intrigued that the two descriptions were so similar.

The police would not tell Imani how Camilla died. That information would be for Camilla's parents, but the officers were thankful that Imani had been at the station reporting Camilla missing at the right moment. If not for Imani, Camilla would have been buried as a Jane Doe since she had no identification when she was discovered gutted on the motel floor.

As Imani told her story, Oliver let go, and his tears poured down his face. He started crying loudly, putting every ounce of energy into letting out the pain. He had a hard time understanding why someone would kill Camilla — kill another one of his friends. He did not have the strength to tell Imani how Camilla was just one of many people close to him who had died recently — murdered. Instead, he just let out his pain through tears and cries.

His crying was interrupted by another knock on the front door. The last thing Oliver wanted was another visitor or to deal with some random solicitor. He wiped his eyes and walked to the front door. He opened the door to see Nicholas standing with flowers — more Gerber daisies. Nicholas could see that Oliver had been crying, so he moved inside and hugged Oliver as tightly as he could, concerned that someone might have hurt Oliver and that he would now have to hurt more people. With the news from Imani, Oliver had forgotten that Nicholas was on his way over.

After a few minutes, Nicholas and Oliver started to move toward the living room. As they entered the room, Nicholas saw Imani on the couch with her back to him. Before she turned around to greet him, he quickly ran out of the living room and headed for the bathroom. She only saw a blur of a figure.

"I am sorry, Oliver, but I need to go," Imani said as she got up, wiped her tears, and hugged Oliver. "I will contact Camilla's parents and tell you about the funeral plans." And with that, Imani was gone.

Nicholas hung out in the bathroom until he heard Imani leave. While unsure, Nicholas believed that Camilla had confided in Imani and that Imani might know what Camilla thought to be true — what was true, and she would expose Nicholas for the murderer that he is. At that moment, alone in the bathroom, Nicholas decided that Imani did have to die after all.

Nicholas came out of the bathroom, and Oliver started crying again before he could say anything. Nicholas held Oliver tightly while Oliver cried for much longer than he wanted. In between letting out some screams, Oliver was able to tell Nicholas that his dear friend Camilla was found dead. Nicholas held Oliver tighter, longer, as if he never intended to let him go. For the first time he could remember, Nicholas, let a tear escape and roll down his face. He was sorry for hurting Oliver this way, but Oliver could never know the truth.

* * * *

Nicholas gave Oliver the space to deal with Camila's death and funeral. He wanted to make sure that Oliver could have the closure he needed. He also wanted to put some distance between him and anything to do with Camilla. With Imani still alive, Nicholas needed to be sure he could not be identified. He had come too far and sacrificed too much, he thought. There was no way Nicholas would allow anyone or anything to come between him and Oliver now.

Oliver did not attend Camilla's funeral. He sent flowers but did not travel to Pennsylvania. He could not face her parents. He felt that, in some small way, he was responsible for Camilla's death. When Imani finally did learn how Camilla died and shared that news with Oliver, he was even more convinced that her blood was on his hands. He knew he should have been there for her more or not let her be alone after everything they went through together, but she demanded her space. He wanted to tell her parents everything so they could make sense — make peace with her death, but he could not. They would bury their daughter, thinking she was randomly murdered for no reason. Oliver was disturbed by Camilla's death and feared that whoever was lurking around killing his friends would catch up to him eventually. Oliver did not want to be the next one to die.

Oliver had never been able to attend funerals in the past. He tried attending the one for Elizabeth but got so upset about losing her that he had to leave the funeral. He was crying too much and moaning too loudly — everyone was looking at him rather than focusing on the service. That experience made him realize that funerals were not for him — at least not the funerals of people he knew. He skipped his own father's funeral completely. His mother was not happy with him then, but she could do nothing to make Oliver attend. He cried alone at home and eventually over his father's tombstone to deal with the loss. Oliver did attend Peter's funeral, but that was because he did not know Peter, and he was too busy trying to figure out why he was at the funeral in the first place.

Because Oliver skipped Camilla's funeral, he could move to New York as planned. He emptied his mother's house—keeping only enough furniture to furnish his new apartment. He sold everything else with the house for a quick sale. He knew he should have taken more time to go through the house and debate what to keep and sell—that is what most children would do when they buried the last of their parents and then struggled with the reality that they were alone, or at least orphaned. But for Oliver, it was quite the opposite. He needed quick closure. He was not one to linger or procrastinate about something—anything, and he was not very sentimental about material things.

With the sale, the move, and the loss of Camilla, Oliver completely forgot to let Nicholas know that he had completed his move. It was not intentional or devious in any way. He was so busy and so overwhelmed—as he felt he always was these days, that he just up and left Greenwich and did not text or call Nicholas.

* * * * *

Nicholas knew that Oliver had moved. He never stopped watching Oliver from a distance. Whether it was a tracking device or a Wi-Fi camera hiding in a tree, Nicholas rarely took his eye off Oliver. He loved him, or maybe he just obsessed over him that much. Nicholas would see it as love. After he left Oliver alone to deal with the death of Camilla, Nicholas contemplated what to do about Imani. He did not want her popping up unannounced anywhere because he was confident she would recognize him—know exactly who he was. He knew that would be the beginning of the end for him, and only Nicholas would dictate how this all ended.

Rather than hastily killing Imani, Nicholas watched her for a couple more weeks after the funeral. Nicholas felt that if Imani or Jackson made any attempt to investigate more about Camilla or keep in touch with Oliver, then Nicholas knew he would have to kill them. Part of him hoped that Imani would just go on with her life and stay away from Oliver. They were not friends. Camilla was the link between them, and with that link broken, she should fade away, as most of those kinds of relationships did. At least, that is what Nicholas was hoping.

Luckily for Imani, that is precisely what happened. She did not seem bothered about Oliver missing the funeral, and Nicholas noticed she never revisited Oliver. Even Jackson seemed to have faded from the picture, although he was by Imani's side at the funeral. Nicholas remembered thinking Jackson looked more handsome when he cleaned up and sank his body into a fitted suit.

Chapter Nineteen

It had only been one month since Oliver moved to New York, and he was already quite comfortable living in the big city. His new apartment was just the fresh start he thought he needed and deserved. Most other residents were older, more affluent, and less friendly than he had expected, especially after meeting several of them during the interviewing process. Still, enough of them said hello when passing in the halls to make Oliver feel welcome. Of all the neighbors he had met, he had two favorites. One was a widow in her 80s, who he would learn as they often waited for the elevator together, had been a Broadway star many decades earlier. She did not speak about her roles but shared lengthy stories about the parties she attended and all the men who fought for her attention.

She introduced herself as Mrs. Pankhurst and never gave him any other name. She only wanted to be addressed by her proper name. Oliver found it endearing that Mrs. Pankhurst was old school and proper, but he was curious to know her first name. He asked many of the residents he encountered in the halls, the elevator, and even the mailroom, and while many knew of Mrs. Pankhurst, and a few even claimed to know her very well, not one of them could tell Oliver her first name. In the mailroom, one day, Oliver found an unclaimed New Yorker magazine, and when he looked at the shipping label, he saw the addressee as "Mrs. Pankhurst." No first name. Oliver knew this was a woman he wanted to get to know. She was a mystery.

Frederick Leyland was the other resident Oliver got the most acquainted with in his early days. Frederick lived on the same floor as Oliver and brought Oliver a plate of homemade oatmeal cookies the day Oliver arrived. Frederick was a 52-year-old single, gay, black man who looked older than he was but behaved like he was much younger. Oliver found Frederick entertaining and funny. He felt confident that Frederick would become a dear friend in the months ahead. Frederick was the most flamboyant gay person Oliver had met, which added to the fascination Oliver had with Frederick. While Oliver did not like the cookies, he enjoyed Frederick's company.

Once Oliver settled into his new apartment, he finally texted Nicholas, letting him know the move was complete. The two had not been texting or talking much while Oliver focused on the move, but Nicholas had watched Oliver from a distance a few times when he was in the city stalking Harold. Once Nicholas discovered that Harold was still alive, Nicholas was obsessed about taking Harold out of Oliver's life, especially now that Harold and Oliver lived in the same city. Nicholas would not compete with anyone for Oliver's love or attention.

When not stalking one of his victims, Nicholas was busy buying assets he thought would be essential for him and Oliver once they were together for good. The financial advisor overseeing the fortune left for Nicholas when Peter died was quite perplexed at the purchases. None of them made logical sense other than being something physical to hold on to rather than stocks or cash. Nicholas was buying different pieces of property, from the 15th-century castle on the Scottish coast to the two-thousand-acre farm in Vermont to an entire island in the South Pacific. He hoped that at least one would be someplace Oliver liked enough to live with Nicholas forever.

The common thread of each property was the isolation they each offered. Nicholas did not want to live with Oliver in a populated area, assuming, of course, that Oliver would eventually want to live with Nicholas; love Nicholas. New York was way too busy, thought Nicholas. Even Greenwich had proven to be filled with too many people connected to Oliver. Nicholas spent so long trying to get Oliver for himself. He feared Oliver would be distracted if they lived in a densely populated place like New York. Nicholas believed that if Oliver got distracted and found someone else to love, then Nicholas would have to keep killing, and he wanted to stop killing. He wanted to live and love in peace and do that with and only Oliver. With his latest purchase complete, Nicholas added a 2500-acre ranch in Montana to the menu of offerings. He then redirected his attention back to Harold. He still had to take out Harold, and he hoped Harold would be the last sacrifice before he and Oliver could be together forever.

Nicholas stalked Harold for a couple of weeks. He was learning where Harold liked to eat, where he wanted to shop, and how often he was going out to different clubs. Nicholas knew that Harold was a creature of habit. He had a handful of places he would go throughout the week before or after work. Day after day, Harold was proving to Nicholas just how predictable he was, which Nicholas liked. This helped Nicholas put together a simple capture-and-kill plan.

In his second week of stalking, Nicholas watched Harold enter the local grocery store near his apartment building on his way home from work. Nicholas had learned this routine as it happened a few times a week. Today Nicholas stayed outside and waited for Harold to come out instead of going inside and watching him more closely. Nicholas had already scoped out the store and knew the only entrance was in the front. He could stay outside and wait for Harold, keeping his distance. Nicholas had to be sure that Harold did not see him because he did not want to be recognized, or worse, have Harold tell Oliver that he had bumped into Nicholas. While waiting for Harold to come out of the store, Nicholas received a text message from Oliver.

"How's it going?" read the text. Nicholas thought it was rather bland and generic, something you send to an acquaintance, not a good friend—not a lover. But then Oliver had not professed his love to Nicholas yet.

"Good," was all Nicholas could think to write back. He started typing, then stopped and erased, and started repeatedly. It took him way too long to come back with one word, but that was the best he could do without looking too excited to hear from Oliver.

A few people came out of the store across the street. Nicholas looked up and noticed that none of them were Harold, so he focused back on Oliver's texts.

"I am all settled into my new place. Next time you are in the city, let's get together. I'd love to show you my new home."

Nicholas typed, "I am in the city now," without thinking through the fact that he was in the city on a mission that he did not want Oliver to know about. This text puts Nicholas in town when he needs Oliver to think he is elsewhere. If Nicholas harmed Harold, now there was the chance that Oliver could connect the dots, Nicholas thought. Nicholas did not know just how little Oliver was thinking about the conspiracy theories he, Camilla, and Howard had conjured up and extinguished. Oliver was too busy trying to settle into a new life. Imani had tried to lure Oliver back in, and the death of Camilla almost succeeded, but in the end, Oliver chose to look forward.

"That is fantastic. Are you free tonight?" Oliver typed back.

"Yes," Nicholas responded, still without thinking. He was so excited that Oliver wanted them to spend more time together.

While Nicholas was deep in thought, texting with Oliver, he did not see Harold leave the store and continue his journey. If he had, Nicholas would have noticed Harold walk in the opposite direction that Nicholas was predicting Harold would go.

"Great, my address is 36 Gramercy Park East, Apt 13S."

"Okay. I can be there in about an hour," Nicholas typed back as he looked up, concerned that Harold had not come out of the store yet. He put his phone in his pocket and decided to go into the store and look for Harold. He was hoping to kill him today, but he believed that the text from Oliver had changed those plans. Nicholas walked every aisle of the store but could not find Harold anywhere. Nicholas yelled in frustration when he was back outside, looking in every direction for any sign of Harold. His scream was louder than he meant it to be, but fortunately for him, the people of New York go about their days ignoring the cries of other people. Once he let out his anger, Nicholas decided to go see Oliver, as promised. He would have to kill Harold another day.

While Nicholas had been busy texting with Oliver, Harold was in the store buying a bottle of wine to bring to Oliver. Harold was thrilled that Oliver was in New York, and he was hoping to get much closer to Oliver finally. Harold had no idea that Nicholas was obsessed with Oliver, not that knowing would have changed how Harold felt about Oliver. When the two met, Harold assumed Nicholas was just a friend of Oliver's. As far as Harold was concerned, Oliver was still single, and Harold was ready to pick up where they had left off over the summer. Harold thought it would be a fun surprise to show up unannounced with a bottle of wine, hoping that Oliver would welcome him in with open arms.

Oliver sat in his new apartment, waiting for Nicholas to arrive. He was nervous and excited about having Nicholas visit. In their little time together, Oliver discovered that he was growing quite fond of Nicholas. Oliver knew he enjoyed the sex and liked the feeling of his body wrapped around Nicholas' naked body, but he felt it was something more. He was not ready to call it love, but he was ready to explore it more, to label the feeling.

Not that he was focused on Harold all that much, but Oliver knew that with Harold, it was just about the sex. He enjoyed it a lot, but he was not interested in a serious relationship with Harold. Oliver thought he had been making that clear the last couple of times he saw Harold and even in their text messages when he shared his address. Oliver believed he was setting friendship boundaries. Harold did not interpret it that way at all.

As Nicholas approached the address Oliver had texted to him, he saw Harold; more like he collided with him as he turned the corner onto Gramercy Park East. The bottle of wine Harold had been holding sailed through the air before it kissed the concrete, making a loud shattering sound as it bled red all over the sidewalk.

"I am so sorry," Harold said as he stepped back to ensure no one was hurt.

"No worries, mate," Nicholas replied.

"Hey, I know you," Harold pointed to Nicholas. The frustration he should have expressed because of the broken bottle was masked by the sound of delight at seeing a familiar face. "You are Olly's friend, right? You are, um… Nicky."

"My name is Nicholas," he responded as he pulled Harold in close to him. Before Harold could ask another question, Nicholas wrapped his hand around Harold's neck and kissed him. He knew that was the best distraction for Harold and anyone who might have seen their collision and paid any attention to them. Nicholas wanted to conceal his face and make sure people ignored them. It was New York City, so people paid no attention.

Harold pulled away from Nicholas momentarily, only to catch his breath. Confused by what was happening, he leaned back into Nicholas for another kiss. Nicholas immediately noticed how different Harold and Shane were at kissing boys. Shane put passion in his kissing, visceral, while Harold was more cautious and curiously excited, like a teenage boy discovering how to kiss. Nicholas could not imagine Oliver kissing Harold. Nicholas thought Oliver was a great kisser and would have only wanted to kiss other great kissers like Nicholas. Maybe sex with Harold made up for the lousy kissing, Nicholas thought. Harold was enjoying the moment; his lips locked and his tongue spastic as if he were an anteater at dinner time.

As much as Nicholas wanted to see Oliver, he was unsure when he would have an opportunity to capture Harold so quickly again. He grabbed Harold's crotch and felt how aroused Harold had become, so Nicholas thought they should have some fun together. Nicholas pulled his tongue out of Harold's mouth.

"Do you have plans right now?" Nicholas asked.

"I was going to visit Oliver with that bottle of wine," Harold said, almost out of breath, pointing to the stained concrete. "But I can be easily persuaded to go somewhere with you, stud."

"This might sound crazy," Nicholas started. "But how would you feel about going to my place right now?"

Harold grinned with excitement as Nicholas hailed a cab. Nicholas knew that he could not wait any longer. Harold needed to die today because Nicholas needed to be with Oliver.

Thirteen stories above, Oliver was looking out the window at the very moment when Nicholas and Harold collided. He felt like a voyeur for watching the tiny specs of men. He was unsure he was seeing Nicholas and Harold, but the figures looked like his friends. At first, he was confused, then Oliver got jealous and angry when he saw the two small figures kiss and then get into a cab. Oliver knew he was being unreasonable in his thinking. He was not confident that he was looking at Nicholas and Harold from way above the street.

In the heat of the moment, Oliver grabbed his phone and texted Harold; then, he sent one to Nicholas. He kept the texts short; non-confrontational. Neither of them responded. Oliver threw his phone at the couch and then slapped himself for being so jealous.

An hour later, when Nicholas had still not arrived or responded to Oliver's text, Oliver yelled at Nicholas as if he were in the room with Oliver. He yelled loud enough that his neighbor, Frederick, came knocking to make sure that Oliver was okay. Oliver thanked Frederick for coming over and explained that he was angry and jealous over a boy and was learning to cope with these new feelings. Frederick wanted to hang around and ask questions, but he explained to Oliver that he had dinner in the oven and a gentleman guest pouring wine. Oliver laughed, the two hugged, and Frederick was gone.

Chapter Twenty

Harold felt lost when the taxi driver stopped in front of a brownstone resembling every other brownstone. He had been so busy making out with Nicholas in the backseat of the taxi that he paid little attention to all the turns the drivers took, zigzagging across Manhattan. Harold was still new enough to be clueless about what part of the city they were now standing in as the taxi drove away. Nicholas grabbed Harold's hand and pulled him down some stairs, then into the basement level of the building that Nicholas had recently started renting. He had not told Oliver about this place yet and was confident he never would. He needed someplace in the city to crash and plan Harold's death.

Inside, the hallway was dark. The air smelled of fresh paint. Harold held Nicholas' hand tightly, almost afraid to let go for fear of getting lost in the black labyrinth.

"Where are we going?" Harold asked. "And can we turn on some lights?"

"Don't worry about it," Nicholas shot back with less interest in his tone. "I just moved in. The power does not get turned on until tomorrow." He was lying.

"Dude, then we should have gone to my place. I have electricity."

Nicholas ignored Harold as they finally stopped in a windowless room. Harold could see nothing, and when Nicholas momentarily let go of Harold's hand, Harold let out a yelp of panic. "I am not a fan of the dark."

"Relax, and do not move," Nicholas fired back.

Little by little, the room started to illuminate as Nicholas lit candles. By the time he had finished, the room was bright, almost romantic. The walls, the floor, and the ceiling were all painted black. Harold noticed that there was no ceiling light and wondered how the room could be lit even if the place did have electricity. Harold also noticed that the walls and ceiling were covered in what looked like padding.

"Is this room soundproof?" he asked Nicholas.

"I am not sure. I have not yet tested it out," Nicholas lied. I just thought this room looked fantastic when I saw the listing online. "The listing called it the perfect, romantic dungeon."

The only piece of furniture in the room was a king-size bed in the center. The bed frame was almost too big for the room and was very ornate. Harold was enamored at the detailed carvings of the posts and the headboard.

"Is this where you sleep?" Harold asked, more confused than aroused at this point.

"No," Nicholas replied, annoyed at Harold now. "It was here when I moved in. It is part of the dungeon decor."

Nicholas walked over to Harold, grabbed both hands, and pulled him toward the bed. He pushed Harold onto the bed, got on top of him, kicked off his shoes, and unbuttoned his shirt. Harold liked the assertiveness. Once Nicholas was shirtless, Harold was no longer focused on the creepy black room. Instead, he started quickly kicking off his shoes and trying to pull his pants down. Nicholas helped Harold get utterly naked while Nicholas kept his pants on.

Harold was panting with anticipation. His skin glowed as the candlelight danced around them. He was aroused, and Nicholas grinned at how much smaller Harold was than he expected. He wondered if Harold's twin brother was identical down there, too. Harold lay on the bed, fully erect, wanting Nicholas to have his way with him. Still, on top of Harold, Nicholas grabbed him, and they rolled around on the bed. The mattress was soft, almost swallowing them.

Nicholas stopped rolling when he was on top again.

"Would you like some, Molly? Nicholas asked as he pulled a little baggie out from under the mattress. He opened the bag and pulled out two little rainbow-colored pills. He put one in Harold's mouth and made it look like he put the other in his mouth all before Harold could say 'No.' Harold swallowed the rainbow without question.

Then Nicholas grabbed Harold's right arm and put it in the handcuff attached to the bedpost. As Harold tried to understand what was happening, Nicholas put Harold's left arm in another handcuff connected to the other post. Harold started pleading with Nicholas to uncuff him. He was no longer having fun.

"Dude, please stop. I am merinthophobic," Harold yelled. "I cannot have my hands tied up. It freaks me out."

"Come on, man. You know you like being dominated like this," Nicholas replied, ignoring Harold's plea. "I am about to rock your world."

Harold liked the idea of having his world rocked but was not comfortable with being tied up. He started to hyperventilate, but Nicholas assumed he was pretending. Harold had done some kinky things, usually with older guys living out a fantasy and paying him well for his uncomfortable service. But Nicholas was not a client, and

Harold had no idea what kind of crazy, kinky sex Nicholas had planned.

With Harold now spread out on the bed, lying on his back and his arms stretched over his head to the right and left, Nicholas started working on Harold's feet. Nicholas kissed and licked Harold's toes, trying to distract Harold from the reality that he was stretched out like The Vitruvian Man. Harold had a weakness and fascination with feet, so to have his licked and sucked by Nicholas not only distracted Harold from what was happening but also kept Harold aroused. Before he knew it, Harold was utterly trapped. Both wrists were tethered to head posts, and both ankles were tethered to foot posts. Harold suddenly felt the pain of his body being stretched out and locked in place. He tried to wiggle, but he could barely move his body.

"Listen, dude," he started in, almost crying. "I like a little kink as much as the next guy, but this is going a bit far. These restraints are hurting me. And what the hell was in that pill? I am feeling a little disoriented."

"Calm down, Harold," Nicholas said, scolding him for complaining so much. "I know you like it kinky. I have seen you in action. Trust me when I say that this is about to get good. You will explode like you have never exploded before."

With Harold secure and a little more sedated as the drugs kicked in, Nicholas poured warm oil on Harold's chest and started rubbing it all over his body. Nicholas was rubbing the oil in slowly, enjoying the feel of Harold's smooth skin. Harold was not as toned as other guys, but Nicholas still thought Harold had a great body. Given different circumstances, Nicholas felt confident that he and Harold could have had great sex together.

"Is that olive oil?" Harold asked, now feeling quite relaxed from the ecstasy. "Man, your hands feel good against my skin."

Nicholas finished covering Harold's body with a generous amount of oil. He even stroked Harold a few times just to keep him excited. Then Nicholas picked up one of the candles and poured hot wax on Harold. Slowly, Harold's nipples were covered with the hot wax mixed with the oil. Harold moaned loudly and bit his lip to keep from screaming at the searing pain. He liked it a little. With Harold's nipples covered in hardening wax, Nicholas poured wax all over Harold's chest while stroking him. Harold's body twitched and twerked at the eruption growing within him and the pain covering his body. He was beginning to believe Nicholas's words about the best explosion ever.

Then, just as Harold exploded, Nicholas released his hand and covered Harold's dick in hot wax. Harold screamed.

"Fuck!"

Nicholas stepped back away from the bed to admire his artwork. Harold was glistening, almost swimming in oil. Nicholas had placed candles on Harold's chest near where he had poured the wax. The wax had hardened, securing the candles to Harold's chest so they would not slip off as his chest rose and fell with his irregular breathing.

As Harold's body slumped, post-explosion, Nicholas grabbed a blow torch off the floor and turned it on. He admired the blue flame that shot out. Then without saying a word, Nicholas touched the bottom of Harold's foot with the flame just briefly. Harold screamed as the oil ignited and the flame swam across his body. Nicholas watched as Harold's body tried to thrash. As the flame spread, the bedding covering caught fire, and Harold was engulfed in flames. Nicholas watched with wonder in his eyes and listened to Harold scream.

Harold could not move. His body was ablaze, and his skin was bubbling over. He was in so much pain, but he no longer had the voice or the words to express this pain. He tried to look in Nicholas' direction, but his eyes hurt. His entire body hurt. He stopped yelling. Nicholas was pleased with how well his plan came together.

The heat from the fire warmed the room so much that Nicholas started sweating. He grabbed Harold's underwear off the floor, sniffed them, then wiped his brow before throwing them onto Harold's body. They burned quickly. Nicholas stood as close to the bed as he could without getting burned. He wanted to watch Harold's face as he slowly burned to death. Nicholas was fascinated with how Harold's skin boiled and burned away. The room's temperature was well over 100 degrees between the candles and the burning body. Nicholas could feel the sweat running down his body. The last time he was this sweaty was when he was at the Monster dancing with Mike. He knew he needed to clean up and get to Oliver, but he enjoyed watching Harold burn.

Harold died in front of Nicholas, but Nicholas let the flames continue to incinerate the body. He knew all the candles would burn out in a few hours, and the flame that killed Harold would also fizzle out. Nicholas contemplated putting the fire out, but instead, he left it going as he walked out of the room, closing and locking the door behind him. Harold's dead body was trapped in a room that grew darker with each minute. Nicholas knew that if anyone found Harold's body, he would be completely unrecognizable.

Nicholas walked upstairs to the main floor of the brownstone. He could feel the warmth of the fire below. He knew the flames would not penetrate the room but wondered how long the house would stay warm. He continued up another flight of stairs and walked into the primary bedroom, where he had new clothes laid out. He stripped out of his jeans, leaving them alone on the bedroom floor. He had not been wearing any underwear, and the rest of his clothes were trapped with Harold. Satisfied with this latest kill, Nicholas enjoyed a long, hot shower that included his own explosion before getting dressed. He never went back to the basement to check on Harold.

Nicholas picked up Harold's phone while sitting on the bed. It was the only thing of Harold's that made it out of the basement chamber. Nicholas had already used Harold's fingerprint to unlock it and turned off the lock feature so he could use it now. He flipped through Harold's emails and then his photos. He was surprised at how many pictures Harold had of his own penis on his phone. Nicholas did not think the real thing was impressive enough to justify that many photos. When he got to Harold's text messages, Nicholas could see how much more aggressive Harold was at pursuing Oliver than Oliver was towards Harold. Nicholas felt better about his chances with Oliver and his decision to remove Harold from the picture.

Nicholas saw the latest text from Oliver. He looked at the time stamp and realized that Oliver had texted him and Harold almost simultaneously. That got Nicholas thinking that Oliver saw the two of them together. He was unhappy about that possibility, so he texted Oliver from Harold's phone.

"Hi, Olly," Nicholas wrote. "I was coming to surprise you with some wine, but I dropped the bottle, so I went to get a replacement, but then worked called, and I had to run to the office. I am hoping we can get together next week if you are around. I cannot wait to see your new place."

Nicholas added a heart emoji since that was what Harold often did with his texts to Oliver. Nicholas threw the phone into his bag and walked through the house and out the front door after texting Oliver. He did not lock the door behind him. As he walked away from the brownstone that he rented under Harold's name, Nicholas looked at his phone and the text from Oliver. He knew he needed to respond. This moment made him think about last year when he pretended to be Eric. Just like then, Nicholas knew what he needed to do. This time would be different, though. This time he did reply to the text from Oliver.

"Hi. Sorry about bailing. A work emergency came up. I must go out of town but I will text when I return. See you soon."

Nicholas did not include any emojis. That was not his style. It buzzed as he was about to put his phone back in his pocket. He looked at the screen and saw, 'no worries. See you soon. smiling emoji.' Nicholas smiled. Two blocks from the brownstone, he dropped Harold's phone into a dumpster and headed to the airport.

Chapter Twenty-One

Nicholas felt at home the minute he stepped off the plane at Heathrow airport. London was his true love, his first home. Ever since Peter told Nicholas about his conception and what happened to his mother, Nicholas has been fascinated with his past and, more specifically, his biological father, Adam. Nicholas had been killing people since he was a teenager, and his kills grew more violent as he got older and fell more in love with Oliver. Nicholas often wondered if his birth father had the same issues. In his late teens, when Peter told Nicholas about Adam and what happened to him, Nicholas started researching Adam. It was hard to find any information, especially from the States. It was not until his college years that Nicholas frequently traveled to London to research more about Adam.

Nicholas learned that his birth father was Adam Burlington. What little information he found through old police records online painted a story of Adam taking his own life when cornered by the police while trying to escape from a police station. Nicholas found the story fascinating. Aside from a few fluff pieces about Adam and Catherine, Nicholas could not find much more about Adam. There were a few more reports that blamed Adam for some murders, but there was not a lot of detail about those cases, which led Nicholas to believe that Adam was never convicted. It became clear to Nicholas that he needed to hire some experts to help him learn more about Adam.

After Peter died, Nicholas hired two university students in London studying to be historians. He pretended to be an up-and-coming author writing his first book, which was all about Adam. Nicholas told Eleanor and Morgan, his historians, that he needed to find everything possible on Adam, going as far back as they could go. Nicholas had received weekly email or text updates from Eleanor and Morgan. Still, anytime the two revealed that they had found a jackpot of information, Nicholas would fly to London to meet with them in person.

Eleanor was older than Morgan. She was a tiny woman, almost dwarfed by the thin lankiness of Morgan when they were side by side, which they were quite often. Both wore glasses and had dark hair that sat unkept on their heads like an old mop—neither looked like they ever combed their hair. Eleanor smoked but never around Nicholas. She did once, and he barraged her with enough insults that she stopped smoking when Nicholas visited. He could still smell the odor on her and found it repulsive. Morgan did not smoke; he never had. He did know how to throw back pints of beer, which Nicholas found amazing. Morgan could drink twice his weight in beer and still behave completely sober.

Morgan and Eleanor never dated. They slept together once, and soon after, they started working for Nicholas. Morgan fumbled with himself, never satisfying Eleanor the way she liked, so they agreed never to talk about the drunken night again and just be friends. Neither of them dated anyone else and instead focused on discovering everything they could about Adam.

Still fueled by the excitement of recently killing Harold, Nicholas arrived in London with a little more enthusiasm in his step. While on his flight to London, Eleanor, and Morgan emailed Nicholas that they had some great news about Adam. He texted that he was going to London and suggested they meet the next day.

"It was not easy," Eleanor told Nicholas when they met up. "This guy was quite a mystery, but we connected several police reports from different parts of the country. This guy might have been the most prolific serial killer in the United Kingdom."

Nicholas smiled at the news, feeling as giddy as a schoolgirl in love. He knew that his father had raped his mother, and he knew that Adam had been connected to some deaths, including his own, but to learn that Adam might have killed so many more people had Nicholas overcome with joy. He wanted to know about every death—how the people died and how Adam was connected to them all. Given that Nicholas had been killing with almost no discernible pattern, he wondered if Adam killed the same way.

"We still have a lot of police reports to read," Morgan added. "But from what we can tell, a man named Adam had been arrested many times for indecent exposure, prostitution, or selling drugs. So far, the reports we have found and reviewed all have similar fingerprints, and mug shots—at least the mug shots are similar enough to make the connection that these are most likely the same person."

"And what is most interesting," Eleanor interrupted. "Is that a week after each of Adam's arrest and release, regardless of where he was in the country, the same police department that charged Adam for petty crimes would open a murder investigation, most of which are still unsolved."

"What makes that so interesting," Nicholas asked.

"For starters," Morgan chimed in. "Each of the unsolved murder cases involves a dead body found in a cemetery. I know that is where you find dead bodies, but these were all above ground. I am not sure how the police never connected these dots, but each time Adam was arrested, he was in a cemetery—the same cemetery as the murder investigation."

"Any idiot could step back and look at the bigger picture," Eleanor continued. "And see that a week after Adam was arrested, a dead body would be found in the same cemetery. But, because these events were happening all over the country, the different police departments never had the option to connect any two cases to see a pattern."

Nicholas could not believe his luck. This information was like winning the lottery, he thought. Nicholas had collected enough information about Adam over the years to see the connections. He knew that Adam was a murderer, so he knew that Adam had to have been the killer in all these unsolved cases.

"How many cases have you found so far?" Nicholas asked.

"So far, we have made 50 connections," Eleanor said. "We are working on a complete report for you with all the details. It should be ready in a week or so."

"And there is more interesting news," Morgan continued. "Adam is not from around here. We were able to find immigration records. He was born in America. We found a copy of his passport and traced his youth to an orphanage in Vermont."

Nicholas could not stop smiling. He felt he would finally know who Adam was—where his story originated. He told Eleanor and Morgan that he was staying in a rented Kensington flat and would only be in town for a month. They assured him that they would have their latest report completed within the week, and then from there, they would start getting more details about Adam's

American roots. They both indicated that they would need to go to America to continue their research. Nicholas told them they could go wherever they needed to go to get all the information on Adam that they could. Neither Eleanor nor Morgan had ever been to America before, and both were excited at the opportunity to explore a new world. They would not have been as excited had they known who Nicholas was or what he would do to them when they finished their research.

Chapter Twenty-Two

Two weeks later, armed with more than 300 pages of information about Adam, and his final few years, Nicholas went on a self-guided tour of the cemeteries around England, Wales, and Scotland. In all his previous visits to the UK, Nicholas never went outside London. The only cemetery he spent any time in was Brompton cemetery — the one where he was created and where many years later, Oliver watched him have sex. Brompton would always be his favorite cemetery, but with his newfound knowledge about Adam, Nicholas was excited to visit the other cemeteries.

Nicholas headed north to Coventry to explore The London Road cemetery. The report listed it as one of the earliest murders Eleanor and Morgan could link to Adam. When Nicholas reached the graveyard, he was surprised to find this cemetery similar in size to Brompton cemetery. He assumed that all the smaller towns would have smaller cemeteries. Nicholas wandered the paths for an hour, trying to imagine how different the landscape might have looked 25 years earlier.

He came upon a caretaker who was tending to some overgrowth. The man looked quite old. He was hunched over, even when standing upright. He wore thick glasses that seemed too big for his face and bristles of grey on the tip of his chin. His skin was leathery — evident of someone who spent much time under the sun. This man, Nicholas would learn, had spent his whole life working in the cemetery.

"Excuse me, sir," Nicholas said. "I am writing a book on cemetery murders, and I was wondering if you could help."

The old man looked up at Nicholas, studying the young face, trying to decide whether he would engage with Nicholas. A few seconds later, the man smiled and told Nicholas that there had been only two murders in the cemetery in the last 100 years. The first was long before the man was old enough to work, he told Nicholas, but the second he remembered well. "I was the one who found the body," he said. Nicholas could not believe his luck.

"Oh, my," Nicholas exclaimed, trying to sound shocked. "Where did you find it, and what happened?

The old man stood up and leaned against his shovel, using it to keep himself from falling over. He pulled some papers and tobacco out of his pocket, rolled them together, and lit his cigarette before telling Nicholas how he discovered a young teenage girl slumped over a pile of older tombstones that had fallen with age.

"Her body was covered in blood and mud," he spat out as he exhaled a large puff of smoke, coughing.

In the report from Eleanor and Morgan, Nicholas would read that it had rained a lot the week leading up to this murder, and the cemetery was quite soggy. He learned the girl was naked, and the police never found her clothes.

Nicholas wanted to ask many questions, but he could see that the old man would have ignored them. He was telling a story while enjoying his smoke break. The man said that a metal cross affixed to the top of a tombstone for decades had been broken off and jabbed into the little girl's chest.

"The poor lass," the old man said. "That cross was so old and rusty. I am sure whoever murdered her just pulled it off without any trouble. The rust and blood that covered her bosom were just too much."

The old man finished his story by telling Nicholas that had he not found the girl, wild animals would have most likely eaten her. He had been making his final rounds before closing the cemetery for the weekend. If they found her body three days later, the authorities might not have been able even to identify her, he said with confidence. Nicholas found it interesting that the man would share those undocumented details.

The man took another big puff of his cigarette, signaling that he had finished his story.

"And that was what happened," he concluded. "I think the police had some suspects but never found the monster who killed the Vicar's daughter. And he was never the same again — the Vicar. Soon afterward, his wife committed suicide. She hung herself from the Charterhouse Bridge on the cemetery's edge." The old man pointed in a random direction, trying to remember where the bridge was in relation to where he and Nicholas stood now.

Nicholas found the old man's story riveting. This was the closest Nicholas had come to hearing a story about his biological father. While Adam was never convicted of this crime, Nicholas made the connection based on all the research that Eleanor and Morgan had been doing for him. He was so excited he contemplated locating the current Vicar's family and seeing if he had a wife and daughter so he could recreate Adam's murder. The idea of copycatting his birth father sounded like the most fun he could have had that day.

The old man told Nicholas he needed to return to work and walked away, leaving Nicholas to admire the blood-soaked tombstones. Nicholas imagined the girl's body draped over them. He could almost see his father tearing the cross from a headstone and ripping open the young girl's chest with it. He could envision himself doing the same thing. Nicholas could feel his heartbeat racing as he let his imagination recreate the old man's story, and within minutes he felt his right leg get wet. Just the thought of how his father once killed got Nicholas so worked up that he ejaculated at the excitement without touching himself.

He was still overly stimulated by the idea of what just happened and knew then that he had to go to every location that Eleanor and Morgan reported on to see if he could hear other such stories. Nicholas hoped every cemetery would have a witness just waiting to share their story. But before he left Coventry, Nicholas knew he needed to leave his mark, too.

Chapter Twenty-Three

Nicholas spent the next week hiding out in his rented flat in London. His excursion to Coventry had not gone as well as he had hoped. The day after Nicholas heard the story of the Vicar's daughter and wife, and all about Adam's kill, Nicholas set out to recreate that scene as best and quickly as possible. He was not very successful. The town's current Vicar was a childless, single woman. There was no way for Nicholas to recreate Adam's work—to kill another vicar's daughter. Nicholas was pumped with adrenaline from the old man's story and desperate to kill anyone. In haste, Nicholas grabbed the first girl he found.

A teenage girl was walking through the cemetery with a bouquet. She passed Nicholas as he was leaving the cemetery. He had been walking in circles around the grounds trying to decide what to do once he learned that killing the Vicar's daughter was not an option. Instead of leaving the cemetery, Nicholas turned around and followed the girl. She had no idea Nicholas was following her. When Nicholas saw the girl stop at an old tombstone, he decided to stop right next to her. He pretended to be grieving with the girl. Thirty minutes later, Nicholas was heading to his car on the main road. The girl was draped over the tombstone with a broken neck, and an old metal cross jammed into her chest. It was the best Nicholas could muster up on such short notice.

Standing beside Nicholas, the girl wore a light blue dress with a white lace collar. She had white ankle socks, also adorned with lace. Her feet were tucked into shiny black dress shoes. When

Nicholas thinks back on the moment, he finds it odd that the girl was alone. She told him that she was only 14 years old. She wore her black hair in a ponytail. She was not wearing any makeup. Nicholas commented on the person buried beneath the tombstone, and he remembers the little girl turning to face Nicholas to scold him for saying what he said. He cannot recall his own words.

The little girl had defended her grandfather when he was alive and continued to do so. Before the girl finished barking at Nicholas, he grabbed her by the neck with both hands, lifting her off the ground. She was a short girl. With her feet dangling six inches above the ground, Nicholas tightened his grip and twisted. Her whole body went limp, and the flowers fell out of her hands. Nicholas dropped her body over her grandfather's tombstone and pulled a metal cross from his jacket pocket. He had pulled the cross off an older tombstone earlier in the day as he walked through the cemetery, contemplating who he could kill next.

He stabbed her a few times before finally leaving the cross in her chest. Her dress was dripping in blood, and in his haste, Nicholas managed to get a good bit of her blood on him. He was not pleased about that and put on new clothes in his car before throwing his bloody clothes in a trash bin at a rest stop on his way back to London.

In the days that followed, Nicholas watched the story unfold—come to life about the dead girl. He was watching Chanel Four news when he saw the old man being interviewed. He told the reporter the same story he told Nicholas. Then he told the reporter about Nicholas—describing Nicholas without enough detail for Nicholas to fear that the police would be knocking on this door anytime soon, but enough to infuriate Nicholas.

"Fuck!" Nicholas yelled to no one as he sat in the oversized recliner.

Nicholas laid low for a few extra days, watching and listening to the story unfold on the television and radio. With each passing day, the story got weaker. Coventry police shared no new information with the public—mainly because they had little to no information to share. The girl had no identification, and no connection could be made between her and the tombstone where she was found. It would be a few more days before her aunt finally identified the girl. Nicholas knew he was sloppy with this recent kill, and he was angry at himself for not taking the time to plan appropriately. He repeatedly told himself that he risks getting caught when he does not plan his kills. And this time was proving that point all too well. He hated that the old man described Nicholas so well to the authorities. For a moment, Nicholas contemplated going back to Coventry to kill the old man, but just as he was starting to think seriously about it, he got a text from Oliver.

"Hi. I hope everything is okay. I have not heard from you in a few weeks. Just checking in."

Nicholas studied the text, forgetting about killing the old man from the cemetery. Instead, he was enjoying the text—the realization that Oliver did care about him. Nicholas convinced himself that if Oliver was taking this kind of initiative, then maybe Oliver was beginning to care for Nicholas the way he had cared about Oliver all these years. Nicholas wanted to fire back his love for Oliver but stopped himself. He decided those words needed to come from his mouth, not his fingers. His love had grown over the years and was deserving of a more romantic reveal.

"Hey," Nicholas typed back. "All is good, thanks."

Nicholas was being cautious with his words. He wanted to show his affection for Oliver's concern but not necessarily give Oliver much information about what he was up to right then. Nicholas knew he still had several stops to discover more about Adam and needed to do that alone. He needed to stay focused.

"I will be back in New York in a couple of weeks," Nicholas typed. "I am looking forward to seeing you again."

Nicholas knew the last line might be too revealing, but he was baiting Oliver. Nicholas was hopeful that Oliver would bite.

"Great," Oliver typed back after Nicholas watched three dots flash on his screen for too long. "I am also looking forward to seeing you again." Oliver closed his text with a hugging emoji and a kissing emoji. Nicholas smiled and put his phone away.

* * * * *

Confident that he could leave the flat again, Nicholas spent the next three weeks crossing cemeteries off his list. He was bouncing around the country in a similar pattern that Adam had taken, which he thought was brilliant. The more Nicholas studied what he believed to be murders committed by his late father, the more he believed that Adam had been quite intelligent. Of course, Nicholas could not prove that his father had killed all these people, but he could not disprove it either. Knowing that the police across the country were baffled about the murders made Nicholas laugh.

As someone who killed with a great deal of frequency, Nicholas felt he was better positioned to know if Adam was the killer. Nicholas believed that, at some level, he and Adam thought the same way about killing. He did not necessarily believe that Adam had killed out of love, as Nicholas did these last few years, but he still felt that, as he learned more about the deaths—heard more stories from people in the towns, Nicholas was sure that Adam was responsible.

Each murder was similar in that the victims were all found in cemeteries, as Eleanor and Morgan pointed out, but they differed in how each body was found and what method was used to kill. Even the victims themselves varied. Nicholas had been to eight different cemeteries over the course of three weeks since getting the kissing emoji from Oliver. He learned that five men and three women were killed. He learned that three men were in their early twenties, one was in his thirties, and the fifth was in his sixties. He learned that three of the men were gay. The three women were all in their thirties. Two were single, and one had been married at the time of her death.

Finding details about each of the victims was easy. The information in the report from Eleanor and Morgan painted a clear picture of each kill—the victim, the location, and even how they were killed. But the stories people shared with Nicholas as he traveled helped him understand the depth of the murders. As Nicholas listened to each story and read each report separately, he could see how it was difficult to connect the murders. He was confident that many people had tried to solve the individual cases, but it was clear how the police could not do so. So many deaths spread out around the country made it difficult, and almost unrealistic, for any one police force to see the connections.

While he did not have the time to recreate every murder, Nicholas was determined to copy a couple of them. He knew of his errors with the Coventry kill, so when he killed at the Histon Road cemetery in Cambridge and the Arnos Vale cemetery in Bristol, he took what he thought were extra precautions. In Cambridge,

Nicholas stumbled into a local gay pub, the Glenfairy. He stopped for a drink after walking all around Histon Road cemetery. His energy was deflated because he could not find anyone in that garden of death who could remember the boy Adam had killed so many decades earlier.

From the report, Eleanor and Morgan shared, the boy's name was Jacob. At the time of his death, he was 19 years old and studying theology at Jesus College. Nicholas noticed a wall of memories in the back corner of the bar by the bathrooms. There were photos and articles of LGBT people killed in the area. Nicholas was surprised at just how packed the wall was with photographs. He noticed Jacob's image from the report Eleanor and Morgan provided.

"That is my brother," a woman said to Nicholas as he looked at the wall.

"Excuse me," Nicholas replied, taken aback by the woman so closely behind him.

"That one there," she continued as she pointed to the photo of Jacob. "He is my twin brother, Jacob. We lost him thirty years ago in a brutal murder across the street."

"I am sorry to hear that," Nicholas said, trying not to smile as he turned around to face a woman who looked older than someone in her early fifties. He studied her cropped pink hair and her nose ring and was very confused by the t-shirt that she was wearing. It was tattered and covered with small photos of the people from the wall—her brother right in the center. She wore more makeup than Nicholas thought a woman her age should be wearing, but the makeup fit the rest of her look.

"Were all of these people murdered?" Nicholas asked, now pointing to the wall behind him.

"Yes," she responded. "Sadly, many of them were brutally killed for being gay. My brother was one of the first of many killed, or at least found dead in the cemetery." She wiped her eye before the tears could escape.

Nicholas had come to Cambridge to find a story about Adam and to kill someone—anyone. But at that moment, as he watched this older woman fight back the tears as she talked about all the gay lives lost—unsolved murders—unnecessary murders, as she put it, Nicholas could not help but think of Oliver. Would he cry if Oliver were brutally murdered for being gay, he wondered. He knew the answer right away. Before he could find time to cry, he would kill anyone and everyone who hurt or even tried to hurt Oliver.

"... and so, we keep this wall to help us remember them all," Nicholas heard the woman still talking while he thought deeply about Oliver.

"Did they ever catch the murderer?" Nicholas asked.

"No," she said with conviction. "Some of us have our suspicions about who he was, but he vanished soon after he killed. The police claimed they were all random hate crimes. A few people were arrested and jailed for a while, but no one was ever convicted and put away for life. So, the killings continue." As she spoke, the woman pinned another photo to the wall. The brown-skinned boy in the picture looked so young and full of life. His smile was big and bright. Nicholas admired the image, remembering the words that the boy had screamed two days earlier as Nicholas stabbed him in the neck.

Nicholas could still taste the boy's blood in his mouth. He remembered how it sprayed everywhere. Nicholas was covered, and the tombstone the two were leaning up against, making out, was forever stained. Yet one more tombstone painted red.

"Excuse me," Nicholas said to the woman as he left the bar. He decided right then that he needed to get back to Oliver.

Chapter Twenty-Four

As he lay in bed in the comfort of his flat, clicking through channels, Nicholas stopped clicking when he saw the Glenfairy bar on the news. A reporter stood in front of the bar talking with the woman Nicholas had spoken with days earlier. She was talking about the recent boy, Abdul Karim, who had been murdered. The case was getting attention because Abdul was an international student from a wealthy Indian family—his father was part of the Indian government. What bothered Nicholas most about the news story was that the woman mentioned Nicholas—not by name. But she described him with an abundance of detail. Nicholas could not believe she had paid that much attention to him in the short time they had spoken together.

Between the old man in Coventry and the woman in Cambridge, Nicholas, the police, and the news stations, were beginning to see a pattern. Nicholas did not like being called out, even just in the description, at two murder scenes. He knew then that it was time for him to return to America.

Nicholas texted Oliver apologizing for the lengthy absence, and asked Oliver to meet for a drink in two days. Oliver responded almost immediately, suggesting that the drink be at his place. Nicholas agreed, packed up, and headed to the airport.

On his way to the airport, he listened to more news stories describing a tall, handsome, white man in his 20s with dark hair and green eyes appearing at different locations where police were investigating the latest murders. On the screen in the back of the black cab, Nicholas saw a fuzzy camera image of him walking out of one cemetery. He was still wearing gloves and carrying a knife. Fortunately, he was wearing a hoodie, so his face was covered, but you could see the blood on him. That image sent a chill down Nicholas' spine. This was one of the few times where he was caught on camera. He was glad he was getting out of the country before he could get caught.

As Nicholas was boarding the plane back to New York, he received a text from Eleanor. It contained a link to their latest report and said she and Morgan were done in America and would return to the UK in two days. Nicholas had forgotten that he had sent them to America to finish their report and was glad they were still stateside. Nicholas was confident they would connect their information and the news headlines if they were in the UK and watching the news. Nicholas was not ready to have his historians bring closure to his story.

"This is great, thanks." Nicholas typed back. "I am heading to New York right now. Let's meet in the city before you and Morgan go home." Then Nicholas typed an address and hit send before turning off his phone.

* * * * *

Nicholas woke to the beeping and screaming sounds of New York. The room was dark, and the sounds quieted a little. He felt the warmth of Oliver next to him and smiled. He had been back in New York for almost a week. When alone, he would search for news stories from the UK about sightings of a man who matched his description and the murders, but for the last few days, he was seldom alone. He and Oliver were spending a lot of time together. Nicholas claimed to have a home to get back to — plants to water, but those lies would get buried in a moment of passion between him and Oliver, and Nicholas would stop thinking about leaving. He was enjoying every moment that he had with Oliver. Years of stalking had finally delivered what he always wanted, and Nicholas could not be happier.

Nicholas thought about his journey to this point as he lay under the comforter, his naked body touching Oliver's. He thought about everyone he killed — he had to kill to find himself right where he was now. Oliver was still sound asleep. His quiet snore and deep breathing were soothing to Nicholas. As happy as he was to be with Oliver, part of him wanted to leave and learn more about his father. Reading the report from Eleanor and Morgan was one thing, but Nicholas wanted to explore Boston and Vermont to see how much more he could learn about Adam, but he did not want to be away from Oliver ever again. The peace he felt being so close to Oliver now, their bodies touching, was a peace Nicholas wanted every day.

When Oliver finally woke, he was pleased Nicholas was still in bed. He was not worried that Nicholas would have left, just that he would not be in bed. Nicholas was sitting up, reading the latest report from Eleanor and Morgan. As Oliver woke, Nicholas put the report down and pulled Oliver in close.

"What are you reading," Oliver asked as he accepted the warm embrace from Nicholas.

"It is a report about my father," Nicholas admitted, surprising himself with his honesty with Oliver.

"Peter?" Oliver asked with some confusion in his tone.

"No. Adam. My biological father," Nicholas said.

"Oh wow. That is cool. I thought you said you did not know much about him," Oliver continued.

"I didn't," Nicholas responded. 'That is until I hired someone to research him. I figured it was about time I knew something about Adam beyond what Peter told me." Nicholas noticed how quickly he had gone from telling Oliver everything to leaving out critical information. He knew that he could not tell Oliver about Eleanor and Morgan. He had killed them both a few days earlier and did not want Oliver to know anything about them just in case their bodies resurfaced.

* * * * *

Nicholas had every intention of killing Eleanor and Morgan. From the moment he met them, he knew they would know more details about Nicholas than he wanted anyone to know. He knew that when he started recreating Adam's killing history, they would be the first to make the connection and point the finger at Nicholas. Once they gave him the stateside report on Adam, Nicholas knew it was time to end their lives.

As the three planned, they met at Brooklyn Bridge Park. Nicholas knew Eleanor and Morgan had never been to the Brooklyn Bridge before and thought it would be an excellent place to kill them—two tourists dying at a popular New York destination.

The three met later in the day when the park was quieter. They sat on a bench at the water's edge, admiring the architectural wonder of the bridge. They talked about the reports and all the work that Eleanor and Morgan had compiled. Eleanor and Morgan still believed they worked for an up-and-coming author, not a serial killer. As the three watched the sunset, Nicholas threw his coffee cup in the trashcan behind the bench. Eleanor and Morgan were still enjoying the drinks that Nicholas had brought with him. By the time Nicholas sat back down, he could see that Eleanor had finally passed out and had slumped over Morgan's shoulder. Morgan was surprised. He knew they were both exhausted, but he had not expected Eleanor to fall asleep watching a beautiful sunset. Morgan tried to wake Eleanor, but she did not respond. Then he realized that he, too, was getting quite sleepy. With Eleanor and Morgan resting on each other's shoulders, Nicholas grabbed the coffee cups from their hands and walked to the edge of the sidewalk to throw them into the water.

Nicholas had planned to leave the two bodies on the park bench to be found by strangers, but as he leaned over the edge of the walkway, looking down into the water, he saw a dock just a few steps away. Nicholas realized then that getting rid of the bodies would be better. He picked up Eleanor and Morgan and carried them like drunken friends down to the dock, where he saw several concrete blocks and rope, which he knew were there for boats.

Nicholas laid Eleanor and Morgan on the dock and tied their legs to different concrete blocks. He hoped the water was deep enough that the bodies would not be found. Once both bodies were securely tied to blocks, Nicholas pushed the concrete blocks off the edge of the dock into the water. The bodies rolled off the dock, chasing the blocks to the bottom. Nicholas watched for a few minutes to be sure Eleanor and Morgan did not come loose and float to the surface. He could not see their bodies in the murky water, so he felt confident that they were far enough below the water's surface not to be found for some time.

Nicholas walked away from the park as if nothing had happened. He did not see the cameras around the park, hiding in plain sight. Nor did he know that it was high tide. Two days later, he would read a story in the paper about how two young bodies were found on the bay floor at low tide. Crabs and birds had ravaged the bodies so badly that the two could not be identified. Nicholas learned about the cameras and the hunt when he read the article. A photo from the video cameras was in the paper and on the nightly news. It was grainy, but to anyone who knew Nicholas, it was clear that the man in the photo was him. Thankfully very few people knew Nicholas. It was only Oliver that Nicholas had to focus on now. He needed to be sure that Oliver never learned of the dead bodies or saw the video image.

* * * * *

"Would you be up for a road trip?" Nicholas asked Oliver.

"Where to?" Oliver asked with some enthusiasm in his voice.

"Vermont," Nicholas responded. "Partially to get out of the city, and partially because I want to see where my dad was born. There is a chance I could have some relatives up there."

"Sure, that sounds like fun," Oliver said, excited that Nicholas wanted to include him.

"I love you," Nicholas said, not needing but hoping that Oliver would repeat the words back.

Oliver was not ready to say those words to anyone, including Nicholas. Instead of saying them back without knowing if he meant it, Oliver squeezed Nicholas tightly before kissing him, then sliding down under the covers.

Chapter Twenty-Five

Nicholas and Oliver were three days into their Vermont adventure before reaching Adam's Burlington hometown. When Nicholas learned where Adam was born, he wondered if Burlington was Adam's real last name or one given to him at the orphanage. For a moment, he thought about changing his last name to London. While Nicholas was on a mission to find his father's roots, he also wanted to make the trip romantic and spend quality time with Oliver. They traveled to Dorset, Montpelier, and Shelburne before settling into the depressing parts of Burlington.

When they arrived in Burlington, their first stop was St. Joseph's Orphanage. Unfortunately for Nicholas, the orphanage was closed — it had been closed for a long time. There was a tall fence around the property with worn down, plastic 'Do Not Disturb' signs dotting the rusty chain-link fencing. A few windows were broken, and the main door was boarded closed; the boards were covered with vibrantly competing graffiti. In the right weather, the place could look like the perfect haunted house, Oliver thought, looking at the abandoned property.

"This is where he lived?" Oliver asked.

"According to this report, he spent more than a decade here," Nicholas said, feeling defeated.

The two sat in the car, looking at the building. The report mentions the orphanage and is where Adam's story begins, but Nicholas wanted to know about Adam's life before St. Joseph's.

"Look over there," Oliver pointed to an old church sitting in the shadow of the abandoned orphanage. "Didn't you say nuns ran this place? Maybe someone in that church will be able to help."

They exited the car and walked to the small white building on an otherwise vacant lot next to the large, abandoned brick building. Nicholas and Oliver tried to open the church doors, but they were locked. As they contemplated their next move, they heard a voice.

"Can I help you?"

Both men turned around to find a nun standing at the base of the stairs. She had a large pair of gardening shears in her hand and was wearing a full habit under the denim gardening apron that looked too big for her.

"Nothing ominous about that," Oliver whispered to Nicholas.

'Yes, ma'am," Nicholas said, smiling at Oliver. "We are enquiring about the orphanage next door. More specifically, we seek information on a resident from many years ago."

"Yes, that building has been closed for a long time," the nun replied, pausing to remember her days walking those old halls. "But all the children's records are stored in our basement. Are you reporters, or are you looking for a relative?"

"Relative," Nicholas responded almost immediately. "I am looking for my father. His name is — was Adam Burlington."

The nun looked at Nicholas, almost questioning his answer. "Adam? Oh yes, I do remember that boy," she said. "He was a troubled child. Poor thing came to us already broken." She waived the shears to signal Nicholas and Oliver to follow her, and she started walking away, still telling her story.

Nicholas looked at Oliver. "Seriously? You know Adam," he asked as he and Oliver followed her around the outside of the church.

"He came to us at such a young age," the nun continued. "Six or seven. I can't recall. He was born into a bad home."

Nicholas could not believe his luck. He was hoping for some written information, at best. He never expected to get the first-hand information about his father he was getting now. He grabbed Oliver's hand in excitement and squeezed it lovingly. Oliver squeezed back.

The nun told Nicholas and Oliver about Adam — at least as much information as she could recall. She was approaching her 85th birthday, and her memory was no longer accurate. She would have days where she could remember the day she gave her life over to God, and then she would have days when she could barely remember what she had for breakfast or why she was holding gardening sheers.

Sister Mary Francis was her name, and she told Nicholas how Adam had lost both of his parents and how he was a troublemaker in his teens. She said that once Adam turned 18 and was no longer a ward of the state, he walked out of the orphanage and never returned. She went on to say that she does not recall ever hearing from him again.

"So, I really could not tell you where he is today," she finished.

"He is dead," Nicholas said abruptly. "He died almost 25 years ago. I knew about his later years, but I am trying to learn more about his childhood."

The three finally made it to the basement, and Sister Mary Francis looked through a couple of large ledgers to determine which of the hundreds of boxes contained Adam's files. When she finally found his name in the log, she, Nicholas, and Oliver discovered that Adam's file was missing from the box. Sister Mary Francis could not say if the files were taken, lost, or returned to the wrong box. This was where her value ended. If this were any other day, Nicholas would have found a way to send Sister Mary Francis to God for good. But, because he was with Oliver and trying to change for him, he let Sister Mary Francis live, but he was not happy that Adam's file was missing.

"I am sorry that I could not be of more help to you boys," the nun apologized, still flipping through boxes, surprised at the disorder.

"You have been quite helpful," Nicholas told her, hoping to ease her conscience. "Thank you, Sister."

Nicholas and Oliver left the church and drove a dozen blocks to find a hotel in the downtown area. They spent much of their day with Sister Mary Francis, which they had not planned, so they decided to stay in Burlington for another day. They found a quaint bed and breakfast in the town square, and once they were settled in their room, the two of them showered for dinner. Nicholas showered first, then Oliver. Oliver thought about getting in the shower with Nicholas but decided that Nicholas needed that alone time to process the news from earlier in the day.

In the shower, Nicholas kept thinking about the missing files. He wondered if maybe Eleanor and Morgan had been to the orphanage and had taken the files in error or on purpose. He only had their final report, so he assumed they had other notes and files in their hotel room waiting to be discovered. While rinsing out the shampoo, Nicholas suddenly felt unable to breathe. He felt sure Eleanor and Morgan had notes, files, and maybe photos and more information on Nicholas in their hotel room. He had no idea what hotel they had checked into and never checked out. He was convinced that the police had that information now and, with it, would begin to connect some dots, some murders together, all of which would point back to Nicholas, eventually. He started crying for the first time in a very long time. He was confident that his life would begin unraveling just as he finally got to be with his one true love.

When Nicholas finally emerged from the shower, all his tears masked by running water, he gave Oliver the biggest, naked wet hug he could without hurting Oliver. Without questioning him, Oliver squeezed back, letting Nicholas's wet body soak him. Oliver thought the hug was because Nicholas was upset. After all, they were unable to discover more about Adam. He had no idea that the hug was all about him. All for him. Nicholas did not want to ever let go. Eventually, he let go, and the two got dressed, but Nicholas spent much of the night holding Oliver's hand.

They enjoyed a semi-romantic dinner at a small Italian restaurant around the corner from the hotel. They relived the new information about Adam's childhood over several bottles of wine. As they talked and highlighted fragments of Sister Mary Francis' story, Oliver studied Nicholas. He could see the happiness on Nicholas' face when he spoke of Adam. He could see what appeared to be genuine love for a father he never knew. During that meal, during those deep conversations about the day's revelation, Oliver realized that he was in love with Nicholas.

Oliver reached out across the table and grabbed Nicholas' hands. He squeezed his hands around Nicholas' and held them tight.

Oliver stared into Nicholas' eyes momentarily, drowning in the beautiful bright green looking back at him.

"I love you," he said, finally.

Chapter Twenty-Six

Nicholas loved everything about the experience he and Oliver were having in Burlington, but he was struggling because he still had the urge to kill. He could not understand why he wanted to kill. He was happy with Oliver. He had spent years convincing himself that if he could be with Oliver, then he would be able to stop killing. He believed that killing was something he had done because something was missing from his life, that Oliver was missing from his life. He had gone almost a week without killing, or even having an urge to kill, until now. He thought that Eleanor and Morgan were the last two people who had to die. He was wrong.

As Nicholas sat in the hotel lobby waiting for Oliver to come back down from the room, Nicholas looked around him. He saw people coming and going, oblivious to Nicholas or anyone else. He realized that life goes on; that people just live their lives. He saw one kid pick his nose and then lick his finger. He watched a pair of glammed-up young ladies as one of them was scratching her ass. The more Nicholas focused on everyone around him, the more he realized that everyone does what they do without realizing or caring that they are being watched. Either way, Nicholas decided then that he could continue to give in to his urge to kill. He just needed to be sure he was not being watched. He felt confident that he could continue to kill people as he had been—planning and being very cautious and still be with Oliver. He thought he could have it all—deserved it all.

When Oliver returned to the lobby, Nicholas was gone. Oliver had been taking much longer in the room than Nicholas expected. Oliver had no idea where Nicholas had gone or for how long he had been gone. He did not know that Nicholas had walked outside and around the block. Nicholas was looking at the buildings and observing all the security cameras. He decided he would kill someone while he and Oliver were still in Burlington. He just needed a plan. He needed to kill without being sloppy, unlike when he killed Harold's brother Shane, Camilla, or even Eleanor and Morgan.

Nicholas finally returned to the lobby to find Oliver sitting by the fireplace. He could see that Oliver was annoyed.

"So Sorry," Nicholas quickly spat out. "I was unsure how long you would be, so I walked around the block to see if there was any place to grab a drink."

Oliver accepted the excuse because he had no reason not to, and they headed out for that drink. Fortunately for Nicholas and his excuse, a bar was around the corner from the hotel. It was a quaint gay bar. They drank into the night, finally eating some food before retiring back to the hotel for sex, then sleep. Oliver liked what felt like an ordinary, routine evening. He was with Nicholas, and he was happy — he felt happy for the first time in a long time. He was in love.

When Oliver was soundly sleeping, the quiet snore telling Nicholas that Oliver was out cold, Nicholas slipped out of bed and got dressed. He headed downstairs and out of the hotel. He was wearing running clothes to present a cover story if he needed. Once outside, Nicholas walked towards the center of the town square, where he found a large park. He walked through the poorly lit park, wondering if he would find anyone at this late hour. It was well past midnight. He just needed to kill and taste blood and feel the adrenaline rush. He knew once he killed, he would feel better — be better, and he could refocus on Oliver.

After walking for a few minutes in the park, Nicholas came upon what appeared to be a homeless man — a young boy. He was sitting on the ground, his body buried in a dirty sleeping bag. There was a shopping cart next to the boy filled with bags of clothes. The kid's entire life fits into one cart. Nicholas thought about his own life and how little he owned — less than this kid if he really thought about it — material things, not including property.

The kid was quietly smoking a cigarette ignoring the world around him. Nicholas studied the boy as he approached him. He was sure that if the boy took a bath and rinsed the filth off, anyone would see how handsome he was. The boy was surprisingly filthy for such a young-looking boy and had a slight odor that clung to his body. Nicholas stopped and asked the boy if he wanted to share a joint. The park was quiet and dark. The boy looked up, smiled at Nicholas, and pointed to the ground inviting Nicholas onto the sleeping bag. Nicholas sat down next to the boy.

"How old are you," Nicholas asked. "And why are you out here all alone?"

"I turned 18 today, actually," he responded. "My name is Bart, and this is not exactly how I thought my 18th celebration would play out, but this park is my home now, well, tonight anyway."

Nicholas pulled a joint out of his pocket and lit it using Bart's cigarette. He took a few puffs and then handed it to Bart.

"My parent's trailer burned down a few months ago. They did not make it out. I was next door in my friend's trailer, getting high on meth when we heard the screaming. I am sure my mother left something cooking on the stove and was passed out drunk. She was good at doing that—a lot. I lost everything that night and have been roaming ever since. It sucks, man, but I am making the most of it."

Nicholas listened to Bart's story thinking about Adam and the harsh life he must have had growing up, too. Nicholas thought about the hard times people face in this part of the country as he and Bart sat on the ground, in the dark, alone together.

Nicholas asked Bart why he was not living with friends, and Bart said no one wanted him around. His friends were not true friends. They all did drugs together, but that was about it. None of the adults in the trailer park where he grew up were any better than his parents, and he figured that a life out of the trailer park had to be better than staying, so he ventured out into the world. They both laughed at the fact that Bart had not made it far. The trailer park was just on the other side of town.

Bart went on to tell Nicholas that he had not finished high school and never even had a girlfriend. He said he got a hand job from a girl when he was 13 years old, but since she gave one to his friend simultaneously, he did not think it was anything special. Nicholas was amazed at the level of detailed information Bart was sharing with him. The marijuana was not so potent that it would make anyone share so much, thought Nicholas. Bart talked about how he lost touch with his older brother, a stepbrother, years ago. He left Bart and his parents so he could try and raise a child with his girlfriend. That was seven years ago. Bart was convinced that his brother and girlfriend had likely died from an overdose. He told Nicholas that everyone he knew depended on drugs, and many had died from an overdose.

As he told Nicholas more and more about his past, Bart found himself crying. The tears carved paths through the dirt on his face as they escaped. He realized he had been utterly alone since losing his parents, and no one talked to or with him. He had not been able to grieve or share his pain with anyone until now. He wanted to hug Nicholas. He wanted to feel the comfort of anyone as he did as a little boy.

"I can help make it all feel better,' Nicholas said as he grabbed Bart's throat and strangled him. Bart was not strong enough to fight back—to defend himself. He had not eaten in two days—his body was weak. When Nicholas felt Bart's body go limp, he let go of Bart and watched him collapse on the ground.

"Happy Birthday," Nicholas spat into the air.

Then he stood up, turned, and started walking away, picking up his pace. Within minutes Nicholas was running, generating the sweat he needed to keep up his disguise. He was confident that he and Bart were the only two people in the park at that late hour and that no one saw what he did.

When Nicholas returned to the hotel room, he found Oliver sitting in bed, his face buried in his phone. Oliver looked up as Nicholas removed his shirt, revealing a sweaty chest.

"I am going to shower," Nicholas said as he walked past the bed and into the bathroom.

"Where'd you go?" Oliver asked, almost yelling so Nicholas could hear him in the next room.

"I went for a run—wanted to exercise while you rested.

"You left your phone here," Oliver replied. "I was worried."

When Nicholas exited the bathroom, still wet from his shower, he walked over to the bed and seductively dried himself off, dancing close enough that his limp dick bounced inches from Oliver's face. He dropped his towel on the floor and got under the covers with Oliver.

"You have nothing to worry about," Nicholas said as he snuggled up to Oliver, kissing him gently. "Let's have some fun, then get some sleep." He grabbed Oliver's rising dick and smiled. "We have a long drive tomorrow."

* * * * *

When Bart's body was found the next day, the police could see the marks on Bart's neck. They knew he had been strangled. Bart had no identification in his pockets or shopping cart, so he was filed as a John Doe, but the police were still determined to find his killer. After a week of collecting footage from cameras around the perimeter of the park, the police were able to follow one figure who appeared in many of the videos. The police saw a hooded figure leave the same hotel where Nicholas and Oliver had stayed. That figure walked into the park at the north entrance and ran out the east entrance and back to the hotel. With the coroner's best guess about when Bart died and the wealth of video footage, the police concluded that the man in the videos was their killer.

Nicholas and Oliver were back in New York when the hotel staff was questioned. Nicholas was not identifiable in the video footage, but the interviewed hotel staff said they believed the man in the video was one of two guests. The first guest was still staying at the hotel.

When two police officers knocked on the hotel door, the woman who opened it was not pleased. She was only wearing a dirty collared shirt that belonged to the guest. She was not registered to the room. One of the police officers recognized the woman but chose not to embarrass her. He did not think his best friend's sister would appreciate being called out as a whore. He could have arrested her, but he knew it would not make any difference. She would return to the streets a day or two later, repeating the offense. She yelled for her John to come to the door. The man who came to the door half naked and red from fury and embarrassment did not have the body of their killer. The man before them was short and fat, unlike the tall, slim, athletic man from the videos.

The police realized that the front desk clerk knew that his guest was not the one in the video and wanted him to be caught for having a prostitute in his room. Regardless, the police still took the time necessary to question the guest to ensure they were correct in their assumptions. They had let a criminal go in a similar situation before, and they were not about to botch another case.

With this man cleared, the police put all their attention on the other guest, the one who had checked out a week prior—Nicholas became the main suspect in the murder of John Doe. Unfortunately for the local police, Nicholas and Oliver paid in cash. They left no digital footprint. But Nicholas did not realize that when Oliver checked them in, he used his real name and phone number—as any honest person would when checking into a hotel. Nicholas never used his real information in these situations.

Chapter Twenty-Seven

Nicholas and Oliver stopped in Middlebury and Manchester before finally cutting over to Albany and back into Manhattan. Oliver was enjoying the time with Nicholas. He felt comfortable around Nicholas—safe. Oliver had never imagined himself as the 'settle down' type of person, but he felt different around Nicholas. He thought that Nicholas could be 'the one.' Their excursion through Vermont provided them the time needed to get to know each other much more. Of course, Nicholas already knew quite a lot about Oliver, but he still learned a few new things about Oliver's past, which he liked. Oliver shared more of his past with Nicholas, specifically about his struggle with his sexual identity and his suicide attempt—something Nicholas was unaware of before.

Nicholas, too, began to share more with Oliver. The more the two learned about Adam, the more Nicholas felt safe telling Oliver about specific moments in his past when he struggled with not knowing his biological parents. Nicholas was finally letting someone get close to him. He talked more about similar struggles he had with his sexuality and how there are times when he still questions it.

Both were discovering what it meant to be genuinely in love for the first time. They had found that one person who brought so much comfort and bliss into their lives. Nicholas had always dreamt that he would have this feeling once he could be with Oliver, and he was so happy he was right. It was a new feeling for Oliver—one he was not sure was real at times, but their time together in Vermont cemented it.

Nicholas was thrilled that Oliver said those three magic words in Vermont. When Oliver said, 'I Love You,' it almost brought tears to Nicholas' eyes, but he held them back then. He was ready to let the tears out as the two sat in Oliver's apartment. Nicholas wanted to cry for joy and happiness, but most of all, for finally having the person he had been chasing for so long. The amount of pain Nicholas suffered on his journey, and the number of deaths that he felt had to happen to get them both in this place — this time in their lives, seemed so necessary at the time, and he felt so vindicated now.

Oliver was sitting on the couch, snuggled under Nicholas' arm. The two had just opened a bottle of Pinot Noir. The fireplace was alive with a soothing array of warm colors, while a collection of Beethoven music was shuffling quietly through the air. Neither could have wished for a more relaxing, more romantic setting. But, as it had always been the case for Nicholas, that moment was brief, almost fleeting, as Oliver's phone rang, and rang, and rang.

"It is ruining the moment," Nicholas said, sounding annoyed. "You might as well answer it."

"No," Oliver replied. "This is our moment, not theirs."

Oliver would not let another outside source ruin his moment of serenity. He felt that he was the happiest he had ever been — could ever be in that moment with Nicholas. Oliver could finally envision a future with Nicholas, and it was a beautiful life.

The phone stopped ringing. A few moments later, the phone beeped to alert Oliver of a voicemail. He ignored it, too.

The two young men finished the bottle of wine and fell asleep in each other's arms on the couch. Both slept peacefully in their confined space. The nightmares each had suffered through over the years were nowhere to be found as they slept, leaning into each other.

Both men slept through the night for the first time in a long time. Even the noisy hustle and bustle of the New York streets below did not disturb them.

As the morning sun filled the living room, their restful sleep was interrupted by the ringing of Nicholas' phone. Nicholas abruptly woke up, and his sudden movements woke Oliver. Nicholas reached for the phone to see that the alarm system he had set up at his rented house was going off.

"I've got to go," he yelled, jumping off the couch and looking for his shoes. "I am sorry, but I need to get back to my place. Someone just set off the alarm."

"Your house alarm?" Oliver asked, a little confused.

"I am sorry. I will call you once I get this sorted out," Nicholas yelled as he closed the front door behind him.

Oliver sat on the couch in the silent room, trying to understand what had just happened. He thought it was odd that Nicholas would not just call the alarm company or why the alarm company did not call him. His mind wandered to the idea that he should probably install an alarm in his apartment. He would ask Nicholas what company he used. Then it hit Oliver—he had no idea where Nicholas lived. He thought he lived in Greenwich, but they never talked about it. Greenwich was an hour away. Nothing was making sense.

Oliver grabbed his phone off the coffee table and listened to the voicemail left the night before.

"Hello, Mr. McPherson. I am Detective Babson of the Burlington police department. I am calling to speak with you about a case we are working on that involves guests of the Hotel Chevaux.

We understand you recently visited the hotel and we have a few questions."

The officer went on to leave his phone number but did not give any more details about why he wanted to speak with Oliver.

Oliver listened to the voicemail again to ensure he was hearing it all correctly. Instead of deleting the message, Oliver hit the call button on his phone. After a few rings, Oliver heard the same voice from the voicemail.

"Babson here," the detective recited.

"Hello, um, is this Detective Babson?" Oliver asked.

"Yes, it is. How can I help you?"

"Hi, yes, well, um, my name is Oliver McPherson. I received a message from you yesterday."

"Ah, yes. Thank you for calling me back, Mr. McPherson," Babson interrupted. "I appreciate your time, and this should not take more than a few minutes. Would you be able to come into the station?"

"What station?" Oliver asked.

"The Burlington Police Station, just off the square."

"I am sorry, sir, but I am in New York. Is there something I can help you with from here?"

"Oh, I see," said the detective. "And how long have you been in New York, sir?"

"Well, I live here, detective."

"Ah, well, okay then. I understand,' the detective continued. "Well, is there any chance you might be able to come up to Vermont, maybe tomorrow or the next day?"

"I am afraid that will not be possible. I have to work," Oliver lied.

"Oh, right. I see. And what line of work are you in?" the detective asked.

"I am sorry, detective, but is there something I can help you with?" Oliver changed the topic. "Is there a way you can ask me any questions here over the phone?"

The detective reluctantly decided that asking Oliver questions right then might be the only chance he had to get some answers, so he waved another officer over and put the phone on speaker.

"Mr. McPherson, I have put the phone on speaker and have one of my fellow officers on the line with us now. I hope that is okay with you."

"Sure," Oliver responded.

"Great. Well, Mr. McPherson, can you please confirm that you were a guest at Hotel Chevaux a week ago, Tuesday?"

"Yes," Oliver said. "I was there with my boyfriend." Oliver could not recall ever using the word 'boyfriend' before and surprised himself when he heard the word escape his mouth.

The detective and Oliver continued to volley words back and forth in their verbal game of ping pong. Eventually, the detective told Oliver that if he and his boyfriend could not come into the police station, then the detective would appreciate it if Oliver would email a full body photo of both he and Nicholas, along with their body stats.

"We are just trying to eliminate all possible suspects in a murder investigation," the detective continued. "You understand, of course." He spoke to Oliver like Oliver was a regular amongst the police and 'understood' the process the police go through with suspects. This was not Oliver's first dance with the police, but the detective did not know about the catastrophic year Oliver had recently.

Before Oliver hung up, he wrote down the detective's email address and assured the detective that he would send photos as soon as possible. Oliver was not about to do anything without talking with Nicholas first.

* * * * *

Two days had passed since Oliver watched Nicholas run out of his apartment to attend to a home alarm issue. Oliver still thought that interaction was odd—different in a way that had Oliver now wondering how well he knew Nicholas. Oliver and Nicholas exchanged some text messages over the two days but they were short—abrupt. At one point, Oliver wondered if it was even Nicholas on the other end texting back because the messages, the capitalization, everything seemed off, different. Nicholas had noticed that his perfect life with Oliver was beginning to come upended and realized that he needed to get better at covering his tracks. Back in Greenwich, Nicholas was trying to understand who set off his alarm. What he did not know was that Juan Diego had caught up to him and was back to causing trouble for Nicholas.

Nicholas had been watching the news for updates on his latest victims, and when he learned that the authorities in Burlington were looking for someone that looked like him, he knew that he needed to get ahead of the story before he found himself cuffed and questioned. He had no idea that the police had already reached out to Oliver.

As Oliver sat on his couch thinking about his relationship with Nicholas and the detective's request, his thoughts were interrupted by the door buzzer. Oliver looked at the small screen on the wall and saw Nicholas standing in the frame, smiling and holding a bottle of wine. Oliver watched Nicholas for a moment, taking in the grainy image on the screen before finally pressing the button to release the front door, letting Nicholas through the door. The doorman must have been in the bathroom or otherwise preoccupied, thought Oliver. A few minutes later, there was a knock on the door.

When Oliver opened the door, Nicholas dove in for a kiss and a hug. Oliver reciprocated, but with less enthusiasm than a few days earlier.

"What happened in Burlington," Oliver blurted out.

"What do you mean," Nicholas responded, a little worried that his life might unravel faster than expected.

"I got a call from the Burlington police wanting to talk with us about a murder," Oliver spat back, furious that death still followed him. "A freaking murder!"

"Oh yeah, I got a call, too," he lied. "Some homeless person was found dead in the park next to our hotel. They were talking to all the guests. I told the police what we were doing and where we were when the person was supposedly killed. I believe I answered all their questions. They said they would call me if they had more. I talked with them yesterday. When did they call you?"

Oliver looked at Nicholas, wanting to believe him. He didn't think there was any reason not to believe him. As far as Oliver knew, Nicholas had always been honest with him. In the end, Oliver believed Nicholas and assumed there was no need to send photos to the police now. For Oliver, the case was closed, but Nicholas did not feel victorious. He felt lucky that Oliver was buying his lie. He also knew that he and Oliver would need to move, or at least he would, but he was not ready to let Oliver go.

Chapter Twenty-Eight

Once Nicholas decided to move away, he started thinking about all his properties. He could not decide which one to move to and was hopeful that Oliver would help make that decision and want to move with him. He did not like that he continued to lie to Oliver. He had hoped that he could change, that being with Oliver would make him whole, but what Nicholas was coming to terms with was that he was not fixable. Much like Adam, he was broken. He was a killer and always would be a killer. Nicholas was beginning to accept that unless he told Oliver the truth about his past and what he had done to all those innocent lives, he would have to lie to Oliver — forever.

The only way Nicholas knew how to deal with this situation was to spend a little less time with Oliver — take a small break while he decided what he would do about Oliver. During this time Nicholas was killing more random people just to fill an urge. For some, a good massage could calm their nerves. For Nicholas, it was a quick, clean kill. The problem was that he was no longer enjoying the kills or planning them out. He would find himself following a stranger, only to stab them in the back, cut their throat, and just leave them on the ground, ignoring them as their final breath escaped. He was hopeful no cameras or people were watching, but he was not taking the necessary precautions that he usually took to ensure that no one was watching. He did not care anymore. The desire to plan the details that went into the killing was gone. He needed to clear his head and get back in the game, and he thought being away from Oliver was the only way that would be possible.

As he was re-evaluating his life, Nicholas was not prepared for Oliver hounding him. With Nicholas gone so much and communicating less, Oliver started thinking that either Nicholas was not 'the one' or he had done something to upset Nicholas. Oliver sent more and more texts to Nicholas. Sometimes he would get an answer—one or two words. Other times he would get the three dots flashing for a long time and then nothing. It was not like Oliver to obsess over a guy not responding to him. Like Nicholas, Oliver had usually been the guy who was being chased. He did not like being on the other end. As he sat around his apartment sulking in what might be his new reality—life without Nicholas, Oliver thought about all the times he ignored other guys, his friends—sometimes even his mother when she was alive. Oliver realized that he could be quite a jerk sometimes.

Through it all, though, he was clear about one thing—he still loved Nicholas. And he decided that he would fight for their relationship, so he continued to call and text. Oliver decided he would not stop reaching out to Nicholas—filling his voicemail box with messages and overloading his phone with text messages until Nicholas returned, for good. He caught himself sending too many hearts and kissing emojis, but he did not care. Oliver decided that Nicholas was worth the fight, even if Oliver was unsure if they were even fighting.

On the receiving end, Nicholas would listen to Oliver's voicemails and cry. He would read the text messages and start to respond but then not know what to say. He wanted to be with Oliver, but he feared that the truth would come out and that Oliver would hate him and never want to speak to him again. That would be the one thing that would put Nicholas over the edge—the one thing that could result in his own death, or so he thought.

Nicholas traveled to Manhattan often to watch Oliver. He was still not ready to speak with him directly. He was afraid of Oliver's questions—the answers he would demand. While in the city watching Oliver, as he had for so many years, Nicholas would continue to take innocent lives to satisfy his thirst for death. And, because he was getting sloppy, Nicholas did not see Oliver watching him for a change. And he certainly did not see Juan Diego.

Nicholas was walking down 15th Street, heading towards Stuyvesant Square Park, when he saw a large coach bus traveling at a speed that Nicholas thought was faster than it should be on a city street. Just ahead, Nicholas noticed a young woman preparing to cross the street, but not at a crosswalk. Nicholas walked past her thinking about how easy it would be to push her into traffic—to kill her in the middle of the day. He refrained. He was still struggling with how to balance killing and loving at the same time. Nicholas, in his dark hoodie walked on, hoping he would come up with a plan to save his relationship.

What Nicholas did see was the other dark hooded man behind him, or Oliver behind that man. The other hooded man snuck up behind the woman and pushed her into the traffic in broad daylight. The impact of the woman's body against the front of the coach made a loud bang, and by the time the bus stopped completely, the woman's body was run over by two of the large tires and was trapped under a third. Nicholas never turned around to see what had happened. The hooded man ducked into the park, getting lost in the beautiful green setting while the woman spilled red all over the black pavement. Oliver saw a hooded man who he thought was Nicholas — caught a glimpse of him out of the corner of his eye as Oliver came out of a store. Oliver decided to follow him. He had called out to Nicholas, but Nicholas did not respond — he had not heard Oliver.

Oliver followed the person he thought was Nicholas for five blocks before witnessing him push the woman into traffic. It looked like he accidentally bumped into her, causing her to lose her balance and walk into traffic, but from Oliver's perspective, it looked clear — Nicholas, or whoever was in the hoodie caused her death. From his perspective, Oliver saw the hooded man purposefully push an innocent woman into traffic. He was horrified at what he witnessed and confused about if it was even Nicholas who pushed her.

As Oliver watched the hooded man walk on as if nothing had happened, his first thought was of how Miles and his friend were killed. Oliver hated himself for pulling that idea back into his head. He questioned if Nicholas might be the killer Oliver and his friends conspired him to be not so long ago. Oliver's mind started racing with theories, and then he stopped. Oliver realized he had lost sight of the man he assumed to be Nicholas for just a few minutes when following him. By the time Oliver saw the hooded man push the woman, multiple dark hooded figures were on the sidewalk, including Juan Diego. There was no way to know if it was Nicholas who pushed the girl, and the more Oliver thought about it, there was no way to confirm that he had been following Nicholas at all. Oliver's mind was racing with a mixture of thoughts. He needed to talk with Nicholas.

Oliver had the urge to call the Burlington police to follow up on the murder that Nicholas said he had already resolved with the police, but he did not. He was not about to make any rash decisions just yet. After all, this was the man he believed he was in love with—the One. So, instead, Oliver pulled out his phone and texted Harold. It had been too long since they last talked, and Oliver needed a friend.

Harold was usually quick to respond, but Oliver got nothing back. So, Oliver called Harold, and the call went directly to voicemail, but Oliver heard an announcement that the voicemail box was full. Oliver realized as he looked at his phone that he had no idea where Harold lived or the name of the firm where he worked. He did not even know Harold's last name or where his family lived in Boston. He knew Shane's name and that Shane had died recently, so Oliver typed 'Shane' and 'obituary' into his phone to see if he could find anything. It took a few minutes, but Oliver found the obituary of Shane Murphy. With this newfound information, Oliver headed home. He was determined to find Harold.

As he left the horrific scene on 15th Street, lit up by flashing red and blue lights by now, Oliver contemplated telling the police what he saw. Still, he decided he needed to be more clearheaded about what he saw—maybe even talk with Nicholas beforehand. Oliver partially hoped that while he thought he saw Nicholas, perhaps he lost sight of Nicholas as they turned onto 15th Street, and it was not Nicholas who pushed the woman under the bus. Or maybe he never saw Nicholas and had followed a stranger the whole time. He was so conflicted—so confused about what he saw or what he wanted to or not to believe. He believed that the distraction of finding Harold was what he needed.

Walking back home, Oliver sent a text to Nicholas.

"Hi," it started. "Are you okay? I miss you and wish you would talk to me. Please tell me what I did wrong."

Nicholas, who had not stopped walking, looked at his phone when it chimed, alerting him of another message. He walked straight through the park and caught a cab uptown.

"I am so sorry," he replied, surprising Oliver. "You did nothing wrong. You are perfect."

Oliver loved the message.

"I wish you would talk to me," Oliver sent back.

"I am in Albany right now," Nicholas sent back—another lie. "I will be back in Manhattan tomorrow. Let me take you to dinner to compensate you for being a total ass for the last couple of weeks."

Oliver sent a smiling emoji response.

"I will call you tomorrow," Nicholas shot back. "Stepping in to see my financial advisor now."

Oliver felt a little better because Nicholas had finally responded, but this had not erased the idea that he thought he just saw Nicholas hurt someone. He decided to give Nicholas the benefit of the doubt and ask him tomorrow at dinner. Right now, though, Oliver wanted to talk with Harold.

Safely in the comfort of his apartment, it took Oliver almost an hour to find a phone number for who he hoped would be Harold's parents. He dialed the number, and a woman picked up almost immediately. Oliver did not even hear the phone ring.

"Hello?"

"Hi. Hello. Yes, hi, is this Mrs. Murphy?" Oliver asked.

"Who is asking?" the woman asked. Oliver was not expecting the sweet-sounding voice to be so abrupt and rude.

"Hi. My name is Oliver McPherson," Oliver continued. "I am a friend of yours... I am a friend of Harold's."

The woman started crying and mumbling words, but Oliver could not understand them.

"Ma'am," Oliver interrupted, a little louder than he had planned. "I cannot understand you. Are you Mrs. Murphy? Do I have the right number for the parents of Harold Murphy?"

There was silence and then a man's voice.

"Who is this?" a baritone voice barked into the phone. Oliver felt like he was getting nowhere.

"Hi, sir, my name is Oliver..." Oliver started before being cut off.

"Son, why are you calling and upsetting my wife?"

"Sir, I am a friend of Harold's and trying to locate him." Oliver felt relieved to get all that out without any more interruptions finally. What he was not so relieved about was the news that followed.

"We are trying to grieve the loss of our son, and I do not need you upsetting my wife," Mr. Murphy yelled back into the phone. Oliver envisioned a large man, maybe with a buzzcut and goatee — ex-military Irish American. He was glad to be speaking over the phone and not in person.

"Yes," Oliver interrupted. "I am so sorry for the loss of Shane. I did not know him..."

Mr. Murphy interrupted Oliver yet again.

"What? Shane? He died months ago," Mr. Murphy said, almost scolding Oliver for his lack of manners or understanding of the situation. "We are mourning Harold now. Two boys in one year. No family — no mother should have to go through that."

Later Oliver would recall thinking that it was interesting that Mr. Murphy said mother and not parent as if Mr. Murphy was above grieving—a man's man who did not show weakness. But right then, Oliver just started crying, almost uncontrollably. Mr. Murphy had Oliver crying in one ear and his wife in the other.

Oliver stopped long enough to apologize and ask what had happened. Mr. Murphy would only say that Harold was dead. He did not know Oliver, so he was not about to share details about his son's death—murder, as he would say to the police. Much later, Oliver would find out how Harold died, thanks to the internet.

"I am so sorry, Mr. Murphy," Oliver offered. "Harold was a friend, a good—special friend..."

Mr. Murphy hung up the phone before Oliver could finish his sentence.

Chapter Twenty-Nine

It had been almost three days since Oliver learned about Harold's death. Nicholas resurfaced and was spending a little more time with Oliver. They were not back to behaving like the loving couple they were during their romantic Vermont adventure, but Nicholas was spending the night again. They both were trying to find the happy place they were once in, together. Nicholas was struggling with whether or how to tell Oliver the truth. Some days he would wake up ready to share every detail—to step into the confessional and let everything out as if it were that easy. Confess all his sins and say a few 'Hail Marys'; to be forgiven.

On the other hand, Oliver had spent most of the last few days debating with himself about asking Nicholas if he had lied to him. He did ask Nicholas a few times, and each time Nicholas fired back questions rather than answers.

"I am not sure how much longer I can play this game," Oliver heard himself say one evening while cooking dinner. He and Nicholas were having a quiet night in. Nicholas was beginning to think that maybe Oliver was hanging up his detective hat, and the two could get back to loving one another rather than constantly questioning and arguing.

"I am not following," Nicholas said, trying to figure out how a conversation about which wine to pair with dinner turned into a 'game.'

Nicholas turned around to face Oliver. He had a bottle in each hand as if to ask which Oliver preferred.

"I can pick the wine if that is a 'game' you no longer enjoy," Nicholas said, not entirely clear what Oliver was trying to say.

"I am so happy I met you," Oliver said, more seriously now. "But I feel like we go hot and cold a lot. And before you say anything, I know that is how many relationships go, especially new ones. I understand that no relationship can always be rainbows and sunshine."

Nicholas put the two bottles on the counter and moved forward to hug Oliver, but Oliver pushed back.

"I am being serious, Nicholas," he said. "You do this all the time. When I try to be serious, you hug me as if I need to be consoled for something. I don't need a hug. I just need the truth."

"The truth about what? "Nicholas asked. "About whether I love you or not? Well, I do."

"No, smart ass," Oliver said. "The truth about who you are. You come in and out of my life. You are here, then go for long periods; sometimes, you are not totally present even when you are here. You are an enigma."

"What is it that you want from me?" Nicholas asked.

"I want the truth," Oliver fired back. "If we are going to have any real shot at a long-term relationship, then I need to know the man behind the beautiful green eyes and wonderful smile, and well..."

Nicholas took that moment to move closer again and kiss Oliver. Oliver accepted the kiss and could feel himself losing focus again as he and Nicholas started making out.

"Stop," Oliver said as he pushed Nicholas away. "You are doing it again."

"Fine," Nicholas yelled louder than he intended. "Let's put dinner on the table, and you can ask me anything you want. I promise to answer honestly. But this is a two-person game. I can ask questions, too."

They set the table and sat down to eat the pasta Bolognese that Oliver had spent most of the afternoon making. They enjoyed the Pinot Noir that Nicholas paired with the meal, and when their dishes were almost empty, Oliver told Nicholas about when he thought he saw him push a woman into traffic. Oliver provided a lot of detail—some of it seemed embellished as he told the story, but he wanted to paint a horrific picture and hear how Nicholas would explain himself out of it. Nicholas was confused. He was not about to admit to killing anyone he killed, so he was perplexed at how to address a story about someone he did not kill. More confusing to Nicholas was who killed the person Oliver believed Nicholas had killed.

Before Nicholas could answer a question that Oliver did not ask, Oliver said that he thought he saw Nicholas and Harold outside his building but never heard from Harold again and then learned about Harold's death.

"And then there was the homeless guy in Vermont," Oliver started in on a third story before Nicholas decided he needed to stop Oliver.

"I can see the bigger picture that these small stories paint when put together," Nicholas said, interrupting Oliver, looking at him, trying to come up with his next words. Nicholas sat silently momentarily, staring into Oliver's deep blue eyes. He wanted to tell the truth. He was preparing a string of lies that would be even more false information he would have to remember.

"And?" Oliver asked, getting frustrated with Nicholas' silence.

"And they have some truth to them."

Nicholas heard his words in the air and could not believe he had finally told Oliver the truth. He felt relieved and nervous at the same time. He felt like a huge weight had been lifted from his shoulders, and now they could return to focusing on their relationship.

"Some truth," Oliver asked. "What does that even mean?"

"Do you love me?" Nicholas had become very good at answering questions with questions. "I mean, really love me. Like, even if I have made some mistakes—some worse than others, would you, could you still love me? I mean, love me for my flaws, and now for my brutal honesty?"

"Now you are just scaring me," Oliver shot back at Nicholas. "What the hell are you talking about?"

"Do you?" Nicholas asked again. "It is important that I know that you truly, deeply, until death does us part level, really love me. Not just some cheap words, but true emotional feeling."

"I think so," Oliver said. "I mean, I want to believe I do. How do you even measure love?"

"Would you love me if I lied about something?" Nicholas asked.

"Probably, assuming the lie was not over the top crazy."

"Would you love me if I hurt someone you loved—emotionally or physically?"

"I am not sure. It depends on who you hurt and how you hurt them," Oliver said. "Where are you going with all of these questions?"

"Do you believe I would do anything in the world—no matter how crazy it might sound, to be with you because I love you that much?" Nicholas asked.

"I do want to believe you, Nicholas," Oliver said. "But lately, you have been distant and quieter than usual, so I am unsure. I want to believe it. I do. I hope you love me as much as I believe I love or at least want to love you, but your 'man of mystery' routine, and now all these questions worry me sometimes—scare me sometimes."

"I have hurt people in the past," Nicholas said, almost whispering now. "I mean, really hurt them. I have anger issues and have been working through them for a long time."

Nicholas understood what he was doing. He knew he was adding more lies but was also about to open Pandora's Box, and there was no going back. He knew that if he said what he wanted, his relationship with Oliver would be forever changed. He did not know if it would be a good or bad change.

"My anger has gotten out of control before," Nicholas continued. "And I have been punished for my actions," he lied again. Nicholas was crying now, almost forcing the tears out, hoping that Oliver would hug him and end the conversation, at least for now. He did not.

"Should I worry about your anger issues?" Oliver fired back, trying not to cry.

"No!" Nicholas said with a tremendous amount of authority. "I could never hurt you. I love you too much to hurt you.

"But sometimes I hurt other people. It is not done intentionally, but sometimes it goes too far. Peter helped me cope with the destruction I caused."

Nicholas could not believe that he lied about Peter, but he was hoping that since Peter was Oliver's biological father, then Oliver would believe Nicholas.

"I have hurt a few people and left them," Nicholas said, wiping the tears from his face. "Sometimes I would later discover that they had died due to the pain I inflicted, but Peter always told me to stay in the shadows and not come forth that I had hurt these people shortly before they died."

The lies were spewing out so easily. Nicholas made up stories to cover up the truth or at least to soften the truth. He was unsure if Oliver could handle the complete truth, at least not right now. Oliver needed to be eased into the reality that Nicholas was a killer. Nicholas reached out to touch Oliver's hand, but Oliver pulled back. Oliver struggled to understand how hurting someone and not coming forward if they died was okay.

"I do not understand," Oliver said through tears.

Nicholas stood up, went around the table, grabbed Oliver, and hugged him. Oliver tried to resist for a moment but gave in as Nicholas' arms engulfed him, warming him.

"I am sorry, but this is all too much to digest," Oliver said. I need to lie down. Oliver wiggled free of Nicholas' grip and walked towards the bedroom. Without turning around, he added, "I think you should sleep at your place tonight," before he closed the bedroom door.

Chapter Thirty

When Oliver woke the following day, realizing that he had slept for almost 12 hours, he sleepily walked into the living room, partially hoping that Nicholas was asleep on the couch. The couch was empty. Oliver saw the kitchen had been cleaned, and a note was on the counter.

Oliver picked up the piece of paper. It started with 'My Dearest Oliver.' That was enough for him to put the paper back on the counter and focus on some tea. He was not prepared to read a lengthy love note so soon after waking up. While the water boiled, Oliver kept finding himself drawn back to the letter. He was trying to resist reading it until he could get some caffeine in him. He was weak. Before the kettle started to whistle, Oliver was halfway through reading the note.

He was partially hoping that Nicholas would confess something in the letter—tell Oliver some truth, but instead, there were too many words about how much Nicholas loved Oliver and how much he wanted him and Oliver to be together forever. If Oliver knew everything about Nicholas, he would know how brilliant Nicholas was with the note. Nothing Nicholas wrote could incriminate him in anything—except for being in love.

Oliver read the note a few times, each time looking for more meaning than was there. He was also trying to retrace the conversation with Nicholas the night before. He thought Nicholas confessed to killing someone or more than one person as if it were okay because he did not mean to kill or intend to kill them. He could not remember. Oliver was struggling with how that justification was okay and if the conversation went how he remembered it now. As he finished his cup of tea, Oliver wondered if he could still love Nicholas, knowing what he now knew or thought he knew. The entire conversation was fuzzy and cryptic then and was even more so now as he struggled to remember.

Talking with Nicholas was the only way to ensure he remembered the conversation correctly. Oliver knew that talking with Nicholas was also a way for Nicholas to control the conversation and remain cryptic, and Oliver was not sure he was ready for that, at least not so early in the day.

By the time Oliver finished breakfast, showered, and was getting ready to head out the door for a long walk in Central Park, Nicholas had left half a dozen text messages for Oliver. The messages were cute, loving, and heartfelt. When Oliver saw the messages, he remembered the Nicholas he fell in love with and wondered if that person was still Nicholas or if he would see Nicholas differently now.

Waiting for the elevator, Oliver was met by Mrs. Pankhurst, who gushed about the lovely young man she had seen coming and going from Oliver's apartment. As if she were channeling Oliver's dead mother, Mrs. Pankhurst was giving Oliver her blessing and hoping that Oliver and Nicholas — she confessed to meeting him one day — would be together forever.

Oliver smiled and thanked Mrs. Pankhurst for her kind words. He knew she was right. He knew Nicholas was a good person, or at least he wanted him to be. Oliver was asking himself now whether the few confessions Nicholas made were all his misfortunes or if there were more.

When Oliver and Mrs. Pankhurst reached the lobby, they were met by a florist with a large bouquet of Gerber daisies. Mrs. Pankhurst assumed they were for her and was a little resentful of Oliver when the skinny tattooed girl with purple hair and a gold ring through her right eyebrow said they were for a Mr. McPherson. Oliver blushed.

Oliver left the arrangement with Tony, the doorman and asked him to send them to Mrs. Pankhurst's apartment. She smiled at the gesture, but Oliver did not see that as he headed to the park.

* * * * *

Nicholas was not expecting Oliver to respond immediately. Still, he was hopeful that all these gestures were going to be enough for Oliver to want to see Nicholas again, to allow Nicholas to finish explaining.

Days had passed since Nicholas sent the third bouquet to Oliver. Each time, the number of flowers increased. Oliver's apartment was beginning to look like a funeral parlor, but Nicholas did not know that—he did not know that Oliver was keeping most of the flowers. Nicholas might not have killed again if he knew that Oliver still cared about him and wanted to be with him as much as Nicholas still wanted to be with Oliver.

The silent treatment from Oliver had Nicholas furious. He thought that he had failed their relationship. He spent so much of his life chasing Oliver, wanting to be with Oliver, and that dream was turning into a nightmare. Nicholas went on the hunt as he always did when he felt defeated. He knew taking someone else's life would help cheer him up or at least dull his pain.

Sitting in the coffee shop across the street from Oliver's apartment, watching — waiting, Nicholas thought about killing one of Oliver's neighbors but then realized that he should not kill anyone close to Oliver. He was trying to win Oliver back. Killing anyone Oliver knew, Nicholas thought, would not be a good idea.

As Nicholas sat, drinking his latte, he saw Oliver come out of his building and head toward Central Park. Oliver was in running clothes, so Nicholas knew that Oliver would be gone for a couple of hours. Nicholas knew he could not get into Oliver's apartment — not with the doorman on duty. Tony knew what Nicholas looked like, and Nicholas did not want to risk any negative exposure.

Before leaving the coffee shop, Nicholas sent yet another text to Oliver, "Hi. I hope you are doing okay. I still think we need to talk."

* * * * *

Nicholas looked at his phone. Over the last two weeks, he had sent more than a dozen text messages to Oliver. Oliver responded to none of them. He never even teased Nicholas with blinking dots as if he were thinking about responding. Nicholas could not determine if Oliver read the messages or just deleted them — or worse, blocked Nicholas.

He grabbed a towel from the motel bathroom and wiped the blood off his face. The boy, a skinny, tall white frame covered in random tattoos, topped off with a short, orange mohawk, had turned 21 the week before. His girlfriend was just 19. She was still a senior in high school. Nicholas learned these and many other details about the two when he met them at a rest stop off Interstate 7 earlier that day.

Vermont held good memories for Nicholas. The time he and Oliver spent in the state together was a pinnacle time in their relationship. Nicholas thought that driving through Vermont would help him remember the wonderful time he and Oliver had on that trip and help him stop remembering that Oliver was not being responsive. As he enjoyed the countryside drive in the old car he paid cash for at a sketchy used car lot in Queens, Nicholas was hopeful that he could resist the urge to kill anyone.

About an hour into Vermont, Nicholas pulled into a rest stop to pee. He saw the girl first. She was sitting on the hood of an old Honda Civic. Her hair was bright orange, her skin porcelain white, and her clothes, what little she was wearing, were all black. She almost blended into the black car. They exchanged nods as Nicholas passed her on his way to the men's bathroom, where he saw the boy. His lips are what Nicholas noticed first, which was not something Nicholas typically focused on when checking out guys. The boy was talking with another boy, arguing about the price the orange-haired kid was being asked to pay for some drugs.

Nicholas pissed into the urinal and then, while washing his hands, used the mirror to watch the two boys arguing. The boy selling the drugs was shorter but looked to have a lot more muscle than the buyer. Nicholas could see the pistol resting in the back of the dealer's pants and knew it was only a matter of time before the dealer swung the gun around. Nicholas wondered if the kid had ever even fired the gun before.

"Sorry to butt in," Nicholas said as he joined the two on the other side of the bathroom.

"Fuck this guy," Nicholas said to the skinny kid, pointing to the dealer. "I have a car full of shit you can have for free if you come to this party with me."

"Shut the fuck up, man," the dealer said to Nicholas as he pulled the gun out of his pants and pointed it directly at Nicholas. "This is my customer. Mind your own fucking business."

Nicholas walked up to the dealer, getting close enough that the gun barrel was almost touching Nicholas' chest. Before the dealer could do or say anything else, Nicholas punched the dealer in the face and grabbed the gun. Blood gushed out of his nose; the dealer fell back and down to the floor. Nicholas looked at the gun and saw it was loaded—something he had not expected from looking at the incompetent dealer.

"Man, I think you broke my nose," the dealer yelled through bloody hands covering his face. "You are a dead man."

Nicholas looked at the skinny kid smiling at Nicholas in that 'my hero' way. Nicholas asked him if he was interested in going to a party. The kid said yes, so Nicholas told him to meet him outside. Once the kid left, Nicholas grabbed the dealer off the floor with both hands, stood him up, pinned him against the wall, then dragged him into the accessible stall. With one hand, Nicholas locked the stall door and pushed the dealer into the corner. Nicholas could feel the rush. His heart was racing as he was thinking about killing the dealer.

Nicholas flushed the boy's gun into the toilet, jamming it in the bowl. Before the dealer could say anything, Nicholas punched the boy with such force that the boy's Adams Apple went into the back of his throat, and he choked to death right in front of Nicholas. As his limp body sat on the floor, slumped over the toilet, Nicholas took any drugs he could find in the dealer's pocket.

When Nicholas emerged from the bathroom, he saw the skinny kid sitting on the hood with the girl—two orange tops. Nicholas could hear the kid telling the girl about how Nicholas hit the dealer.

"Still game for a party?" Nicholas asked, waving a bag of drugs in the air. Both kids smiled and slid off the hood of the car. "The party is just up the street if you want to leave your car here."

Nicholas was surprised when the kids agreed to get in the car with him. Five miles later, the three of them were in this motel room. Nicholas gave them the baggie he stole from the dealer, and the boy and girl swallowed a handful of pills. They washed them down with some beer Nicholas had picked up when he first crossed into Vermont.

Soon after taking the drugs, the girl started taking her clothes off and getting frisky with the boy. She was trying to remove his clothes, but he was a little shy with Nicholas in the room. The boy looked up at Nicholas as the girl was on her knees unbuttoning his jeans. Nicholas smiled, and the boy smiled back. He pushed the girl away and stood up. He kicked his shoes off and then pulled his t-shirt over his head. Nicholas got a good glimpse at just how skinny the boy was. His pants slid down, and he kicked those off, too.

Still leaning up against the TV, Nicholas watched as the girl grabbed the growing bulge hidden in the tight white briefs—the only clothing still on either. The boy was looking at Nicholas, almost ignoring the girl. It was clear to Nicholas that she wanted to blow the boy, but Nicholas could see that the boy was more interested in Nicholas—curious.

The girl pulled off the boy's briefs, getting smacked in the face with his extra-large penis. She was used to it—she had often played with it. Nicholas was surprised at the boy's size but liked what he saw. As the boy fell back onto the bed, he propped himself up on his elbows and watched the girl go down on him like a lion on a wildebeest. Nicholas took advantage of the moment and moved over to kiss the boy. He accepted the kiss — his first one from a guy.

After an hour of three naked bodies fulfilling several positions of Karma Sutra Nicholas was growing bored. He found the two kids repulsive suddenly. Their bodily fluids were everywhere. As the girl and boy lay on the bed, passed out from all the sex, Nicholas looked at both and remembered his youth and the first time he had a threesome. He remembered all the good times he had with Juan Diego, wondering for a moment what Juan Diego was up to these days. Nicholas grabbed a knife from his jeans that were still on the floor. As he stood over the two kids, all the three still naked, Nicholas put his hand over the boy's mouth and began stabbing the girl's back. She was on top of the boy, so he could not escape as Nicholas pushed down on them both. After a few dozen deep stabs into the girl, Nicholas started to stab the boy in his sides, still covering his mouth. The girl was dead before Nicholas finished stabbing the boy. Nicholas pushed her off the boy so Nicholas could get on top of the kid and keep stabbing him. Nicholas removed his hand from the boy's mouth as the boy spit up a lot of blood, letting out his last breath.

Moments later, Nicholas climbed off the boy and stood at the side of the bed. The girl's face was on the floor, but her body was against the bed, and her legs were in the air. Her blood was soaking into the filthy carpet. The boy had spewed blood and semen all over the sheets. Nicholas grabbed the boy's large, limp penis with his left hand and swung the knife with his right. With one clean slice,

Nicholas now stood above the boy holding the detached penis as more blood dripped everywhere. He slapped the dead boy's face a few times with the penis before shoving it into the dead boy's mouth. Nicholas stood back and admired his latest destruction and then took a shower, dressed, and left the motel room, putting the 'do not disturb' sign on the door.

When the police found the bodies three days later, they counted 125 stab wounds on the two bodies. The police were convinced that these murders were not the work of a single person and that they should be looking for a violent drug gang as they began investigating another murder they would never solve.

Chapter Thirty-One

Nicholas did not stick around to watch the police discover his latest kills. By the time the police found the couple in the motel and the dealer in the rest stop, Nicholas was back to watching Oliver and sending him flowers and text messages. Nicholas had spent the last decade watching and wanting Oliver and refused to allow anything to come between them. If only Oliver could forgive him.

"Okay, I give up," said the most recent text Nicholas sent to Oliver. "Whatever you want to know, I will tell you. I am an open book. I love you."

Nicholas put his phone away and started looking at the latest collection of properties his financial advisor had emailed for review. He was not excited about buying any of them because he feared Oliver would not see them. Then his phone buzzed. Nicholas quickly pulled his phone out of his pocket, hoping it would be Oliver.

"I think I see you at the coffee shop. Look up." Oliver could not really see Nicholas 13 stories down, but he could see enough to assume that he was looking at Nicholas far below, often looking up.

Nicholas was still spending a lot of time at the coffee shop across from Oliver's building. He wanted to be close when or if Oliver changed his mind. He looked up but could barely see Oliver in the window waving.

"If that is you, then come on up," was the following text.

Excited to finally be seeing Oliver again, Nicholas abruptly left the coffee shop and ran across the street. The doorman looked at him as if to ask, 'seriously, do you ever give up?' as Nicholas shot past him. He was so excited; he ran up the 13 flights of stairs. He could not wait for the elevator.

When Oliver opened the door, standing before him, Nicholas was bent over, breathing heavily.

"Sorry... I... ran up... the... stairs," he finally got out.

"Come in," Oliver said, stepping aside to let Nicholas pass. His tone was flat, almost loveless.

Once inside and breathing regularly again, Nicholas dove at Oliver to give him the longest, tightest hug he could without hurting Oliver. Oliver could hear 'I love you' mumbled into his chest.

Oliver pushed Nicholas away after a few minutes.

"I have been thinking a lot," Oliver started in. "Thank you for all the flowers. It was overkill, but all my neighbors enjoyed getting fresh flowers for their apartments."

Nicholas started to speak, but Oliver stopped him.

"It is still my turn," Oliver said with authority, holding his finger up to signal Nicholas to be silent. 'I want to understand your anger issue and help you overcome it, or at least control it. I am not saying that I condone hurting people. I do not, just to be clear. But if you have a neurological issue that causes you to lash out, that is something entirely different, and I need to be there for you, with you... to help you get better."

Nicholas was trying to remain calm. He did not have any neurological issues. He could see that his lie had led Oliver down the wrong path. The last thing Nicholas wanted was doctors examining him.

As Oliver continued to talk, Nicholas made himself at home. He picked out a bottle of wine and opened it. Oliver watched Nicholas move about the apartment—opening cabinets and drawers as if he lived there. Oliver said nothing about it. He liked it—missed it. For as mad as Oliver was with Nicholas, he was finding it hard to stay mad at him. Deep down, Oliver still loved Nicholas.

"I love you," Nicholas interrupted Oliver's dribble of a lecture, handing Oliver a glass of the Old Vine Zin that he selected from the makeshift wine closet. "And I cannot promise that I will be better overnight, but you make me want to be a better person every day. I can work on my 'anger' issues if you can promise to love me no matter what, even as you learn more about my past. Please promise me that you will never stop loving me."

Oliver looked at Nicholas, sitting on the couch. His green eyes were shining back at Oliver, and before Nicholas could say anything more, Oliver put down his glass and moved closer, sitting right next to Nicholas, so close he was almost on top of him. Then they kissed.

When Oliver pulled away, he said, "I will always love you—no matter what."

* * * * *

The next few weeks were total bliss for Nicholas. He spent almost every hour with Oliver. He did not have any urges to kill anyone or hide away in one of his properties trying to plan a murder. The weeks were packed with a perfectly wonderful mundane life—buying groceries, doing laundry, and dining out. Nicholas loved every minute of every day. He never wanted to wake up from this new life.

They were not together 24/7 during this time—Oliver went on his runs, and Nicholas visited with his financial advisor, but the two were finally living the life Nicholas had dreamt about for years. He found himself cooking dinner for the two of them, and on a couple of nights, they even invited different neighbors over for drinks. Nicholas was in heaven.

Unfortunately for Nicholas, a dark cloud was hovering above all the bliss. Nicholas was not aware that Oliver was still talking with the police. After Oliver pushed Nicholas away weeks earlier, he reached back out to the Burlington police and told them that he had some information that might help their case. In the weeks since then, the Burlington police, Rutland police, and now the Vermont State police were all talking with Oliver about open investigations. They were all isolated cases until Oliver connected the dots.

The Burlington police had the mystery man in a hoodie on camera, and thanks to cameras at the rest stop, Rutland police also had someone who resembled Nicholas on film, but in those images, Nicholas was very visible. There was no mystery if you knew Nicholas. To anyone else, it was a fuzzy image of a young, good-looking man. To Oliver, it was Nicholas — it had to be Nicholas. That affirmation then connected the rest stop and motel murders. They did not want to spook Oliver or have him scare Nicholas.

Since New York was outside the jurisdiction of the Vermont police, they had to start the red tape process involving the New York police department. It was then that it started getting too real for Oliver. He did not think about his actions when he called the Burlington police to tell them about Nicholas. At the very least, he was not thinking about how he might get sucked into the case or suddenly be considered a suspect or an accomplice. Oliver certainly did not believe that one call could potentially connect Nicholas to so many deaths—so many more than Oliver expected. And, like so many other decisions Oliver had made in his life, he had moments of regret weeks later, which is why he was welcoming Nicholas back into his life now.

Oliver knew that he needed to tell Nicholas what he had done. He knew it was just a matter of time before Oliver was called again or the police just showed up at his apartment. Oliver felt confident that with all the departments involved, one of them had to be getting closer to identifying Nicholas, maybe even watching them both right now.

So, just as Nicholas was drowning himself in the peacefulness of their relationship, Oliver came clean. He and Nicholas were lying in bed. They had spent the evening watching a movie in the comfort of Oliver's apartment. The fireplace was alive with color—warmth, and they had enjoyed a bottle of Cabernet Sauvignon from Paso Robles, one of Oliver's favorite regions. The mood had been set, and Oliver thought this moment would be the best time and way to tell Nicholas.

"I have to confess something to you," Oliver said, his head resting on Nicholas' bare chest. "I was mad at you, outraged. I was confused by your words and mad at you for sharing them with me, even though I asked you to share them."

"It's okay, babe," Nicholas said, shocking himself using that word, 'babe.'

"It's not. I mean, it is okay that I had those feelings, but because of those feelings," Oliver continued. "I called the Burlington police back."

"You did what?" Nicholas yelled, sitting up in bed. Oliver rolled off his chest in the process. "I told you I had taken care of that situation. Why would you call them back?"

Oliver could tell that Nicholas was agitated and a little worried that Nicholas might lash out, so he jumped out of bed. He stood at the edge of the bed, naked, studying Nicholas—waiting for his whole reaction. Nicholas sat in bed, silently thinking about his next move and words.

"What did you tell them?" Nicholas finally asked Oliver, who had grabbed a robe and wrapped it around himself by this time before sitting back down on the edge of the bed.

"I told them that we were at the hotel and described you and sent a photo of me to them. I did not have a photo of you. They wanted to eliminate us as suspects. They were asking this of all the guests."

Nicholas calmed down and pulled Oliver back into the bed. He was trying to convince Oliver that what he did was okay—that he was not mad. Oliver contemplated telling Nicholas about the other police interactions but was afraid of what Nicholas' reaction might be, so he stayed silent. After a few more minutes, the two were back under the covers together. Oliver fell asleep quickly, his head resting on Nicholas' chest, listening to the rhythm of his heartbeat. Nicholas lay there pinned down by Oliver, thinking about how he would undo a potentially big mess that Oliver had created. Nicholas knew he could not be mad at Oliver. After all, the mess was created by Nicholas first. Nicholas knew it was time to put his big plan into action.

Chapter Thirty-Two

The next few days were not as blissful as a few weeks before. Nicholas was not pleased that Oliver had talked with the police, but he knew he needed to keep his frustration bottled inside for fear that Oliver might reject him again or call the police again. Nicholas wore a less-than-genuine smile around Oliver while planning his next move.

Nicholas was spending every night with Oliver and had been since Oliver broke the news about the Vermont hotel investigation. He was doing it partially because he felt he needed to keep a closer eye on Oliver—watching him and protecting him. Nicholas was also spending more time with Oliver because he knew that if the two of them were going to spend the rest of their lives loving each other, he needed to show Oliver that he was a good person—not a killer and that he was committed to their relationship.

Instead of letting Oliver go on his long runs around Central Park, Nicholas suggested that they walk the path together, hand in hand. It was not the level of exercise Oliver felt he needed to maintain his physique. However, spending more time with Nicholas and rediscovering why he fell in love with him in the first place filled Oliver with excitement and joy.

One day, two weeks after they reconnected, they were walking through Central Park. Nicholas was a little nervous about being so exposed. He knew his last few kills were sloppy. With the news that Oliver shared, Nicholas was confident that the police were catching up to him and that it would only be a matter of time before he found himself in the same situation his father, Adam, did all those decades ago.

They held hands, enjoying the sun's warmth that blinded the clear blue sky. Feeling the tenderness of Oliver's hand in his, Nicholas thought about the first time they talked on the park bench in Greenwich.

"Let's take a vacation," he blurted out, drunk with love.

"Where would we go?" Oliver asked.

"I know a quiet little island near Fiji where we can escape to enjoy nature and each other," Nicholas responded. "A nice place to escape the hustle and bustle of the big city."

Oliver liked the idea but did not realize Nicholas was suggesting the change of scenery to stay ahead of any police. He assumed it was to spend time with each other, and while it was, Nicholas had an alternate agenda, too.

"You still love me, right?" Nicholas asked. "I mean, even after everything I told you about my past and my issues?"

Oliver squeezed Nicholas' hand, then leaned in and kissed him.

"Yes. We all make mistakes, and we all have demons," Oliver spoke a little more seriously than he meant. "And I want you to feel comfortable telling me anything, even if it means more stories about where people got hurt.

"I want to help you get better—to be better, and sharing in your pain and your experiences is a way to do that. I love you and want to be the one person you can trust—the one you can confide in and know that you are safe with me."

Nicholas smiled and knew immediately that he would share more stories with Oliver once they were safely isolated on Vomo

Island. Oliver did not know about Nicholas' land purchases over the last few years and was still in the dark about all of Nicholas' true wealth. Nicholas knew that he would finally tell Oliver the truth once they were on the island. Oliver would be a captive audience, and he was confident Oliver would still love him after the truth came out.

"Let's leave today," Nicholas said, stopping and turning to face Oliver. He reached for Oliver's other hand, looked directly into Oliver's beautiful, ocean-blue eyes, and smiled. "Come on. Nothing is keeping us from jumping on a plane and getting away now, is there?"

Oliver thought about what Nicholas said and was surprised at how quickly he agreed. He smiled back at Nicholas and shook his head in agreement.

"Sure, why not," Oliver exclaimed. "Let's do it!"

The two abruptly turned around and headed back to Oliver's apartment. When they arrived, Oliver started packing while Nicholas sat on the bed and watched Oliver run around the room excitedly.

"Don't you need to pack, too?" Oliver asked Nicholas.

"No, I plan to walk around naked the whole time," Nicholas laughed. "The island is that deserted, and the estate is very isolated."

Oliver studied Nicholas' face to determine if he was being serious or not, but he could not tell. He liked seeing Nicholas naked but then started thinking about how unrealistic and uncomfortable it might be to run around in your birthday suit constantly.

"I am kidding," Nicholas said when he saw the confused look on Oliver's face. "I bought the island years ago and have plenty of clothes there already."

"You what?" Oliver asked.

"You don't think you were the only one Peter left money to, do you?" Nicholas asked with a chuckle. "My mother came from money. I never knew I was born into wealth until Peter died. It turns out I am filthy rich."

As those words leaked out, Nicholas knew he was already beginning to expose the real Nicholas to Oliver. He was getting excited at the idea of revealing his true self. He just hoped that Oliver would remain as open-minded as he claimed he would be.

* * * * *

Oliver laughed when Nicholas walked across the bedroom naked. They had been on the island for a week, and Nicholas spent much of the week with his dick swinging in the ocean breeze. Each time he walked into any room, Oliver heard himself giggle. Nicholas did not mind the laughing because it was often followed by their two bodies twisted together. Nicholas knew what he was doing each time he appeared naked. He knew that Oliver would get aroused, and they would have sex. It was all part of Nicholas' master plan to make Oliver so comfortable—so relaxed that when Nicholas confessed more about his past, Oliver would be accepting of the news.

As the two watched the sunset over the Pacific Ocean, admiring the beauty of nature before them, Nicholas decided it was the right time to share more of his past with Oliver. Their bodies were so close together, lying in the hammock swing. They were exhausted from an afternoon of sex and were intoxicated enough without being drunk.

"I have a confession to make," Nicholas started. "You know I love you, and I would do anything to protect you and never hurt you, right?"

Oliver kissed Nicholas to indicate, 'yes, silently.'

"I have seriously hurt a lot of people." Nicholas momentarily let his words linger in the dry air, waiting for Oliver to react. He didn't. Instead, Oliver continued to enjoy the warmth of Nicholas' body, practically glued to his own — two naked boys together as one.

"Did you hear what I said?" Nicholas asked after a few moments of silence — the only sounds being those of the island and ocean — nature providing a symphony of sounds as the score to the adventure Nicholas was about to reveal.

"I heard you," Oliver whispered into Nicholas' ear. "And I love you. You've already told me you hurt people in your past, and I have come to terms with it. That was your past. I am your present and your future."

Nicholas loved hearing Oliver say those words but was a little angry that Oliver was not taking him seriously. He wanted to confess, to come clean about the dozens of people he killed over the years. He was not ready to give names but was prepared for Oliver to hear some truth.

"What happens if the police decide that I should be punished?" Nicholas asked Oliver as he adjusted in the hammock to face Oliver now. "What if I am arrested and imprisoned for the rest of my life? Will you still love me then? Would you visit me?"

Oliver gave Nicholas another kiss. He was impressed by how calm he was as he listened to Nicholas. His conversations with the Vermont police were rushing through his head. Oliver wondered if Nicholas knew he was not telling Nicholas everything about his conversations with the police. Oliver thought about those conversations and suddenly realized that maybe Nicholas did know, which was why they were isolated on this island, far from any police.

"Of course, I would still love you," Oliver heard himself say as he kissed Nicholas again and rubbed his crotch against Nicholas. Oliver was unsure he liked where their conversation was going, so he tried to distract Nicholas with more sex.

"I am being serious, dude!" Nicholas said, almost yelling. Oliver could not recall Nicholas ever using the word 'dude' before. It did not fit the personality that Oliver had come to know. It is something Eric would have said, Oliver thought.

"I want to be with you forever," Oliver said. "And if that means loving you through bulletproof glass, and confessing my love through a dirty phone receiver, then so be it. But you are not going to jail, so please stop talking silly."

"I have killed people!" Nicholas tried to pull the words back as he heard them mix with the symphony of birds flying overhead, spooked by his scream.

Oliver stopped trying to excite Nicholas, going limp himself. He could feel goosebumps covering his body, almost forming a wall between him and Nicholas. In a way, Oliver already knew Nicholas had killed people. His conversations with the police made it quite clear that, while the police did not have any hard evidence, Nicholas or someone who looked like Nicholas was the prime suspect in several murders.

Oliver did not know what to do next, so he gave Nicholas another kiss, this time on the chest, just above his heart. Nicholas could feel Oliver's soft lips touch his skin, but he could not determine how Oliver felt about the news or what he was thinking.

"Did you mean to kill them?" Oliver asked.

"Some of them, yes," Nicholas replied, concerned about how this information would sit with Oliver. "I told you before. I am not a good person. I mean, I am—with you, but..."

"Would you hurt me like that?" Oliver interrupted.

"I could never—would never hurt you physically, but I worry about hurting you emotionally and verbally, especially as I share my life with you. I worry that you will feel hurt and grow to hate me by telling you about this part of my life."

"I will admit that this is not the reveal I was expecting from you," Oliver shared. "But I love you more for being honest with me. Of course, I need time to understand this side of you, but please know I want to understand. I am not going to push you away. I just need time."

Nicholas pulled Oliver in close. Their naked bodies once again entangled as one. The sun had set, and the cool ocean air swam around them. Nicholas held Oliver tightly, keeping him warm and safe.

"Thank you, my love," Nicholas said as the two fell into a blissful slumber.

Chapter Thirty-Three

Oliver sat at his kitchen counter, waiting for the tea kettle to whistle. He was wearing a pair of Nicholas' boxer shorts, enjoying their warmth. He was thinking about their recent trip to Fiji. It had been a month since they returned, but the conversation still sat heavily on his mind. He loved Nicholas and appreciated that Nicholas finally felt comfortable enough to expose more of himself to Oliver, but some part of him was not satisfied. Oliver was feeling the pressure from Nicholas, even though he was thousands of miles away, and Oliver was still feeling the pressure of the police.

Soon after he and Nicholas returned to New York, Nicholas had to head off to Scotland because of some unfinished business with the property he bought there. It would be a quick trip. Oliver was exhausted from the last trip, so he stayed behind and was looking forward to some alone time, some quiet time. Unfortunately, his time was taken hostage by Detective Babson and the other officers in Vermont. They felt they were finally closing in on their cases and were more convinced than ever that Nicholas was their man. They just needed to bring him in for questioning. Eventually, Oliver had to take their calls. They had been leaving so many messages, and he feared they would show up at his front door if he did not talk with them.

Oliver agreed to meet with the police again. By this time, the Vermont state police and the New York state police were jointing working on several cases that they believed were all linked. Oliver went into a precinct not far from his apartment, and that is when he realized just how close the police were to capturing their killer; if they could conclude that their killer was, in fact, Nicholas. With all his new knowledge about Nicholas and his killing spree, Oliver became increasingly convinced that the police were close to capturing Nicholas. As the police shared more information than they should share—Oliver thought about Jennifer—he was putting the puzzle pieces together, and it was not looking good for Nicholas.

"We are going to make this simple for you, Mr. McPherson," said one of the officers. "We have solid evidence that your boyfriend committed several crimes across multiple states." Oliver knew that the officer was not as confident as he sounded. Sure, he made a good case, but pinning their crimes on Nicholas was still a stretch based on the information they shared with Oliver.

"So, you have a choice to make," said another officer.

"Should I have my lawyer present," Oliver asked, surprising the officers with his defensive response.

"If you feel that is necessary," said the first officer. "But the bottom line is that we can charge you as an accomplice, or you can help us bring your boyfriend in for questioning. It is that simple."

Oliver did not like those options. He loved Nicholas and had promised him that he would keep his secret, but at the same time, Oliver was not prepared to go to jail for something he did not do. As the officers continued to lay out their case, Oliver knew that his only option was to help them. He had to protect himself—take care of himself first.

Once he agreed to help the police, they wanted to know where Nicholas was. Oliver lied, saying he did not know where Nicholas was but that he would be coming to his apartment the next day. The police decided to stake out Oliver's building so they could bring Nicholas in as soon as he appeared. The police told Oliver to go about his day as if nothing was wrong. He was instructed to talk with Nicholas normally and not to alert Nicholas that the police were watching. The police were hoping to capture Nicholas outside the building so as not to disturb or upset any of Oliver's neighbors.

Oliver went home and cried. He knew that what he was doing was right. But it was also wrong to set Nicholas up after everything they discussed in Fiji. He cried himself to sleep only to be woken by a phone buzzing. Nicholas had landed.

Oliver heard the buzzing but quickly realized that it was not his phone. He was lying in bed looking at his phone, but the buzzing continued. He eventually found a flip phone in the drawer of his bedside table. It was dancing around the mostly empty drawer. Oliver picked it up and answered it.

"Hi, babe."

Oliver heard the voice but was unsure what or who he was hearing.

"Nicholas?" he asked.

"I do not have time to explain," Nicholas said. "I want you to listen to me very carefully. I know that the police threatened you. I know what they are trying to do, and you cannot let them bring me in. Not now, and not like this, okay?"

Oliver was confused about how Nicholas knew and was more confused by the phone.

"Holly shit," Oliver yelled, finally understanding. "Is this a burner phone? Oh my god, you are in trouble. I am in trouble. Oh crap, this cannot be happening."

"Oliver, please calm down," Nicholas said. "I have been in this position before. I know what to do, but I need you to listen carefully. Can you do that for me?"

Oliver was nodding his head, holding back tears.

"Oliver?"

"Sorry, yes, yes, I can. What do I need to do?"

"I am going to send you a text message in an hour. That message will tell you where to meet me. I am pretty sure your phone is tapped at this point, so hopefully, the police will take the bait. You will need to leave your apartment and head towards the address I give you, but I want you to take the bus first, switch to the subway, and finish the trip in a taxi. Do you understand?"

"Yes," was all Oliver could say.

"Bring the burner with you. I will call you when I know you are about to get in the taxi."

Chapter Thirty-Four

Oliver sat in his apartment waiting for the text from Nicholas. He could not believe what was happening. Was this going to be his life now, the thought. He certainly did not want to end up in jail. He thought about his mother and how she would not have approved of this new life, not approved of him being an accomplice to a crime or being involved with the police in any way. Oliver was thankful that his mother was not alive to see him now, but at the same time, he missed her more. He needed a hug from her.

He was dressed and ready to go when the text came through. He wondered if the police were also seeing the text; Nicholas said they would. Oliver looked out his living room window and saw what he believed to be the unmarked police cars drive away. He was surprised that it was that easy to sway the police.

A few minutes later, Oliver was walking out of his building, beginning Nicholas's planned journey. He was unsure why he needed to make all the stops and changes if the text had already sent the police on a wild chase. But to be safe, he followed Nicholas' instructions exactly.

Oliver left his phone in his apartment and traveled only with the burner phone. He always thought these were things you see in the movies and never expected that he would be using one. For a moment, he thought it odd that Nicholas was so prepared that he already had the phone sitting in Oliver's apartment. He wondered how often Nicholas relied on such devices and how long this phone had been sitting in his drawer. His mind wandered back to his conspiracy theories with Howard and Camilla. He snapped back into focus when the bus stopped abruptly. He looked out the window and noticed it was the stop Nicholas mentioned.

Normally, Oliver would be oblivious to the world around him, but today, as he sat on the bus, he studied each person, wondering if they were undercover cops. He felt he was in a frenzy of panic and conspiracy theories. As he exited the back of the bus, he noticed two men getting on the bus. They were in suits. Oliver was convinced they were the FBI, which did not make sense since he had only been talking with state police. He exited the bus and blended into the crowd on the street, but he stopped long enough to watch the men who got on the bus flash their badges. He was right. Maybe not about them being FBI, but they were cops and most likely looking for Oliver. He ducked further into the crowd, getting lost again.

As Oliver emerged from the depths of the subway, he was greeted by two officers. They called Oliver by name, which he found very discomforting. He suddenly concluded that he might not be good at this game of cops and robbers.

"Mr. McPherson," one of the officers said. "We are so glad we found you. We are close to capturing your boyfriend, and we need you to identify him so we can be certain that we have the right guy. We certainly do not want to arrest the wrong person now, do we?"

Oliver was perplexed at how they found him or even managed to follow him if that was what they had done. Oliver had been unaware of a girl on the bus sitting behind him. She got off at the same stop and followed Oliver since he left his apartment. Oliver had been so focused on men in uniforms or suits that he did not think twice about the young-looking girl with blue hair. Undercover cops and burner phones? Was this his new life? He wondered as he agreed to go with the police.

The police were not arresting Oliver. They never even blamed Oliver for trying to allude them. They just cornered him and gently forced Oliver to go with them. At that point, Oliver was only worried about them finding the burner phone on him and having a direct link to Nicholas.

When Oliver and the police arrived at their destination, Oliver noticed that it was an East entrance to Central Park. He had not paid any attention to the text that Nicholas had sent. He just knew that Nicholas would try to point the police in a different direction.

"Where is he?" one of the officers asked Oliver as they all got out of the squad car.

"Where is who?" Oliver asked with a spark of sarcasm in his voice.

"Don't play games with us, Mr. McPherson," another officer said. "I will arrest you for these murders if we cannot locate your boyfriend, so you better smarten up."

Oliver did not like the officer's tone, nor did he appreciate his threat. Oliver loved Nicholas but was not about to go down for something he did not do. Oliver did not know that just before the police arrived at this location, another text was sent to his phone with instructions to meet Nicholas under the Brooklyn Bridge. As the officers and Oliver stood around, he could see the officers start talking with each other about the new text.

"What the hell is your boyfriend doing," one of the officers yelled to Oliver as he ran towards him with his hand on his gun.

"Stand down, Jim," Oliver heard another officer yell.

"I am sorry," Oliver said. "But I do not know what any of you are talking about. I told you my boyfriend would be home soon. I went out to take care of some errands, and now I am wrapped up in some... I don't even know what this is."

"Where is your phone?" an officer asked Oliver.

"I left it at home," Oliver responded. "Why?"

"Your boyfriend... well, someone is texting cryptic messages, sending my team all over the city."

"How would you know that without tapping into my phone?" Oliver asked with some authority and anger in his voice. "I do hope that you have a warrant for that tap. If not, you will be hearing from my lawyer. All I know is that my boyfriend will be home shortly. May I please finish my errands and return home?"

After hearing the response, one officer shouted some words into his walkie-talkie, then told Oliver that he could go home. To be sure he would not be followed this time, Oliver jumped into a taxi and got out of it four blocks later, only to get into a different cab and head in a different direction.

"Hello?" Oliver said into the burner once he got out of the taxi. "What the hell is going on, Nicholas? You have me running all over the city, and the police are riding my ass, not in a good way."

"Sorry, Oliver," Nicholas said. "I love you... Please forgive me, but I need to get out of town. The farther I am from you, the safer you will be."

"What? No way!" Oliver yelled into the phone. "I love you, too. You cannot abandon me now."

"Just until the police settle down," Nicholas replied. "I have a few tricks up my sleeve, but I need you to go on with your life. Keep the burner for now. I will let you know when to get rid of it. We need to make it look like you, and I are done, and you have no idea where I am."

"No, no, no!" Oliver yelled as tears filled his eyes. "Please just come home. Meet with the police and prove you are not the man they seek. I can help. Please, Nicholas. Just come back to me!"

"I've got to go," Nicholas said. "I will call you soon. I love you."

"I love you, too," Oliver said into the phone, but Nicholas had already hung up.

Chapter Thirty-Five

Almost a month had passed since Nicholas said goodbye to Oliver. Since that day, Oliver had kept the burner phone in his pocket. He took it everywhere he went, hoping that Nicholas would call again. He did not. Oliver would flip open the phone open a dozen times a day, looking to see if he missed a call or text. He had not.

The police visited Oliver multiple times since the last day Oliver spoke with Nicholas. They questioned him in his apartment and had him visit the police station, too. They, as much as Oliver, were trying to figure out what had happened to Nicholas. Oliver never told the police about the burner phone, but he did say that he had talked with Nicholas the day they all ran around the city. He told the police that Nicholas only said he was leaving and would not say if or when he would return. To show that he was cooperating, Oliver officially signed off on allowing the New York and Vermont state police to 'monitor' his phone. He knew that meant tapping it and tracing every call in and out of it, but he did not care. He had stopped using the phone. Oliver knew that Nicholas would not reach out to him on that number anymore unless he wanted to antagonize the police.

As hard as it was to accept that Nicholas had left, possibly for good, Oliver returned to living his mundane life. The police tracked down a few other people who looked very similar to Nicholas, hoping that maybe one of them could be the killer they needed. One of them, a guy from southern Vermont, was still in custody. He had been in custody for a few days before Oliver knew about him. He looked eerily like Nicholas, had a lengthy police record, and had no alibi for any of the murders. From the update the police provided to Oliver two days ago, it sounded like Nicholas was no longer a suspect. Oliver was relieved but not convinced. Until this new suspect was convicted and jailed, Oliver would not stop worrying that Nicholas was still in trouble.

* * * * *

The trial of Samuel Hornbill, the latest Nicholas doppelgänger to be arrested for several of the murders committed by Nicholas, was six weeks into his trial when Nicholas finally resurfaced. The trial was being held in Burlington. Oliver knew about the trial but had no interest in watching it. He was not sure if Nicholas had set Samuel up or how the police came to find Samuel, but Oliver was not convinced that Samuel was who the police were looking for at this point. Oliver felt quite confident that Nicholas was the man responsible for the murders that Samuel was being accused of. Oliver had grown confident that the man he loved was a killer, but he was not about to let the police know that detail. He knew that if he attended the trial, the authorities would question whether Samuel was their man, or worse, it would pull Nicholas out of hiding. Oliver did not know Nicholas was back; he was watching the trial in person.

On the other hand, Nicholas was a narcissist and was fascinated that someone was taking the fall for his murders. He was also furious that someone else was taking credit for his work. To be clear, Samuel was not taking credit for anything. He and his lawyers argued every day that Samuel was innocent. His lawyers were getting testimonials from anyone and everyone who knew or interacted with Samuel. He was a 25-year-old, uneducated farm worker with three kids, all under five, from two different women. Neither woman was his girlfriend or his wife. Samuel dropped out of high school in the tenth grade so he could work, so no one could believe that he was smart enough to commit all the murders. Back then, he, his parents, and three siblings lived together in a two-bedroom mobile home on a corner of the farm where they all worked. Today he shared a smaller mobile home with one of his brothers. They lived four trailers down from their parents. His kids lived with their mothers, and Samuel rarely got to visit with them.

As Nicholas listened to the trial, he was stunned that anyone could believe that Samuel killed any of the victims. The more he listened to the story of Samuel's life, the more Nicholas was convinced that he needed to stand up in the courtroom and admit to the murders himself. Nicholas had a long-haired, blonde wig pulled back in a ponytail. He was unshaven and wore a pair of tortoise shell glasses with no prescription. Oliver might not even recognize Nicholas in his current state, just as he did not realize that Eric and Nicholas were the same person all those years ago. Nicholas had become quite good at disguising himself.

With all the media attention the trial was starting to get, Nicholas decided that he had seen enough to know that he might have to keep running. He got out of town and headed back to Greenwich. On the journey south, he did reconnect with Oliver briefly.

"Hey, handsome," his text to Oliver started. "Watch the trial. There is no way they will convict this guy. I think I need to stay away a little longer."

No sooner did Nicholas send the text did his burner start ringing.

"You have to come home," Oliver pleaded. "Or let me come to you. This is getting ridiculous. I miss you."

"I know, but it is not safe," Nicholas said. "Have you been doing what I said to do? Do you feel like the police have finally left you alone?"

"Yes, and yes, I think so. My life is dull, so maybe they just got bored," Oliver said, laughing, trying to lighten the mood.

"I have a plan," Nicholas said with confidence. "But it means we must wait a little longer before we are together again. I just bought a large property outside of Timber Cove in California. It will be the perfect place to meet in a month.

"A month?" Oliver yelled louder than he meant to but was frustrated that even more time would have to pass before he could see Nicholas again. "How will I know where to go?"

"I am having a package sent to you this week with instructions," Nicholas replied. "If you are in your apartment, go to the bedroom and lift the light on the bedside table on my side of the bed. You should see a key.

Oliver was home, so he followed the instructions and was surprised that he had never noticed the key. It made the lamp tilt slightly, but he never paid any attention to it. The key had a number engraved on it.

"What is 379?" Oliver asked, looking at the key in wonder.

"That is a key to a storage unit in Greenwich. You know the post office on Main Street, right? Five doors down from the post office is an off-brand storage facility. Melissa, my stepmother, had used this place to hide things from Peter. When she died, I emptied it and have been using it. That key will open unit 379. You will find information about where we should meet and when.

"This all sounds too cloak and dagger for me," Oliver said with some hesitancy in his voice. "Is all of this necessary?"

Their conversation went back and forth for many more minutes, with Nicholas assuring Oliver that it was a solid plan and nothing could go wrong. Nicholas was confident with the plan, but he needed Oliver to believe that he was confident in the plan; otherwise, he knew Oliver would not follow through. When they finally hung up, Oliver left his apartment and headed for the train station. He wanted to get to Greenwich today.

Chapter Thirty-Six

As Oliver headed to the train station in New York, Samuel was found not guilty on all accounts of murder in Vermont. Unlike Nicholas, Oliver did not know as he was not following the trial. Nicholas knew this news might have the police knocking on Oliver's door again, looking for new answers. He knew it was time to implement his plan and hoped Oliver was heading to Greenwich.

A handful of people were on the platform, but Oliver was not paying attention to them. He focused more on why the train was a few minutes behind schedule. He was getting nervous about Nicholas' latest plan.

"Mr. McPherson," Oliver heard from behind him. When he turned around, he saw two officers walking toward him. Oliver felt his whole body get warm.

"Hello, officers," Oliver replied, almost whispering. "How can I help you, and more importantly, how do you know my name?"

"We are going to have to ask that you come with us down to the station," one of the officers said. "There are some people there who have questions for you."

Oliver knew at that moment that Samuel must not have been convicted. Nicholas warned him that this might happen. Oliver knew he needed to get to the mailbox but knew that if he refused to cooperate with the police, he would be delayed even longer. He decided that he could head to Greenwich tomorrow and went with the police to show that he had nothing to hide.

At the station, Oliver was met by the detectives who had been making his life a living hell for weeks. They were, once again, asking Oliver for information on Nicholas. Oliver remained calm and answered their questions as honestly as he could. He had no idea where Nicholas was, which was part of the plan.

After hours of questioning Oliver, the police concluded that he had no new information to help their case. They were still hell-bent on finding Nicholas or someone who fit his description. They had to accept that it would take longer than they had planned. The next time the police handed someone over to the district attorney, they knew it had to be 'the' one, not just anyone.

Nicholas had anticipated that the police would detain Oliver. That was his chance to get an envelope into the storage unit and tie up some loose ends so the two could start their new life together, far from New York. He had spent much of the previous week making several purchases and transfers. He wanted to be sure that even his backup plan had a backup plan.

* * * * *

Oliver waited another week before going to Greenwich after his last visit to the police station. He decided he would not do anything that might lead them to Nicholas or give them any reason to pull Oliver back for more questions. Oliver was not even sure if Nicholas was in Greenwich. For all he knew, Nicholas was already in California. He reached out to Nicholas once on the burner, but Nicholas did not reply. Then, as Oliver sat in the coffee shop around the corner from the storage unit in Greenwich, debating whether to open the envelope there or wait until he got home, he got a call from Nicholas.

"Hey babe," Nicholas sang into the phone. Oliver was still getting used to being called babe. "I see that you have the envelope."

"Wait, what? You can see me?" Oliver asked. "Where are you?"

"No, I cannot see you, but I know the envelope has been picked up, and you are one of only two people with a key. If you do not have it, we have a bigger problem," Nicholas continued with a laugh.

"There are three envelopes in the larger envelope. Please only open the first one now. It has your ticket and flight information and instructions to the property. The other two envelopes have instructions on them as to when you can open them," Nicholas lectured. "I trust you will follow these instructions exactly. I love you, but I must run. See you soon."

Before Oliver could say anything back, the phone went dead. Oliver put the phone back in his pocket and looked at the large envelope. He could not believe how his life was unfolding. A few years back, he never thought he would be in this position. Evading the police and living under a blanket of secrecy was not the life he wanted. His thoughts were interrupted when Imani sat in the chair across from him.

"Hi, Oliver," Imani said with excitement in her voice. "How have you been? It has been a minute."

Oliver greeted Imani but was immediately drawn to her belly.

"Hi," he said. "Are you..."

"Pregnant?" she interrupted him. "Yeah, can you believe it?" Imani started with the story of how she became seven months pregnant. Oliver was only partially listening to Imani go on about how Jackson was the 'one' for her and how they wanted to get married first, but then the next thing they knew, she was 'preggers,' as she put it. She told Oliver how Jackson stepped up and how he would be such a good dad. The more she gushed about Jackson, the less Oliver found himself listening. Her monologue was interrupted by Jackson walking into the coffee shop. She waved him over to the table.

"Hey boo," Imani said to Jackson.

Jackson kissed Imani right after acknowledging Oliver, "Hey man, sup?" Oliver did not bother to respond because Jackson's mouth was devouring Imani's as soon as the 'sup' left his lips. Oliver did not find it tasteful or attractive at all.

Imani talked a little longer and then was pulled away by Jackson. They had to meet his parents for dinner, and Oliver was only too relieved when they were gone. If he had not been so preoccupied with the envelope, Oliver might have paid more attention to Imani and been happy to see them both alive and well. But none of those thoughts filled his head now. It would be a long time before Oliver understood the importance of seeing Imani and Jackson when he did. He never knew that Nicholas contemplated killing them both, but one day he would learn just how much restraint Nicholas had to prove his love for Oliver.

Alone again, Oliver finally opened the large envelope, and just as Nicholas said, he found three smaller envelopes inside. One was white, one was yellow, and the third was blue. There was also a new burner phone. The white one had a note to open immediately.

The yellow envelope had the words 'open only when instructed by Lawrence,' and the blue envelope had the words 'open only if you do not hear from me for 90 straight days.'

Oliver shook his head, frustrated at the continued game. He had no idea who Lawrence was or how he would receive instructions, but he accepted that if this was how Nicholas wanted to play the game, and if he loved Nicholas, then this was the game he had to play. He did not care for the blue envelope message at all.

* * * * *

One week later, Oliver was heading to JFK airport. He organized his apartment in a way that indicated he would only be away for a short time. He arranged with the doorman to have mail collected and put on his dining room table. He arranged for the house cleaner to come once a month instead of weekly and asked her to water his plants. He had no idea how long he would be gone or if he would ever return. That level of detail, if already planned out by Nicholas, had not been shared with him.

Oliver cried as he sat at the gate, waiting to board a plane. It was a quiet cry, one for himself, not one to attract attention. He was upset with his life and how it was unfolding. He always wanted to love and be loved, but he was struggling with the idea that this was the way for all that to come true. This was not how he envisioned his life even just a few years ago.

He felt better once he got the cry out as if he was sending all the negative vibes and the bad energy out of his body through the tears. A little more clearheaded, Oliver was ready for his new adventure. He had not been to California before but trusted Nicholas and his plan. Love will make you do crazy things, he thought to himself.

As he settled into his first-class seat, Oliver sat back and welcomed the glass of champagne that was handed to him by a passing flight attendant. Twenty minutes later, he was sound asleep.

Chapter Thirty-Seven

When Oliver's plane landed at the San Francisco airport, he was greeted by a text message as soon as he turned on the burner phone. The buzzing sound made him smile because he knew it was from Nicholas.

"Drop this phone in a trash can in any bathroom before you leave the airport. I will reach out to you soon on the other one."

There was no 'hey babe' this time, and no 'I love you' either. Oliver thought it was odd that after all the three-word bombs Nicholas had been dropping, this text was so cold, so matter of fact. He thought about texting back or even calling Nicholas but decided that Nicholas probably would not answer. He had a plan, after all.

Oliver walked through the terminal and stopped in the first bathroom he found. He relieved himself, washed up, and then dropped the phone into the trash can before heading to baggage claim to start his new adventure.

Four hours later, Oliver was getting out of the car he rented at the airport, per the instructions detailed by Nicholas. He had to rent the cheapest, smallest car in the lot. It did not matter what brand, so long as it was small and inexpensive. The smaller ones are more disposable; he would learn one day.

Standing beside the car, Oliver looked at the house on the hill overlooking a large pond, or was it a lake? Oliver could never remember how to differentiate between the two. As far as he could see, there was nothing but rolling hills covered in trees. No other building was in sight. Once he turned off the main road onto the property, even the three-mile drive revealed no other structures. He was going to be as isolated as he had ever been, as probably anyone had ever been, he imagined.

The house was a good size. It was more than a shack and less than a mansion, and it fit the surroundings. Oliver counted four chimneys, and one had smoke coming out of it. For a moment, Oliver was excited at the idea that Nicholas was already here, but he quickly learned that George, the caretaker, lived on the property, too. When traveling by ATV, George lived in a much smaller cottage twenty minutes across the property.

George came out of the house, greeted Oliver, and gave him simple instructions about the property. George said he would come by the house once every couple of days. Oliver learned that the estate was called Redwood Manor, and it spanned 8500 acres. Enough space to get lost and stay lost, he thought. George explained that all the food Oliver would need is shipped in once a week, and there was a notepad for Oliver to add anything special he would like delivered. There was no internet and no cell service. The estate was utterly isolated from the rest of the world.

"No internet or cell service?" Oliver asked George with worry in his voice.

"There is a satellite phone in the kitchen if you have an emergency," George replied, unaware of who Oliver was or why cell service was so important.

George had been the caretaker of Redwood Manor for two decades, and before him, his father was the caretaker. George's family took care of the property for more than six decades. George's mother still cleaned the main house once a month. It took her longer these days, but she managed quite well for a woman in her 70s. Sometimes George would help.

His grandparents moved to California from Mexico when Jorge, George's dad, was a baby. They found themselves in Timber Cover and were taken in by the family that owned the property before Nicholas purchased it. Jorge passed away a couple of years ago, leaving George and his mother to tend to the property on their own for the previous owner. George has not met Nicholas but has clear instructions on how to care for Oliver until Nicholas arrives.

Once George had finished giving Oliver the tour and instructions, George left Oliver to settle in. The first thing Oliver did was try to contact Nicholas. The phone number that Oliver had for Nicholas returned a 'not in service' message when Oliver dialed it from the satellite phone. He knew he had no service on his burner, but he tried texting anyway and received a failed message. Oliver threw the burner phone across the kitchen, frustrated that he was completely alone and isolated from the world.

"FUCK!" he yelled at no one.

"Discúlpeme, señor," George's mother said as she knocked on the kitchen screen door. Oliver was not expecting anyone to hear him.

"Oh, shit," Oliver said. "I am sorry. I did not see you there.

"Te traigo unas flores para la casa," she continued as she walked in and placed the flower arrangement on the kitchen table.

Oliver did not understand what she was saying and just nodded and thanked her as he watched her walk in and right back out. He fell back into a chair at the table, put his hands on his head, and started to cry again. Isolated and unable to communicate with the help, Oliver felt completely defeated.

After thirty minutes, Oliver heard a sound he had not heard before. He looked up and saw the satellite phone light up.

"Hello?"

"Hey babe," Nicholas said. Oliver had never been so happy to hear Nicholas' voice as he was at that moment. "Sorry I did not get to call you on the new burner before you got to the estate. Are you settling in, okay?

"Hi. When are you getting here?" Oliver asked. "I am not settling in. I've only been here a few hours. The woman only speaks Spanish, and this place is in the middle of fucking nowhere." Nicholas could hear the frustration in Oliver's voice.

"I hear you, babe," Nicholas said, sounding condescending. "This is something new for you. It will take a little getting used to, but I assure you it will get easier. I am hopeful that I will be on a plane within the week. Please settle in and get comfortable.

"A week?" Oliver screamed.

"Did you meet George yet? He will get you anything and care for you until I arrive. I must run, but I will call or text you soon. I love you."

Before Oliver could respond, he heard the line go dead.

* * * * *

It has been six weeks since he last talked with Nicholas. At least once a day for the last five weeks, Oliver tried calling Nicholas, but no one would pick up each time.

Every day was the same. Oliver would wake up early and run five miles around the estate. When he returned home, he would find George's mother in the kitchen making breakfast. She would appear to make meals and then vanish. Oliver rarely heard her in the house cleaning or saw her outside of mealtime. He enjoyed the hot cooked meals but was tired of being cared for by two strangers.

Today, as Oliver finished his run, he noticed a car parked in front of the house. It was the first vehicle he had seen since he arrived. George had taken the rental car away the day after Oliver arrived. Oliver assumed he returned it to the airport or a nearby rental place but never asked.

Oliver noticed a man sitting in one of the rocking chairs as he approached the house. He did not look familiar. The man was drinking from a glass, so Oliver knew that George or his mother had greeted him.

"Hello," Oliver said, a little out of breath, as he approached the porch. "Can I help you?"

"You must be Oliver," the man said. His suit was well-pressed, and his black shoes shined in the morning light. He wore a brightly colored bowtie, and for an older, round man, Oliver thought the man was attractive.

"Yes," Oliver responded. "And who might you be?"

"My name is Lawrence," he replied. "I believe you have an envelope for me."

"An envelope?" Oliver asked. "Oh, right. Lawrence. You are the yellow envelope guy."

Oliver ran into the house and came out a few minutes later, holding the yellow envelope. He handed it to Lawrence and sat in an empty rocking chair.

Lawrence opened the envelope to find a mini cassette. Oliver looked at it and laughed.

"What year are we in?" he heard himself ask Lawrence. "Is that really what I think it is?"

Lawrence pulled a mini cassette player from his briefcase, put the tape in, and pressed the play button. Lawrence put the player on the table between him and Oliver. It was not an ordinary cassette player; it had a small digital screen. Before the tape would play, Oliver heard the device speak.

"Please enter your code."

Lawrence entered a six-digit code.

"Thank you. Please enter your birthday."

Lawrence looked up at Oliver and pointed to him and then to the device. Oliver was perplexed but tapped his birthdate into the keyboard.

"Thank you. One moment."

Oliver looked at Lawrence, then around the porch. He was unsure if he was being Punked or in some weird science fiction movie dream, and he needed to shake himself awake. Before he could ask Lawrence a question, the device started playing the cassette.

"Hey babe." were the first two words spoken, and immediately Oliver started to cry.

"If you hear this recording, my plan has been delayed or changed beyond my control. It also means that you have met Lawrence. He has been my lawyer for a long time. He is with you because I need you to sign several documents that will give you the authority to act on my behalf, especially if the authorities detain me.

"I know this is not how you hoped our future would start but believe me when I say these are all critical steps to preserve our future together. Lawrence will represent me in court if it comes to that, but by signing the documents he has for you, you can conduct some business for me, which may include accessing the necessary funds for bail.

"Yes, my love, I have been arrested if you are hearing this recording. I knew this day would come, and I was hoping to have had more time with you before this, but these documents will help ensure we have plenty of time together again soon.

"I trust Lawrence with my life, and now I trust you with it, too. Be safe, be strong, and know that Lawrence will keep you abreast of my case. But please promise me that you will stay on the estate. It would be best if you were not arrested as an accomplice to anything. If you cannot be found, you cannot be charged. Please promise me you will stay put.

"Lawrence will update you, and George is there to take care of you. I love you and will see you soon."

Once the tape stopped, Oliver started crying again. He wanted Lawrence to play it again, just so he could hear Nicholas' voice, but before Lawrence could do anything, they both listened to the device make a loud whizzing sound before ejecting the cassette with the dark tape vomiting out of it. There was no recovering the tape and no way to replay it.

"What the hell happened?" Oliver yelled through his tears.

"He turned himself in," Lawrence said. "He called me yesterday and told me that he was going to turn himself in, then clear his name so you two could be together, forever, and without having to always look over your shoulders."

"What do you mean he turned himself in?" Oliver cried. "He was supposed to get on a plane and join me here weeks ago. I don't understand all the games and the mystery."

"I understand," Lawrence said. "But I need you to be strong, and I need you to focus. As I said, Nicholas called me yesterday, and I immediately flew out here. Then this morning, on my way to see you, I got the call that he had called the police and was waiting for them to arrive."

"Arrive where?" Oliver asked. "He never told me where he was hiding out."

"He has been in a rented house in Greenwich," Lawrence responded. "But there was an accident."

"What?" Oliver pounded his fists on the arms of the rocking chair.

"I sent one of my staffers over to the house just so someone would be on the scene when Nicholas was arrested," Lawrence continued. "The neighborhood was swimming with police, and there was an explosion."

"An explosion?"

"Yes," Lawrence said. "My staffer was injured and is in the hospital now. Once I get more information about her and where Nicholas is, you will be the first person I update."

After dropping that devastating news on Oliver, Lawrence left. He had a long drive back to the airport and was not about to miss his flight because Oliver wanted to ask more questions for which Lawrence did not have answers.

Chapter Thirty-Eight

When Nicholas called the police, he expected quite a significant turnout. Still, he did not expect to be trapped in the back of a police car when the gas tanks and home explosives ignited in the basement of his rental—of Oliver's home. He had hoped he would have already been on the way to the police station. The explosion was part of his argument about the stupidity of the police. He and Lawrence were going to blame the explosion on the police and their inability to manage a suspected crime scene. He knew it would be a long shot, but he did it anyway. Still being at the scene when the house exploded was an unexpected setback, and being pinned in the car, covered in his blood, was much more problematic.

Fortunately for Nicholas, he had no broken bones, unlike those of the officer who involuntarily became a human shield for Nicholas as he slammed into the car. The officer's back and neck snapped as he hit the side of the vehicle. Nicholas could hear the bones crack. He knew the officer was dead on impact. And, because he was in the backseat of the car, nothing was available to jab or pin him down, unlike the officers who were on the porch when the explosion happened. Paramedics pulled many pickets out of officers' bodies, who sailed through the air and landed face-up on fence spikes.

When Nicholas woke up, his ears were ringing, and he felt quite dizzy. Most of the blood he was losing was from gashes where the broken glass was logged in his skin. Most were small, and he pulled those out, but he looked down and saw that one of the security bars from the window had broken free and punctured his leg. He pulled it out and used his shirt as a tourniquet to control the bleeding.

By the time the police could make sense of the violent scene and get to the police car down the street from them, Nicholas was gone. He got out of the car and hobbled to another rented house three blocks away, where he had a car parked in the garage. He was worried about leaving a trail of blood in the snow, so he made sure to drag his feet and walk erratically, so the snow looked worn down—not like it had been freshly walked on. Once he was blocks away, safely in the garage, he bandaged up all his wounds, got into the backseat of the car, and went to sleep, buried under many blankets to keep him from freezing.

Nicholas slept for 15 hours. That was much longer than he wanted to sleep, but he accepted the rest. He had slept so little recently. He knew that by now, Lawrence was on his way to see Oliver, if not already there. He did not like that he had kept Oliver in the dark so much over the past few months, but it was the only way Nicholas believed he could protect Oliver. After spending a decade trying to get Oliver to love him, Nicholas was not about to take any chances of losing him now.

Rested and ready to reunite with Oliver, Nicholas left the garage to see if the police were patrolling the area. He could still hear sirens, so he knew the hunt for him was on, but he could not see the depth of destruction he left a few blocks over. Believing he was in the clear, Nicholas opened the garage and drove farther from the scene. He was expecting roadblocks, airport checks, and the typical protocols for when a wanted fugitive was on the run, and he had a plan for how to get through them all.

Chapter Thirty-Nine

Sitting in the back of the Greyhound bus, Nicholas was glad to finally be out of New York and heading to see Oliver. It took a train ride, three taxis, and hitchhiking to finally get into Philadelphia, where he bought his one-way ticket west. In her raspy, cigarette-stained voice, the grandmother behind the scratched bulletproof protector told Nicholas the trip would take three days. He smiled, nodded, and accepted the ticket and receipt for his cash purchase. He wanted to get to Oliver quickly, but he knew the safest way west was in small steps. He had no intention of staying on this bus for three days. He fully intended to get off in St. Louis and jump on a train for a few states.

Nicholas had not traveled by bus in a long time. The last time was in high school when his class went from Greenwich to Stowe for a ski trip. He remembers being swallowed up by the large seats back then, sitting alone. Now, he feels the seats are smaller, almost cramped, as he sat next to a man in his 80s. Nicholas had the window seat, which he liked on this trip because the old man repeatedly stood up to use the bathroom two rows behind them. When not urinating, the man tried to talk with Nicholas, who only wanted to close his eyes and wake up in Missouri—no such luck.

The 22-hour journey to St. Louis seemed much longer to Nicholas since he had little chance to sleep. His neighbor shared stories of his children, his grandchildren, his dead wife, and that one time he kissed a boy in college. Nicholas was unsure why the man shared his gay experience with him but acknowledged that it was fantastic. The man was going to see his daughter in Las Vegas and her new baby twins she had with her wife last month. The level of detail the man shared overwhelmed Nicholas, especially since he always gave so little detail about any part of his life, even to Oliver.

Once in St. Louis, Nicholas decided to spend a day in the town to get some sleep. An old hotel was attached to the bus station, so he put down some cash and headed to his room for rest. The room was not any nicer than many of the dumpy motels he hid out in over the years. There was an odor in the air as he walked the hallways. It was not quite death but close, and Nicholas almost gagged at the stench. Fortunately, his room was less foul—tolerable at best. But he was so tired that he did not care. He collapsed on the bed and slept for nine hours.

Nicholas woke refreshed and ready to continue his journey to the love of his life. He did not have any burner phones, so he took a risk and called Oliver's satellite phone from the hotel room. It rang many times before Oliver finally picked up.

"Nicholas?" Oliver whined into the phone.

"Hey, babe!" Nicholas sang back, refreshed but still sounding a little worn out.

"Where the hell are you?

"I am making my way to you," Nicholas said. "Things have not gone according to plan, so I was delayed some."

"Some?" Oliver asked sarcastically. "I have been waiting here for months. I am all alone in this forest prison. I was about to give up on you."

"Please do not give up," Nicholas heard himself plead. "I am a couple of days away from you. Before you know it, we will be in each other's arms again for good. I promise."

"Okay, but please get here. I am going stir crazy."

"You can explore," Nicholas said. "You are not trapped on the estate. Just do not travel far. It is the safest place for you to be."

Oliver was trying to keep Nicholas on the phone. He liked finally hearing his voice again and hated being alone and feeling all alone. But as much as Oliver wanted to keep talking, Nicholas wanted to get off the phone. He was tired and ready to get to California.

"I need to run so I can catch my train," Nicholas finally said, interrupting Oliver's ramblings of his days. "I love you and will see you soon."

"Train?" Oliver asked, but the line had gone dead again. Oliver was getting tired of Nicholas hanging up on him. He gave up his whole life or somewhat changed the trajectory of his life to be with Nicholas. He thought the least Nicholas could do was stop cutting him off and out.

* * * * *

Two days turned into four days and then into two weeks, and Oliver was still waiting for Nicholas. He had no idea where Nicholas was when they last talked. All he knew was that Nicholas was getting on a train, assuming that was true. Oliver did not know if that meant a metro train in some city, an Amtrak train, or a freight train.

Sitting at the kitchen counter, Oliver thought about how he got to this point—how an envelope sent him on this wild adventure. He remembered that there was still one envelope to open. He pulled that out of a kitchen drawer and read the note, 'Open only if you have not heard from me for 90 straight days.'

Oliver started thinking about all his and Nicholas's conversations since he left New York. He realized Nicholas had been reaching out often enough not to require this last envelope to be opened. Oliver contemplated opening the envelope but was interrupted by a knock on the front door. Oliver opened the door to see a police officer standing a few feet back.

"Hello, officer," Oliver said. "How can I help you?"

"Sorry to bother you, sir," the officer started. "But there have been a series of murders along the coast recently. We are going house to house to be sure people are safe and to see if anyone has seen or heard anything."

"I'm sorry, but did you say murders?" Oliver asked as he thought to himself that this could not possibly be happening again.

"Yes, sir," the officer responded. "The latest one, a young woman hiking up the coast, was found at the edge of your property two days ago. She had been missing for a week."

"Do I even want to know how she died?" Oliver asked, almost afraid of the answer.

"It appears that she was crucified," he said.

"Crucified?" Oliver asked.

"Yes. Unfortunately, I cannot go into details, but she was one of many people killed violently recently. We are checking with all residents to see if they have seen or heard anything or have any security camera footage that might help us."

"I understand," Oliver said before telling the officer that there were no security cameras on the property. "Is there anything I need to be worried about or watch more closely?"

"Please keep your doors locked and report any suspicious activity you see," the officer said before heading back down the driveway. Oliver watched the officer drive off. He leaned against a porch column, looking out across the property. He was not looking for anyone but wondered if he was being watched. The satellite phone was ringing in the kitchen. It took a few rings for Oliver to realize the sound, and he quickly went inside, hoping to speak with Nicholas.

Chapter Forty

When Nicholas finally reached San Francisco, he stepped off the bus, trying not to gain the attention of the police officers patrolling the bus station. They were there looking for illegal immigrants, not rich white guys, but he did not know that then. He was exhausted, but he knew he still had a few more hours of travel before reuniting with Oliver. Once he was out of the station and walking through the city, Nicholas searched for a phone store to buy a new burner to call Oliver.

"Where are you?" Oliver yelled into the phone like a parent verbally scolding their child.

"I am finally in San Francisco," Nicholas responded, trying to hide his exhaustion. "I will get a car and head up the coast. I should be to you in a few hours."

"Ok, well, just so you know, the police have been coming around here, so be careful," Oliver shot back, a little tired of Nicholas' promises of arriving. He was not going to hold his breath that they would be together in a few hours.

"What? Why?" Nicholas asked.

"There have been several murders, apparently," Oliver said, starting to sound like the nightly newscaster. "The latest one was on the property, or at least on the edge. I must be honest with you. I thought it was your work. I was so angry."

Nicholas was silent for longer than he meant to be, but Oliver's words stung. Since sharing more about his past, Nicholas could tell that Oliver was still unsure how to deal with it. He was just happy that Oliver had not left him. Not many people would stay in a relationship knowing their partner was a murderer.

"You still there?" Oliver asked, breaking the silence.

"Sorry, yes. I am here," Nicholas said. "I just got into town and have not killed anyone in a long time." Nicholas knew he was lying to Oliver, but he did not care. He needed to see Oliver, hold Oliver, and do anything possible to ensure that Oliver still loved him.

"I am on my way," Nicholas said just before he hung up. 'I love you."

Oliver listened to the dial tone for a few seconds before hanging up. He was relieved Nicholas was so close, assuming he was telling Oliver the truth. He was also relieved that Nicholas had not already been in town killing people again. His thoughts were interrupted by a knock on the front door. Oliver knew it was not George or his mother. The two of them always came in through the kitchen door. For an estate so remote, he was getting a lot of visitors; lately, Oliver thought as he went to the door.

Oliver opened the door to find a young, olive-skinned man. He was wearing jeans and cowboy boots. His belt was fastened by a large, silver buckle with a man riding a bull. The man wore a flannel shirt of red and black with a hint of yellow in the pattern. On his head sat a black cowboy hat. The man was clean-shaven, making him look more like a mature teenager than an adult man. He was not tall. Oliver guessed 5'7", dwarfed by Oliver's 6'2" frame.

"Can I help you?" Oliver asked, looking at the stranger before him, thinking he was remarkably handsome.

"Yes, hello, sir," the man responded. Oliver could pick up a slight accent, like George's, when speaking English. "Would you like to give yourself over to Jesus?"

Oliver looked at the man and found him less attractive suddenly. Then he looked out beyond the man to see if others were outside.

"Did you just walk the three-mile-long driveway to ask me to give myself to Jesus?" Oliver asked. "Are you fucking with me right now? You cannot be for real." Oliver found himself speaking so disrespectfully to this young man but could not stop. It was as if all his frustrations with Nicholas were pouring out at this man while the young man just stood, staring at Oliver and smiling. Oliver was trying to figure out if the guy was smiling because he was just some smart-ass kid or if he was smiling because he had no idea what Oliver was rambling on about.

Oliver finally stopped his rant and looked at the young man, staring into his beautiful hazel eyes.

"I am so sorry," Oliver finally said. "That was rude and uncalled for. I apologize. It has been a hell of a day.

"I understand," the man sang back, but he did not. "I was only kidding about Jesus. Sorry if that hit a nerve with you. My name is Juan Diego. Nice to meet you." He tipped his hat with one hand, leaving the other holding his belt buckle."

"Oh, well, um, hi. Yes, nice to meet you, too," Oliver stuttered out. "I am Oliver. Are you looking for George?"

"No, my friend," Juan Diego said. "I just wanted to meet you finally, Oliver."

"I am sorry, but how do you know my name?"

Juan Diego, still smiling, looked into Oliver's eyes, staring longer than Oliver appreciated. Oliver looked away, then back. Juan Diego was still staring at Oliver.

"Hello, I asked you a question."

"I have been watching you for a long time," Juan Diego finally said. "I am hoping you can help me find Nicholas."

Be sure to check out more
adventures of Nicholas & Oliver
by John Paul

The Garden of Death
Published 2022

The Shadow of Death
Publishing 2023

www.ingramcontent.com/pod-product-compliance
Lightning Source LLC
LaVergne TN
LVHW011949060526
838201LV00061B/4261